Kong

2018

16. 2018

To Norman,

Best wishes from
your daughters Friend!

THE HANDOVER MURDERS tells a gripping story with a dose of history. The main events are set against the volatile political situation in 1997 Hong Kong. Intertwined with this, a story from the past unrolls against a changing backdrop: the Japanese invasion and occupation of Hong Kong during WWII, the influx of refugees from mainland China, and 1960s and 1970s corruption in the Hong Kong Civil Service.

DAMON ROSE was born in Derbyshire, England in 1971. He currently lives in Alicante, Spain, with his wife Ieva and his two children Adam and Lucy, He enjoys history, travel and Spanish studies. Damon has lived and worked in numerous countries, including Hong Kong, the Philippines, Thailand, Australia, Indonesia and New Zealand. As a young man, he witnessed first-hand the melting pot of cultures that was colonial Hong Kong. In *The Handover Murders*, he draws on his twenty years as a professional diver and thirteen years working in Hong Kong including at the time of the 1997 handover, an event which changed the course of Hong Kong history, and his own life. *The Handover Murders* is Damon Rose's first novel.

Acknowledgements and note on the cover images
The narrative of *The Handover Murders* is set in two periods of time against three "handovers": the surrender of Hong Kong to the Japanese on 25 December 1941, the formal surrender of the Japanese in Hong Kong on 2 September 1945, and the handover of Hong Kong to Mainland China on 1 July 1997. All three were pivotal events in the fate of the fictional characters of this story, as well as in the actual history of Hong Kong.

The cover top photo, combining two images of Central Hong Kong taken at different dates, one during the Japanese Occupation of Hong Kong and one in more recent times, is provided courtesy and by permission of Willie Kristofer Chan.

The cover bottom photo was taken on 30 August 1945, i.e. after the Japanese surrender. For a more detailed explanation of this photo and its background, see: https://gwulo.com/atom/14034.

Care has been taken to respect and acknowledge the rights of all. If, nevertheless, the rights of any have been infringed, this will be remedied in later editions if notification is received.

THE HANDOVER MURDERS

Damon Rose

A Proverse Prize Finalist 2017

Proverse Hong Kong

The Handover Murders
by Damon Rose.
1st edition published in paperback in Hong Kong
by Proverse Hong Kong under sole and exclusive licence,
15 November 2018.
Copyright © Damon Rose, 15 November 2018.
ISBN: 978-988-8491-47-6

Distribution (Hong Kong and worldwide):
The Chinese University Press of Hong Kong,
The Chinese University of Hong Kong,
Shatin, New Territories, Hong Kong SAR.
Email: cup-bus@cuhk.edu.hk; Web: www.chineseupress.com

Distribution (United Kingdom):
Christine Penney, Stratford-upon-Avon, Warwickshire CV37 6DN.
Email: chrisp@proversepublishing.com

Distribution and other enquiries to:
Proverse Hong Kong, P.O. Box 259, Tung Chung Post Office,
Tung Chung, Lantau Island, NT, Hong Kong SAR, China.
Email: proverse@netvigator.com; Web:
www.proversepublishing.com

The right of Damon Rose to be identified
as the author of this work
has been asserted by him in accordance with
the Copyright, Designs and Patents Act 1988.
Cover image and design by Artist Hong Kong.
Colour image by and © Willie Kristofer Chan; b/w image from Gwulo.com

.

British Library Cataloguing in Publication Data
A catalogue record is available from the British Library

Preface

This story uses the 1997 Hong Kong handover not as the subject of the story itself but as a great cover-up, a moment where all manner of wrongs can be swept under the carpet to allow OBEs and Knighthoods to be claimed, and interestingly-obtained extraneous income to be salted away while nobody wants to look too closely.

A Hong Kong cop once told me that in the 1960s policemen would find an extra package of money in their locker in the morning. If they did not take it, they would find their careers blocked. And when a new "gweilo" arrived to take a police position, he would find three presents in his desk: an envelope with money, a bottle of whisky and a picture of a naked woman with a phone number. His reactions to these would be closely watched and it would determine how he was going to be controlled. One big lesson of History is that it takes an awful long time for the effects of old behaviour to dissipate.

The hero of *The Handover Murders*, Alex Torrence, is a Eurasian with the Manchester Police, sent to Hong Kong to pick up the body of a murdered British National. There the history of his father, a Scottish Hong Kong policeman, catches up with him and embroils him in an investigation he was not authorised to deal with.

As a son of a copper myself, with twenty-four years of Hong Kong residency under my belt, I recognise all the characters in this story as people I have met. *Though I wouldn't swear to that in court, guv. Strictly off the record, if you know what I mean?* But they do remind me of a few I've drunk with at official receptions much loved by Hong Kong's élites, and of course in a few Wanchai bars. For that matter, as a guy with a PADI diving certificate – much despised by the divers in this novel – I can say I have dived with some scary characters who were hard-core military-trained professional divers, and yep, I am still traumatised by the experience and feeling like a weak softy in comparison.

Just to add a little extra weight to my recommendation of this book; I ended up in Hong Kong because I was writing TV Cop Shows and had a writing position on one that was set in Hong Kong. Knowing nothing about Hong Kong at the time, my "Asia's Finest" were angels from Planet Z with the moral authority to blow away the bad guys with the biggest pump action bananas known to mankind. They said things like, "Hey, I gotta bad feeling about this!" And then went crazy with a hail of gunshot yelling, "Now it's personal!" Happily, the author of this fiction never once says such a thing, and probably never ever contemplated slipping in the typical cop show line, "Sit down, I want a word with you!" The Handover Murders may be genre fiction right down to the romantic interest and final confrontational reveals, but it is classy genre fiction eschewing clichéd dialogue and unrealistic characterisation.

The author picks up on something few people outside of Hong Kong understand about the place: there are few barriers between the higher-ups and the lower-downs, and consequently the gossip mill churns freely. Nobody really believes official pronouncements because they think they know the real story. And, this being Hong Kong, everyone's nose follows the smell of the money. Corruption is easily slipped into as friends and favours in a society built upon refugees, fugitives, chancers, and the odd F.I.L.T.H. (Failed in London, Trying Hong Kong) component, can in a moment of distraction place anyone in a compromised position. A few of Hong Kong's political and corporate élite currently under lock and key will testify to this.

I do hope the author, Damon Rose, is writing a series featuring Alex Wu Torrence, Triad Liaison officer for the Manchester Metropolitan Police force, as I am certain that there is a TV Production Company somewhere looking for the next Detective show. And I am sure that after a chat with the amiable Black Tooth and a quick special handshake, something could be sorted!

Fans of Detective fiction are in for a treat with this well written, classically structured, and superbly characterised narrative. There are few novels that one can say are hard to put down, but this is one of them.

Lawrence Gray
Founding President, Hong Kong Writers' Circle
Author of the novels, *Cop Show Heaven*
        and A*dam's Franchise*
and the short story collection, *Odds and Sods*.

To Lindsey & Chris

PART ONE

CHAPTER ONE

January 1997

The fasten seatbelt sign pinged into life as Alex looked out of the window of the Cathay Pacific 747 flight, CX252 Manchester to Hong Kong. With the sun just rising over the South China Sea, he could make out the New Territories coastline and the outlying islands near to his boyhood home of Sai Kung.

Detective Alex Wu Torrence, Triad Liaison officer for the Manchester Metropolitan Police force, had received a call at his desk late the previous day. "Torrence, got a case for you in Honkers, you'll need to catch the red eye tonight," Chief Inspector McGregor barked down the line.

Alex sipped a mouthful of coffee. "What's the story?"

"A British construction worker has been found dead at the new airport overnight. Seems like he's pissed off a triad by the looks of it, they've got a suspect in custody. Should be a straightforward bag it and tag it." McGregor paused. "Get your bag packed, I'll send somebody down with tickets and details as soon as possible."

Clunk. The line went dead. McGregor wasn't known for his small talk and Alex didn't expect any. In the eight years since he had been seconded to the Hong Kong Liaison department, he had made the routine trip to Hong Kong numerous times and actually had a ready-packed shoulder bag under his desk. *Bag it and tag it* had become synonymous in the office with the four or five-day return trips to Hong Kong to repatriate deceased British nationals to the UK. With less than six months left to the Handover of the British colony to communist China and over 30,000 Brits still there, these visits seemed to be coming more and more frequently.

The jumbo arched right as it went into its holding pattern before the scheduled landing. In the distance, Alex could only just see the nearly finished airport bridge in front of the massive landfill that was soon to be Chek Lap Kok, Hong Kong's new airport, and currently the biggest construction site on the planet. It was viewed by many as Britain's 'last hurrah' before waving goodbye to Hong Kong and giving the keys back to China. With billions of Hong Kong dollars flowing into the project and the deadline of June 30th, 1997 looming, the pressure was on both Britain and China to have the airport completed on time. With thousands of site workers from all over the world in a relatively small place this was also bringing in problems on the ground; violence, triads, theft, and in the case of *Mr Bag it and Tag it*, murder.

A copy of a fax and a one-way ticket arrived on Alex's desk late afternoon. His colleagues viewed the Hong Kong trips as a bind, but being half Chinese, half British, and with his Chinese mum still living in Hong Kong, Alex actually looked forward to these trips and subsequently had become McGregor's first port of call when the need arose. The fax headed 'Royal Hong Kong Constabulary' gave few details other than the victim: Darren Meakin, 28 years of age, from Salford, Manchester. The approximate time of death being somewhere between six pm and midnight on Saturday 13th of January, and the details of the suspect in custody: eighteen-year-old Kwan Yo Hang.

The two pretty, slightly-built Cathay Pacific stewardesses started to make one last walk down the aisle before landing, repeating in their sing-song voices, "Seats upright, tables, thank you, seatbelts," switching between flawless Cantonese and patchy English depending on the passenger in front of them. Six-foot-tall, dark haired, mixed race and Hong Kong born, Alex often found Chinese people usually plumped for English when in doubt about his ethnicity but in truth either language was fine with him having been brought up by a stubborn Scottish policeman and an equally stubborn Hong Kong Chinese mother, Lily. No doubt at this very moment she would be cleaning her home from top to toe and complaining to anybody within hearing distance that her Detective Inspector son, who is doing very, very well, and will probably be getting another promotion soon, will be arriving on very, very important business and probably won't have much time to visit his old '*ma ma*' and eat some proper noodles, not like that rubbish he eats in England when he's not working doing his very, very important work, but does he tell me long time before? No, the day before...

His late father, former Superintendent Jock Torrence, had passed away seven years earlier in dreary England and not in his beloved Hong Kong, the place he and Lily had previously called home for over forty years.

Alex smiled inwardly and made a mental note to call his mum once he had completed his initial briefing. He then looked out of the window for one last time as the famous red and white Kowloon checkerboard came into view, signalling the pilot to bank right and head over Kowloon City, almost touching the skyscraper tops, before lining up on trusty old airport Kai Tak, coming into view with its runway protruding out to sea. Thousands of pilots over the years had been 'dining out' on 'the hardest landing on earth' and even the most seasoned travellers, Alex included, always seemed to marvel at this unique landing into this unique city. Of course, everyone knew Hong Kong had outgrown Kai Tak, but Alex for one would miss the old girl when she was gone.

On arrival, Alex was quietly ushered off the plane before the other passengers and as usual the two things to hit him were the humidity and the smell. The *nullah* is a stagnant stretch of water between the runway and Kowloon Bay. Alex remembered one of his Dad's bar stories about the American comedian Bob Hope landing in Hong Kong and asking what that smell was.

"It's shit," someone replied.

"Yeah, I know that, but what have they done to it?!"

Just landing in Hong Kong stirred memories both good and bad for Alex, so much so that he hardly noticed the two plain clothes detectives, one Chinese and one European, standing by the unmarked police car, near the terminal building. Normally he would have been collected by uniformed officers but today it looked like he was getting the red-carpet treatment. He briefly shook hands with the detectives, both of whom he knew from previous visits; Detective Inspector Jackie Shuen and Senior Inspector Karl Roberts. Alex had worked quite extensively with Shuen on several cases and found him to be a good, reliable and thorough detective. He didn't know Roberts as well as he did Shuen, but looking at him once more, Alex couldn't help thinking that he couldn't look more like an expatriate copper if he tried; slightly overweight, sunburnt neck and the tell-tale red cheeks of a drinker, probably in one of Hong Kong's numerous expat clubs.

Shuen went straight into work mode as they got into the air-conditioned vehicle. "We're going straight to headquarters now. The suspect in custody is being interviewed as soon as we get there."

Roberts turned to face Alex and added, "Looks like an open and shut case. He admitted it to the arresting officers overnight."

This didn't surprise Alex as Hong Kong's "finest" in uniform had a reputation for being able to get criminals to admit to pretty much anything given enough time and a locked room. Built on the British model, the Royal Hong Kong Police (soon to be just plain Hong Kong Police) had a reputation of being Asia's finest when it came to crime prevention, but some lower ranking officers were known to have a culture of heavy handedness. With the Handover less than six months away, one of the many unanswerable questions was, would the overall discipline and structure of the police force remain intact once China took over? The mantra coming from Beijing was, "No change for fifty years", but Alex certainly couldn't see foreign officers like Karl Roberts, with their expat perks taken away and little or no Cantonese, hanging around for long after June 30th, 1997.

Shuen looked at Alex in the rear-view mirror. "The accused is a low-ranking member of the Sun Yee On Triad and was on the building site taking a dry salary."

Alex knew that "taking a dry salary" was a widespread practice on construction sites where a triad gang would offer "services" to contractors in return for a percentage or a bung. In reality, this meant that the contractor's machines and belongings wouldn't get smashed up or stolen. The triads sometimes placed a foot soldier or two on site as well, to check that other triad gangs didn't encroach on their territory. Shuen continued. "It seems like the victim had been drinking in the city and was murdered on returning to the building site on Saturday evening."

"Why was he on a building site on a Saturday evening?" asked Alex.

Shuen replied, "The airport is way behind schedule so more and more contractors are housing their workers on site."

"Fucking gulags," Roberts interrupted. "Two thousand hairy arsed gweilos living in glorified sheds."

Alex noticed Shuen's eyebrows raised slightly in the rear-view mirror. Gweilo is old Cantonese slang for describing foreigners, meaning white ghost or white devil. Educated Chinese generally wouldn't use that word but some expats sometimes referred to each other in that manner.

Roberts continued. "Looks like your man came back full of beer and bravado and chop-chop, goodnight Vienna."

"The victim had chop marks to his arms and his throat," added Shuen. "We'll be visiting the morgue after the interview with Kwan."

Lovely, thought Alex, just what you need after a twelve-hour flight and an airline breakfast. He noticed how Shuen seemed to be dealing in facts and Roberts mostly in opinions and wondered what these two thought of how the other operated. Even at this early hour Hong Kong was starting to warm up, and he noticed beads of perspiration on the back of Karl Roberts's sun-burnt neck.

"Rugby," Roberts touched his neck self-consciously.

Alex didn't realise he had been staring, must be the jet lag, he thought.

"Played for nearly an hour Saturday morning before all this kicked off. Didn't think to put sun-cream on in bloody January, did I?"

Rugby, gin and tonics at the club, expat salaries and private schooling would all be changing at the stroke of mid-night in June. Alex knew, from talking to other officers on previous visits, that all foreigners had been offered local contracts after the Handover, but the perks would certainly be fewer. Jackie Shuen, he guessed, would carry on the same as before, or indeed fill the ample boots of a fleeing *gweilo.*

The car pulled up at the grand colonial Central Headquarters and the three detectives got out into the humid chaos that is Central District.

"Just one more thing," said Roberts. "The chief wants to talk to you at some point today."

Wow, I really am getting the red-carpet treatment, thought Alex.

*

Alex and Karl Roberts were already in the darkened room behind the one-way mirror, Styrofoam coffee cups in hand, when the alleged murderer was led into the room by a uniformed officer, followed by a sharp-suited lawyer. Hand cuffs removed and seated, Alex got his first look at the accused, slouched in the standard plastic chair used by police the world over. Kwan Yo Hang was doing the standard 'not bothered' act of the average juvenile defendant. Instinctively Alex looked straight at Kwan's arm seeing immediately the tell-tale tattooed wings of the phoenix poking out from under his t-shirt sleeve. Hidden from view would be the dragon's head – the sign of the Sun Yee On, one of the leading Hong Kong triad groups.

Of the fifty or so triad groups in Hong Kong, the Sun Yee On was an established gang in the top five or so in terms of membership and revenue. They had also recently moved overseas to Canada, Australia and on to Alex's patch in the northwest of England – specifically Manchester. Traditionally the Sun Yee On had been involved in gambling, prostitution and counterfeiting, but with so many rich pickings to be had at the Chek Lap Kok airport project, Sun Yee On had moved into the protection and extortion rackets also.

Kwan stirred in the interview room and in Cantonese he addressed his lawyer. "What's happening, brother?"

"Shsssh..." replied the lawyer whilst gesturing at the mirror.

By addressing him as brother this confirmed what Alex already knew; the lawyer was either a member or on the payroll of the Sun Yee On. By the nineties larger triad groups were beginning to diversify and behave more and more like businesses, with lawyers, accountants, stock brokers, estate agents and numerous other professionals at their disposal. In response, the outgoing Hong Kong Government, the police, and organised crime bureaus worldwide, were now having to step up their game.

As the lawyer began to pick something out of his teeth nonchalantly, Jackie Shuen and an attractive female officer entered the room. Pressing the tape recorder Shuen said, "Detective Inspector Jackie Shuen and Senior Constable Heidi Lim attending."

The two officers sat down facing the accused. The lawyer continued to look uninterested and Kwan flicked his fringe nervously, his tough veneer evaporating rapidly.

"How old are you Kwan?" Shuen began.

"Eighteen," he replied.

"Been in trouble much before?"

"I don't talk to turtles!" countered Kwan aggressively, his eyes darting from side to side nervously.

"Turtle" is a common nickname for the police used by triads, implying they only put their heads out of their shells when they want to. The lawyer whispered something in Kwan's ear.

"I've done a few things," said Kwan.

Alex and Roberts behind the glass had a copy of his record in front of them, juvenile crime, mostly theft.

"What's the longest you've been inside for so far?"

"Three months la, easy like a holiday with my brothers," replied Kwan.

"Murder, you'll be looking at twenty years, maybe more for killing a foreigner," Heidi Lim spoke for the first time.

Jackie Shuen let out an exaggerated whistle. "Twenty years is a long time for a young 49er. Long, long holiday."

"49er" being the name for the lowest ranking triad, Alex knew that Shuen would normally have a job on his hands making a scared young triad break his brotherhood vow of silence, especially since his lawyer seemed in on the act. To make things easier, whenever possible the police always tried to get a court appointed lawyer, but for whatever reason somebody further up the Sun Yee On ladder had sent for this lawyer and his very expensive suit.

The lawyer spoke for the first time. "It is our intention that my client will co-operate fully with the police on this matter."

Roberts whispered to Alex. "He'll be singing like a fucking canary in ten minutes." Senior Inspector Roberts obviously did know a bit of Cantonese.

Something stirred in Alex's antennae; he'd seen lower-ranking triads sit for hours, even days at a time, not saying a single word, and Kwan was going to fully co-operate with hardly any coercion whatsoever. His two Chinese counterparts sat pokerfaced on the other side of the glass.

"Go on," said Shuen.

"It is our intention to co-operate fully with investigation and we have prepared a written statement signed by Mr Kwan."

"Bingo," whispered Roberts slightly too loudly.

"For the purpose of this interview..." Shuen addressed the tape recorder. "...My colleague Senior Constable Lim shall read out the statement."

Lim cleared her throat. "On the evening of Saturday the 13th of January 1997, I, Kwan Yo Hang, Hong Kong Identity Number C688688E, was working as a security guard at the Chek Lap Kok construction site. At around 10pm I came across a foreigner whom I now know to be Darren Meakin from England, stealing some copper wiring from behind a container. I shouted at him to stop and he replied in English, something I didn't understand. The foreigner then started to attack me. I had a kitchen chopper nearby as I had been preparing vegetables earlier, and I hit him twice on the right arm with the chopper but he continued to fight, so I went to strike his other arm. I missed and cut his throat by mistake, I then fled the scene. I did not mean to kill him, it was self-defence. This statement is true and correct. Signed, Kwan Yo Hang."

"Do you agree with this statement?" Shuen asked.

Kwan crossed his arms sullenly, his lawyer again whispered in his ear.

"Yes, it's true," replied Kwan.

"Where did he attack you?" Shuen asked.

"On the building site," replied Kwan.

"Where on your body, Kwan?"

"Oh, he punched me on the head, here." Kwan pointed to his temple.

"Was he a big man, the foreigner?" Shuen asked.

"Yeah, normal fat gweilo," shrugged Kwan.

"For the record..." interjected Lim, "the deceased was six foot two and weighed approximately sixteen stone."

"How much do you weigh, Kwan?"

The lawyer interrupted. "This is not relevant...."

Shuen ignored him completely and looked directly at Kwan. "What do you weigh, Kwan? Eight, nine stone tops, five foot nothing? And yet you say this sixteen stone builder punched you and fewer than forty-eight hours later, you sit here and don't have a mark on you? You're lying!"

Kwan crossed his arms once more, sullenly. Alex knew this to be a good move on Shuen's part, by commenting on any adolescent's manhood this was likely to provoke some sort of response.

"It's true," muttered Kwan.

"What's true?"

"It's true, the statement is true," repeated Kwan.

"You want us to believe that an eighteen-year-old boy overpowered a grown man twice his size and killed him with three blows. You're not strong enough!" Shuen said.

"Fuck you, turtle."

Heidi Lim asked calmly. "Where's the weapon, Kwan?"

"Eh?"

She repeated. "Where's the chopper, what did you do with the weapon?"

The lawyer whispered in his ear once more.

Kwan paused. "It's in the water, it was near to the sea. I threw it in the water."

Behind the screen, Roberts stirred and whispered something to a uniformed officer who walked away swiftly. Alex assumed, rightly, that the police divers had been called out by Roberts.

"Tell me about the copper-wiring, Kwan," asked Shuen.

"The gweilo, the fat gweilo, he was stealing it. I chopped him, he deserved it, that statement is true."

Thou doth protest too much, thought Alex in the darkness.

"How was he carrying it?" Shuen continued.

The lawyer interrupted. "Is this really relevant?"

Again, Shuen looked directly at Kwan and ignored his lawyer. "How was he carrying it, Kwan?"

The young boy looked confused.

"It's a simple question, Kwan, the big foreigner that you killed single-handedly, how was he carrying this hundred kilo reel of wiring that you hadn't mentioned until today!"

"I can't remember," said Kwan.

"My client is obviously in a state of distress," said the lawyer.

"You can't remember," carried on Shuen, "because it never happened, he wasn't stealing the wire, even a sixteen-stone man couldn't possibly carry that weight. You're lying, Kwan."

The boy slapped the desk. "Enough...."

"Why don't you tell us what really happened, Kwan?" Shuen asked calmly.

"My client stands by his statement," said the lawyer.

"You need to help yourself here. Tell us what really happened, Kwan!"

Kwan looked at the floor.

"My client stands by his statement," repeated the lawyer.

"Start from the beginning Kwan. Were you on your own?" continued Shuen.

"Finished, no more talking to the turtle," cried Kwan in a visibly distressed state.

The lawyer looked directly at Shuen. "My client stands by his statement and will be making no further comment."

Shuen lowered the paper onto the table, paused and addressed the recorder, "Interview adjourned."

*

In the antiquated colonial corridor five minutes later, Alex stood aside as Roberts addressed the two Chinese officers, Shuen and Lim. "OK, so we've got an eighteen-year-old triad with form, a written *and* spoken confession. We just need the forensics and the weapon and we should be able to wrap this one up."

Alex spoke. "Can we get a stooge in the cells with him tonight?"

"What for?" replied Roberts.

"He's obviously holding something back and is under the thumb of his lawyer. Maybe he'll spill something else to an undercover?"

Roberts looked slightly irritated, "Such as?"

"I don't know, he's obviously scared stiff but something doesn't add up," said Alex. "Maybe he had an accomplice, maybe it was him stealing the wire, I'm not sure. But either way the Sun Yee On hierarchy certainly don't want their 49ers knocking off foreign workers. It's bad for business."

"I can put one of the constables in with him tonight in the bugged cell," offered Jackie Shuen

Alex added, "It might just tie up a few loose ends."

"I'll run it by the Chief, he wants an update anyway," said Roberts grudgingly. "In the meantime; Torrence, Shuen, you get down to the morgue and hurry them up. Lim, get a written transcript of the interview straight away." Roberts barely acknowledged the young female detective as he gave out the orders while the other two detectives entered the nearest lift. Looking at his reflection in the lift doors, Alex was conscious that he hadn't eaten, slept or washed in a considerably long time, but the adrenalin of the chase seemed to be kicking in. He was glad of some time alone to gauge Jackie Shuen's thoughts also.

"What do you reckon, Jackie?" Alex asked.

"I'm not sure," replied Shuen slightly lost in thought. He continued. "We'll see what they say at the morgue and then I'd like to run out to the new airport for another look before it gets dark. Are you alert enough or is the jet-lag kicking in yet?"

Alex liked Shuen. He'd met dozens of officers in the past in both the UK and Hong Kong who just wanted a closed case; Jackie Shuen was different, like him. He wanted to dig deep and get to the bottom of things.

"I think I'll survive, although a coffee and a sandwich wouldn't go amiss," said Alex.

"Sandwich!" tutted Shuen. "I'll get us some fish-balls after we've seen the body."

The lift doors opened and the two men made the brief walk to the Hong Kong Mortuary in the adjourning building. On arrival, they were quickly robed and masked into the standard green scrubs by an assistant. They were then met by a slightly-built bespectacled man.

"Dr Rufus Chan, Director of Pathology," said the man in English, not offering his latex gloved hand.

Shuen replied. "This is Detective Alex Wu Torrence; he is the Triad Liaison Officer from Manchester, England."

Chan nodded. "Through here gentlemen..." Chan pushed the two swing doors with his shoulder and the three men entered the artificially-lit pathology room.

Darren Meakin, deceased, lay on the metallic mortuary trolley with his upper body bare and his lower half covered by a crisp white sheet.

Other than the victim's injuries, Alex's first impression of him was that he would not have looked out of place on a deckchair on Blackpool beach. Caucasian, shaven-headed with a goatee beard, random cheap tattoos, t-shirt marks leaving brown forearms and calloused working-man's hands.

"What was his job on site?" Alex asked no-one in particular.

Shuen replied. "What do you call the man who melts metal together?"

"A welder," replied Alex. "Do they make good money here?"

"Around thirty to forty thousand Hong Kong dollars each month, which is about three to four thousand of your British pounds. I'd say this is extremely good money. More than a detective, that's for sure," said Shuen.

"More than a pathologist," added Chan with a raised eyebrow above his surgical mask. He coughed and pointed at the victim's skull, ignoring the slit throat and arm wounds. "The cause of death was a blunt instrument to the parietal B part of the skull above the right ear. Look here." Chan pointed to an indentation on Darren Meakin's thinning shaved head.

Shuen asked, "Could it be the blunt side of a chopper?"

The chopper had been the triad weapon of choice for decades. Used domestically to chop and dice vegetables, the chopper takes on a different role in the hands of a triad.

"Doubtful," said Chan. "If it was it would have had to be a very large chopper. The width of this indentation is 1.6cm and is angular, like a corner. I estimate a standard kitchen chopper to be no more than one cm wide." Chan re-iterated his point by putting his little finger into the groove.

"Two more things," he continued. "Number one, if it was a chopper even the blunt side would almost certainly break the skin because of the sharp 90-degree angle on the corner. I think whatever caused this was slightly rounded."

"Like what?" they asked in unison.

"I don't know. I've never seen an impact like this before," continued Chan.

"Could he have fallen on something, like a kerbstone? We know he had been drinking," Alex suggested.

Chan paused and thought for a second. "Again, this is doubtful. The injury was sustained on the top to the top/rear of the skull. If he had fallen, for example, the impact would normally be completely to the back or to the side. From this trajectory, my theory is that he was struck with great force by an object to the top of the head from behind."

Shuen and Alex's eyes met across the table.

"How tall was the victim exactly, Mr Chan?" Alex asked.

"Six foot two *exactly*," replied Chan

"And Kwan Yo Hang is around five foot four," mused Alex aloud. "And the second thing, Mr Chan?"

"Sorry?"

"The second thing you mentioned, regarding the weapon?"

"Yes, the second thing. It's not entirely to do with the autopsy or the weapon itself but...the victim was a foreigner."

"And?" Alex asked.

"Like I said it's not exactly in my remit as a pathologist, but from experience I've only ever seen one expatriate chopped to death in the last ten years. And the perpetrator of that crime was out of his mind on drugs; cough medicine would you believe..."

Alex did believe it, as he knew the case well from 1991; the "Blue Pool Road Murder". Such was the rarity of a gweilo getting chopped in Hong Kong; they had studied the case extensively during police training.

Shuen broke the silence. "But the victim does have chop marks does he not?"

"In my opinion, no," countered Chan.

Chan then placed his gloved hand on the victim's throat and opened the wound slightly. "Look closely gentlemen, the skin here is jagged and lacerated...."

At this point, Alex was beginning to think that the fish-balls later would not be such a great idea.

Chan continued. "Generally, a chop wound is clean and the impact direct or semi-direct. This wound is from the victim's left to right; you can tell by the depth and angle, also note the serrated edges with the crowns roughly half a millimetre apart at the right side of the wound...."

"Which means?" Shuen asked.

"Which means," continued Chan. "That this wound wasn't made by a chopper, but by a knife or a saw of some sort, with a fine serrated edge. Furthermore, gentlemen, as I said before, the cause of death was almost certainly the blunt object to the head – I believe the lack of blood on the victim's clothes proves that he was either dead or very close to death when his throat was slit, with the time of death between 19.00 to 22.00 hours."

The words and their implications hung in the air momentarily before Chan, who was now getting into his stride, continued. "Now here is the really interesting part; look at the two cuts on the victim's upper right arm."

The pathologist tapped each wound as if to re-enforce his point. "These two wounds were inflicted minutes after the heart had already stopped. There was virtually no blood here, but again look closely; see the indentations point five of a millimetre apart again, but this time inflicted by a direct impact rather than a slicing motion."

"So, let me get this straight and in the correct timeframe," said Alex. "Darren Meakin here was hit on the head by a blunt object from above and slightly to the rear with a single fatal blow. He then had his throat slit with a saw-type blade whilst he was dead or nearly dead."

Alex collected his thoughts and made a chopping motion with his hand. "And then minutes later, the murderer (or murderers) took the same saw or knife and chopped his arm twice. This doesn't make sense."

Shuen asked Alex, "You obviously understand the normal significance of the chops to the arm?"

Alex, like any other police officer involved in Hong Kong crime, knew that a chop mark to the arm, hand or any extremity was either a warning delivered from one triad to another, or occasionally delivered by one of your triad "brothers" as a badge of honour; not dissimilar to the Japanese yakuza's chopping off of digits. Indeed, younger triad members possibly in need of recognition opted for vests rather than t-shirts to show off their war wounds.

Alex nodded the affirmative but still continued to think out loud. "Darren here almost certainly wouldn't know the reason for chop-marks on the arm and besides, we now know he was dead when it was delivered, so what was the point?"

"I'm not sure," mused Shuen, "but this is very strange."

CHAPTER TWO

Wednesday, November 16th 1941

Lily stretched and yawned as she pulled up a chair to the breakfast table. "Good morning, Father; good morning, mother."

"Good morning, my little Water-Lily," smiled her father.

"Good morning, Silly Lily!" said her sister Ah-Lam, good-naturedly.

Her mother simply nodded.

Lily had always been called Lily from an early age, as it was a simple transition from her Chinese name of Li Lai. An American business associate of her father's had once commented to her father that Li-Lai was a beautiful little "Water Lily", and the name had stuck long before her christening. Ah-Lam (or Helen, as the nuns had christened her) still tended to be called Ah-Lam, her Chinese name, as all the family had trouble pronouncing the letter H and it came out sounding more like Alan, the English boy's name.

Lin Lin, the family amah, placed a plate of fried eggs and toast in front of Lily with her right hand, whilst clipping the back of Ah-Lam's with the other.

"Be respectful to little sister," she barked. Lin Lin almost certainly wouldn't have understood the English or the reference, but the tone of Ah-Lam's voice probably decided the matter.

Ah-Lam lowered her head whilst smiling, "Sorry, auntie."

The line between servant and family member had blurred over the years, and in fact it had been Lin Lin who had been both girls' wet nurse, their mother had never in fact wiped clean, held or nursed either of her daughters; perhaps seeing not delivering a son as a failure on her part. Their father, on the other hand, with his fine three-piece suits and western values and ideas, had fallen head over heels with each of his princesses from the moment they were born and thanked Lord Buddha, Confucius, and the little baby Jesus for his blessings.

"Father, when can we go kite-flying again?" Lily asked, forking a piece of egg into her mouth.

Her father lowered his *South China Morning Post*. "I have to take a business trip to Macau for a few days. I promise to take you both when I return."

Jiangou Wu, the girls' father, was a self-made man; the classic rags-to-riches story, from a teenager arriving in Hong Kong from China with just the clothes on his back – to one of Hong Kong's most successful traders.

The family driver, Mr Chan, beeped his horn outside. "I have to rush or I'll miss the boat from Tsim Sha Tsui," said their father, kissing both daughters on their foreheads.

On the breakfast table, the upturned newspaper headline read, "Japan takes further Chinese Territory."

As their father pulled on his jacket and headed out through the patio doors into the beautiful-smelling rose-garden, neither girl could have known this was the last time they would ever see their father.

*

The lunchtime bell rang out and one of Corporal Jack Torrence's chums slapped him on his bare back.

"Come on Jock, grubs up!"

The 2nd Battalion Royal Scots and the Royal Rifles of Canada regiments were fortifying the existing 'Gin Drinkers line', a 15-mile defensive line based on France's Maginot Line from World War I. The Scots and the Canadians had arrived in Hong Kong three weeks earlier, and had immediately been given orders to run additional barbed wire fencing four feet to the north of the trench. It was said that, should the Japanese be foolish enough to invade the New Territories of Hong Kong over land, the line would hold for up to six months or at least until re-enforcements could arrive from Singapore or Malaya.

It was back-breaking work, not helped by the heat, humidity and mosquitoes, so the lunch-time bell and the chance for a bit of shade were always received with great cheer. The normal cries of "not rice again" were said in jest and had become part of the daily routine and general bonhomie. The first week had been a struggle between some of the Scots and Canadians even to understand each other, but some middle ground had been reached, mainly by the Scots slowing down their speech patterns, miming words, and as a last resort writing the words in the dirt when needed. Spirits were high, even with the clouds of war hanging over them, and a belief that the Japanese wouldn't waste resources on Hong Kong at present as they were bogged down in mainland China, mainly due to the courage and tenacity of the Chinese defence forces.

One of the Canadians asked in passing, "Any word from home yet, Jock?"

"No," replied Jock. "We haven't had any letters since Singapore."

"No news is good news, buddy," said the man.

Jock had really taken to the openness of the Canadians and their general good nature, particularly the officers, who seemed content to leave them to their own devices, which was a blessing especially when compared to their rather staid British counterparts. The Canadians had arrived straight from Newfoundland and were struggling with the heat, which was a novelty for the Scots who were more acclimatised after four months in Singapore. Neither group of soldiers had engaged in any combat action as yet.

Jock had also taken a liking to the Asian food on offer. Some of his fellow Glaswegians had refused even to try rice with meat and vegetables back in Singapore at first, but Jock had wolfed down everything in front of him from day one and had even mastered chopsticks after a lesson from one of the chaps in the Chinese Regiment. He'd also been trying his hand at a few Cantonese words and phrases.

For a young mechanic from the shipyards of Govan, Scotland, Singapore and Hong Kong were an exotic adventure and Jock devoured every experience possible whilst writing daily to his sisters and father back in Glasgow about the new and amazing things he was encountering. Even the monotonous hammering of fence-posts into the ground gave Jock a sense of well-being; the fresh air, the sun on his back and the camaraderie lifting his spirits so much that the young man barely had time to be homesick for cold, grey, dreary Scotland.

The group had found a cool pond and waterfall the previous day. One of the Scots put down his rice-bowl. "Who's for a swim?"

"Aye, go on then," said Jock. "There might be a wee mermaid in there!"

*

Friday, November 28th 1941

Lily sat on the wall outside the Saint Benedict School for Girls, kicking her heels and facing the warm autumn sun. Lin Lin had warned her about getting brown and looking common like some "Hakka girl" but Lily couldn't resist possibly the last of the year's warm rays. She knew Ah-Lam would be five or ten minutes behind her as she was on book-monitor duties all week.

Lily had in her hand a copy of *Pride and Prejudice* by Jane Austin, which her favourite teacher, Miss Francis had lent her, Miss Francis's "very own personal copy" in fact; *and* for a whole two weeks, as a reward for coming first in the English exam. Lily beamed inwardly with pride and couldn't wait to tell Father if he was home already. Miss Francis was quite possibly the greatest person in the whole wide world, other than Father obviously, certainly the greatest *lady* in the whole wide world that was for sure. Miss Francis seemed to know everything about everything, and seemed to glide around the classroom effortlessly rather than walk. If Lily could wish to be anything in the future it would be to be like Miss Francis, with her grace, beauty and her sing-song voice.

Ah-Lam sneaked up behind Lily and pulled her pigtails. "Boo! Got you!"

The two girls clutched their books to their chests and set off at a swift pace towards Dunbar Road and home, sharing the day's gossip as they went. They were both hoping that father had returned after nearly two weeks' business as he always brought the girls presents such as silk, purses or trinkets. Even if he was away only for one or two days he always brought a souvenir for his two princesses.

Mother had said that because of the fighting with the Japanese in China, communications were terrible at present and the family had heard nothing from their father all the time he had been away. Normally one of the boys from Father's Hung Hom trading office would deliver a message or a telegram every two or three days with basic news, a greeting or a return date, but nothing had arrived from this trip as yet. Lin Lin told the girls not to worry, as their father was quite possibly the cleverest man in Hong Kong, and would be sending a message or simply turning up on the doorstep any day now with yet more silk dresses and more tailor-made Western suits for her to wash and iron. Their mother was more reserved and carried a worried expression. Unbeknown to the girls, father had given hand-written instructions to their mother in case the fighting escalated as far as the border or Hong Kong itself and Father couldn't return from Macau. Privately, Jiangou Wu was extremely concerned that Japan had completely surrounded Hong Kong by taking Canton; and whilst he was doing business in the Portuguese enclave of Macau, he was also looking at all available options to evacuate his family should Japan attack Hong Kong. His instructions included the code for the safe at home and the one in the office, bank account details, and names and addresses of people to contact if they needed help. Illiterate Lin Lin had also received clear concise verbal instructions on who to see and where to go should the need arise and should madam and the girls need assistance. Jiangou Wu was not a foolhardy man and neither did he wish to alarm his wife unnecessarily, but in these uncertain times every base needed to be covered, as the Americans say.

The girls passed the cricket pitch on Shek Ku Street and turned into Dunbar Road with their beautiful house being the second on the right. The gates were open and Chan the driver was polishing the black Mercedes-Benz 770 whilst wearing an apron over his driver's uniform. Chan was a man of few words and hardly ever spoke to the girls, but had been in the service of the family since before either of them was born. The house was truly beautiful and the Indian summer had afforded the garden late roses and chrysanthemums, giving it both colour and fragrance. Number 2a Dunbar Road should have been called number 4 Dunbar Road by rights, but Father, like a lot of Chinese men, was extremely superstitious about the number "four", which in Chinese sounds like the word for "death". Father had enrolled the girls at St Benedict's Catholic School for Girls from an early age and had even visited Church with the girls on numerous occasions, where he professed to liking the English singing and the stories. One time Father brought a large porcelain crucifix from an antiques dealer in Shanghai which had a "handsome Jesus" with a white robe and "not the horrible one with the rose thorns and the blood". The crucifix took pride of place in the lobby of number 2a Dunbar Road next to a green Jade Buddha and a Tin Hau statue, in front of which Father placed fresh garlands and offerings every morning.

Lily told her father once that Miss Francis had said that there was only one true God. Her Father had paused and then replied, "Religion is like horse-racing, the more horses you bet on, the more chances you have of winning."

Lily and Ah-Lam automatically crossed themselves in front of the crucifix and instinctively headed towards the kitchen where they knew Lin Lin would be waiting with a glass of milk and a biscuit. Lin Lin had to adhere to her boss's instructions on diet, and served some western foods as well as cow's milk daily, which he said would give them strong teeth and bones but Lin Lin had told the girls privately it would make their sweat smell sour, like foreigners.

"Wash hands, eat snack, do homework," said Lin Lin as she did every day, adding, "and don't make a mess for me to clean!"

"Is Father back yet?" Ah-Lam asked, reaching for a biscuit.

"No, he's too busy in Macau, making money for ungrateful girls to eat biscuits with dirty hands," said Lin Lin.

Ah-Lam replied in English. "A simple no would suffice."

Lin Lin tapped Ah-Lam's knuckles with a wooden spoon. "Wash hands!"

Lily laughed as she ran her hands under the water. – Ah-Lam never seemed to learn that speaking English to Lin Lin invariably ended with a clout.

*

With the additional fortifications completed and deemed adequate by the "powers that be", Jock and his comrades essentially split half of the time on manoeuvres and training at the Sham Shui Po barracks in Kowloon and the other half on duty at various stations along Gin Drinkers Line. No Japanese had been spotted as yet, and the only action was the lengthy card games, or the occasional large snake or wild boar to liven things up.

The troops were usually given one or occasionally two evenings off a week, and most of Jock's colleagues then took the Star Ferry over to Hong Kong Island and the bars and brothels of Wanchai. Jock had reluctantly accompanied his friends one evening and had two beers before an older Chinese woman was deposited on his lap in a smoky, dimly-lit, flea-pit of a bar by his drunken colleagues.

"Go on Jock, have one on us. It's all paid for! You might get your bloody virgin head blown off next week!" shouted Ernie, one of his more drunken and exuberant chums.

More shouting and wolf whistles ensued until the young twenty-one-year-old, who was now blushing bright red, let the prostitute lead him through a pair of red drapes to an adjoining back room.

Someone shouted from the bar, "Hurry up Jock, I'm next!"

"Give me ten more dollars, Tommy," said the woman.

Jocks eyes grew accustomed to the dimly-lit room with a dank single bed in one corner. Jock was not a big drinker, and the two warm beers he had drunk previously had not summoned up enough Dutch courage to go through with this whole situation. If truth be told he wasn't 100% sure how the whole thing worked anyway, and he had never envisaged being in a position like this.

"Ten dollars!" she repeated, offering her outstretched hand.

Jock noticed the woman's yellow decaying teeth and the dark coldness in her eyes. He fumbled about in his green military-issue trousers and gave her the note. Two pictures rushed through his mind simultaneously; the talk on venereal disease given by his sergeant-major back in Singapore, and his father standing in the pulpit at their little Baptist Chapel back home in Glasgow. As an elder of the church, his father, Jack senior, who had never left even Scotland, had taken the pledge against drinking alcohol and had certainly never been in a situation remotely close to the one now facing Jack Junior. The woman started to undo his uniform jacket. Jock placed his hand on her bony manicured ones.

"Stop, please. I dinnae want this."

"I'm keeping the money. No refunds, Tommy!"

"Aye, keep the money, I dinnae want that either."

Jock turned to leave, but the woman stopped him.

"Wait five minutes, that is better," she said.

Jock sat down awkwardly on a plain wooden chair next to the bed. He still couldn't read any emotion in the heavily-made-up face of the woman. She walked over to the cabinet and took out a long thin pipe which she lit and inhaled in one swift motion. It smelt sweet and sickly to Jock, similar to the smell of the joss-sticks placed outside numerous bars and shops all up and down Lockhart Road where they currently were.

She said something that Jock didn't quite catch.

He said, "Pardon?"

"You a virgin?" she repeated, her mood suddenly seemingly happier.

"Aye, Aye, I guess I am," he said quietly lowering his head.

"That OK, Tommy. It good thing. Find good girl, not old woman like this."

Jock tried to interrupt but she raised her hand and sat on the bed next to him.

"You know how to do it?"

Jock didn't answer but shrugged.

"Ayah, let me tell you..."

And so, for the next four and a half minutes, the fully-clothed old prostitute explained in broken English what to do when his pee-pee got hard and where to put it, how babies were made and where they came from.

Jock thanked the woman awkwardly and returned to the bar to a chorus of cheers from his chums. He left twenty minutes later still a virgin but a little bit wiser. He never went back.

*

Tuesday 2nd December 1941

Miss Francis sat with her knees together, sitting upright and facing her class. She had just introduced Captain Penham-Smythe of the Hong Kong Volunteer Defence Corps (HKVDC for short), who was currently pacing up and down in front of the blackboard and the aforementioned Miss Francis with a riding-crop under one arm.

"Now girls, the Japanese, as we know, is a ghastly beast, erm, yes, quite ghastly..." Captain Penham-Smythe appeared to be addressing the far wall behind the girls' heads.

"Now as we know he is currently, ahh, erm, committing, yes committing, all sorts of devilish behaviour over the border in Canton, in Shanghai and in Taiwan etcetera, etcetera. Terrible, terrible state of affairs, simply dreadful....er....yes where was I? Anyway, as you know; the Prime Minister Winston Churchill has recently sent for the three Canadian Battalions, the Royal Scots Battalions, the Royal Indian Army Corps etcetera, etcetera to re-enforce his Majesty's Colony of Hong Kong...."

Captain Penham-Smythe paused as if to catch his thoughts and then continued, whilst now using his riding crop to re-enforce specific points.

"Now...er...as you know, the average Japanese is no match for his Majesty's fighting man and er..." Swish went his riding crop. "Er....yes, the average yellow peril is no match for His Majesty's fighting man...er...and as we know, and intelligence tells us...er...that a British soldier is equal to four Japanese..." Swish.

Lily was sitting in the fourth row. She wondered where exactly the Captain's horse was.

"And...er...where was I? Yes, in the unlikely, unlikely that is, event that the Nips did declare war, not that they ever would...er...er...now girls, that is, girls you see, young ladies...er and the Japanese...er..."

Lily noticed that the Captain was sweating and wondered if he was sick.

Miss Francis interrupted politely with a cough. "May I, Captain?"

Captain Penham-Smythe swished his riding crop once more and said, "Yes, over to er...Miss....er..."

"Miss Francis, Captain Penham-Smythe," said the teacher calmly and politely.

"Yes, I shall pass you over to Miss Francis," said the officer, as if he had suggested this in the first place.

"Now girls. As Captain Penham-Smythe has so kindly offered his time to explain certain aspects of the conflict to us here at St Benedict's...."

Miss Francis's voice seemed to flow like silk to the young Lily Wu and she was immediately attentive to every word of her heroine.

"...however as with Shanghai, Tai Pei and other Chinese cities, there is an outside chance that we may get attacked or even invaded if Japan were to declare war on Britain. Now as you may have read or heard, the Japanese are a ruthless race and have committed countless ungodly acts on civilians, women and children. Far too ghastly in fact to describe to a group of young ladies such as yourselves. However the Government in conjunction with the armed forces has drawn up a set of contingency plans should in fact atrocities take place inside our Colony. It is important that we share these with you, and you in turn, share these with your families and your servants."

The teacher then spent the next thirty minutes taking a point by point look at the pamphlet, *What to do in the Unlikely Event of Invasion*, which had been brought by the Captain to her class, writing key points on the black-board, such as; never engage the enemy, hide whenever possible, do not wear feminine or attractive dress, do not go out after dark, and other instructions.

Captain Penham-Smythe, for his part, sat quietly admiring the young attractive school teacher. He had another six schools to visit that week as well as his day job at the

Ministry, and wished he could take this fine filly with him. He wondered if she might be susceptible to the idea of tea at The Peninsula.

He smiled at the teacher and stroked his waxed moustache as she thanked him once more and ended the lesson with a short prayer and a polite round of applause for their guest. Yes, he thought, tea at the Peninsula would be just super.

For her part, Miss Penelope Francis looked at her beloved class and then at the army volunteer. God help us she thought, may God help us.

*

Thursday 4th December 1941

Jock had finished his mechanical engineering apprenticeship at the shipyard just before he had enlisted. Technically he shouldn't have been signed off until his twenty-first birthday but his bosses knew of his intention to enlist and gave him his papers whilst he was still only twenty. Shipbuilding, like coal mining and steel works, was seen as a reserved occupation and vital to the war effort, but Jock had made his mind up early on that he wanted to fight the Germans. He never envisaged being held upside down by his ankles in a Hong Kong trench trying to fix a diesel pump, however.

"Hurry up Jock, it'll be dark soon and we'll need the power for the lights! How else will I be able to see my winnings from cards tonight!" said Billy McCray, the man holding him by his ankles.

"Two minutes Billy, hold still will ye', it's the cam belt, it's slipping wi' all the humidity," said Jock.

Billy replied, "Och, it's probably nae' helping that you are sweating all over it, Jock!"

One hundred and fifty metres down-wind from the trench, hidden in a small Bauhinia bush, a heavily-camouflaged Sergeant Koji Nishimura from the 38th Imperial Japanese Infantry Division was watching and listening to the exchange, catching snippets of their talk. He wasn't sure however if it was English or not. He'd seen Charlie Chaplin in the cinema once in Nagoya but it was a silent movie. He wondered if Charlie Chaplin's hair was orange like the skinny white man holding the other soldier's legs.

Koji Nashimura had been checking for weak spots in the British defence line since the previous night and would report back to his commanding officer as soon as the sun set and it was dark enough to move again. He thought the best place for an attack would be near here in a place called, according to his map, Shing Mun, if indeed his superiors should decide to liberate the Chinese from these western oppressors. If he got to kill one of these white men he thought, he would cut off some orange hair to show his little brother when he got home to Japan.

*

Lily and Ah-Lam sat obediently in their father's reception room at his Hung Hom office. They could hear their mother raising her voice at Mr Lee, the office manager, through the glass partition.

"Hunan, Hunan! He was meant to be in Macau, why was he in China!?" shrieked mother.

Their father's secretary, Elsie Chan coughed and asked politely if the girls were sure they wouldn't like any tea. The girls declined and tried to listen whilst sitting impassively.

"He didn't want you to worry, Madam Wu. He had some business in Macau and then wanted to get to Hunan and then check on his family and complete some other business. Don't worry Madam, he will be home soon."

"Ayah, home soon, home soon? It's three weeks and we find out only today he is in China with Japanese invading more and more every day!" Mother started to cry.

"Hunan is in Chinese hands, Madam Wu. Of course, it's well north of Canton, but Mr Wu has very experienced guides with him. I'm sure he'll be home soon," added Mr Lee kindly.

Lily liked the scarlet lipstick Elsie Chan was wearing and her fashionable bob haircut. She might ask Father if she could get hers cut like that when he came home.

CHAPTER THREE

January 1997

Two brown paper bags containing takeaways and the customary coffees were on DI Shuen's desk by the time they returned. Heidi Lim stood up to greet them from an adjoining desk. "The car is out front. Detective Wu Torrence's overnight bag is with the driver. I thought you'd want to eat on the run."

"Thank you, Senior Constable Lim," said Shuen politely in formal Cantonese.

"Yes, thank you," added Alex.

"You speak Cantonese?" Lim enquired.

"Badly; if you ask my mum," half joked Alex.

Shuen interrupted with a raised fish-ball skewered to a cocktail stick. "Senior Constable Lim, please grab a camera, notepad and your coat."

Lim immediately got the notepad and camera from her top drawer. She had obviously been expecting this. Very efficient, thought Alex.

"I've arranged for the arresting officers to meet us on-site also, I hope that's OK," she added

"Absolutely. Excellent work," said Shuen.

"One other thing," continued Lim. "The Chief Inspector has gone with Senior Inspector Roberts to the new airport already."

Even Alex, who only visited just a few times a year, knew that Chief Inspector Mark Hayton had a reputation for a "hands-off" approach and a liking for his air-conditioned office.

She added, "I heard that Government House have been on the phone. They want this one solved and shelved as soon as possible."

Great, thought Alex. Politicians getting involved is just what we need.

Moments later the three officers were being driven through the Cross Harbour Tunnel to Kowloon side.

Shuen spoke. "We'll just miss rush-hour and the new bridge is now partly accessible so we should be able to get there with one or two hours' daylight remaining. I visited the site just after 1am this morning but it was dark when the forensics were there. Kwan had been arrested about an hour previously by uniformed officers."

"How exactly?" Alex asked.

"Apparently, he knocked on the door of a legitimate security firm and asked the guard to call the police. The guard didn't believe him at first but he insisted. By the time the police had arrived, so had the lawyer from this morning. They gave a statement to the effect that he had murdered Meakin and would offer details at the interview that you witnessed this morning. Kwan then slept apparently until he was briefed by his lawyer first thing this morning. Inspector Roberts felt there was no point in interrogating him until you arrived as he had confessed anyway."

Alex gave his mother a brief call from his Hong Kong mobile phone, shielding questions and advising her that he might be late tonight, before losing the phone signal as they went over the new bridge.

Heidi Lim smiled at Alex in the rear of the police car. "Your mother lives in Hong Kong and is expecting you, by the sound of it?"

"Yes, Sai Kung. I only really get to see her on these visits nowadays and it's usually pretty busy when I'm here on business. I should come for a holiday really," said Alex thoughtfully.

As the new airport came into view, the size of the reclaimed land was instantly impressive at ground level even by Hong Kong standards. Alex had read in one of the in-flight magazines that it was eventually going to be three and a half miles long by two and a half miles wide and the reclaiming of the land was being done partly by dynamiting existing small islands and levelling the ground off to make the runway, along with tons and tons of reclaimed rubble.

Having been waved through the barrier, the police car travelled a further five minutes over the soon-to-be-runway to the sea's edge. The crime scene was taped off and a uniformed officer stood guard whilst a handful of press milled around near what appeared to be a container. As they all got out of the car, Alex could see Roberts and Chief Inspector Mark Hayton walking and chatting near the water's edge as two police divers entered the water. Hayton, in full green Royal Hong Kong police uniform, beckoned them over. "Torrence, my boy, how are you? Good flight?" Chief Inspector Mark Hayton didn't wait for an answer. "I knew your father back in the day. Did I ever tell you that?"

The Chief Inspector had indeed told Alex that he had worked with his late father, Jock, on numerous occasions, the last time being at a rather drunken black-tie event at the Hong Kong Jockey Club.

"Bloody good officer was Jock. Old school, salt of the earth type. I was very sorry to hear of his passing."

"Thank you, Sir," replied Alex.

Alex distinctly remembered that the Chief Inspector's compliments weren't reciprocated by his late father. In his Scottish brogue, Jock had more than once referred to him as, "that pompous, effeminate public schoolboy gadgie."

"Anyway, onwards and upwards so to speak," continued Hayton. "I'm getting a bit of heat from Government House on this one; the airport is way behind schedule and the papers are full of doom and gloom stories with anything remotely connected to Chek Lap Kok. I've spoken to Inspector Roberts already but I'm going to have to talk to the press in a minute and they'll want an update. Inspector Shuen, what's the latest?"

"As you know we have the suspect in custody: an eighteen-year-old Sun Yee On member, Kwan Yo Hang. He confessed on site to the arresting officers last night and has issued a written confession also via his lawyer...but..."

Just then the detectives were interrupted by one of the divers' support crew. "Excuse me Sir," he said, addressing

Chief Inspector Hayton. "Sorry to interrupt, but we've found a weapon, Sir."

"That was quick, good job, let's see it then," replied Hayton, immediately turning his back on Shuen and walking towards the two police divers on the break wall, who were beginning to de-kit their diving gear.

As the group approached, one of the divers handed Jackie Shuen a stainless-steel chopper which he had placed in a zip-locked bag. Alex could hear the shutters of the press cameras in the distance.

Hayton said, "Excellent job, chaps, very quick, where was it?"

"Just here, Sir," replied one of the divers pointing to the large boulders that made up the break-wall. "We actually saw it from the surface; it was very easy."

"Excellent, excellent! So, we have a suspect in custody, a confession, and a murder weapon. Very good indeed," smiled Hayton.

Shuen looked visibly frustrated; Alex took his cue. "Excuse me, Chief Inspector, I believe what DI Shuen was about to say was that the pathologist told us earlier that the murder weapon was a blunt object, and the cut marks were made with a serrated edge...."

"Rufus Chan!" said Hayton sharply.

"Sir?" Alex replied.

"Rufus 'bloody' Chan, by the sounds of it, in the morgue," continued Hayton. "Making things frightfully complicated as normal, bloody busybody!"

Roberts spoke for the first time and rather condescendingly he said, "The Inspectors would also like us to put the suspect under surveillance in the cells overnight, Sir."

"What on earth for? So he can confess again?!"

"With respect, Sir," continued Alex, "there are some major discrepancies between what the suspect has said and what we can actually see here."

"And with *respect'*, Detective Torrence you are here as a liaison officer and not an investigating officer."

Alex met the Chief Inspector's eyes momentarily.

"Detective Inspector Shuen," Hayton continued, "you have forty-eight hours to complete the formalities, charge the suspect and close this case, understood? And in the meantime I'm going to tell the press over there we have the murderer in custody, before ringing the Governor and telling him the same thing. And then I will be going back to my office and having a rather large whiskey. Forty-eight hours, Shuen. Forty-eight hours."

With that, Chief Inspector Mark Hayton walked briskly towards the pack of press, closely followed by Senior Inspector Karl Roberts.

Shuen inspected his shoes silently. Alex broke the silence and placed a hand on both Shuen and Lim's shoulders "You heard the man, we've got forty-eight hours to complete the formalities, how about we get to it?!"

They both nodded in unspoken agreement. Alex started walking back towards the divers, muttering to himself, "I'll liaise you, you pompous, effeminate public schoolboy gadgie!"

Alex approached the two well-built Chinese divers who were beginning to help each other out of their diving suits. "Good job, guys. Pretty lucky it was sitting there on the rocks eh?"

The taller of the two responded. "Yeah, sometimes it's like that, other times it can take hours or days. It's a good job it wasn't five or ten more metres further out as the water visibility goes like soup where they are preparing for landfill."

Alex noticed hoses that appeared to be dive-related on the side of the container. "What are those used for?"

The diver replied, "That's commercial diving equipment, it's not ours. They're doing mostly inspection work all around the reclaimed land."

His colleague added, "Part of our job is to check their permits and licences every now and again. We know this crew," he nodded towards the container.

Shuen and Lim had joined Alex by now. The police diver continued. "Coniston Marine, mostly British divers. Very professional at work, absolute lunatics when they are not, especially when they are drinking – which is most of the time. Crazy foreigners. No offence, Sir," he nodded at Alex.

"None taken," smiled Alex. "Where are they now, by the way?"

"They're in the workers' accommodation which is about five minutes' walk that way. Their hut has a British flag on a pole, you can't miss it. We saw a couple of them earlier today and they wanted to know if they could work on Monday. No diving means no pay."

The officers thanked the police divers, and began to walk away from the water's edge. They could see Roberts and Hayton getting into the back of a police car as the press began to disperse.

Jackie Shuen pointed to the large roll of copper wire which was about the size of a lorry tyre, lying on its side about ten metres in front of the diving container. "This is the murder scene; there are samples of the victim's blood and his fingerprints on the wire itself. Judging by the way the body was found, he was either leaning or kneeling over the roll, or he fell over it when he was struck from behind."

"Any of Kwan's prints?" Alex asked.

"Not on the wire, but plenty around the site. According to the constables on site today, he'd been hanging around here selling marijuana and collecting horse-racing bets for the site-workers, small time stuff. He'd been here for a couple of weeks apparently."

"Any sign of a blunt weapon?"

"Nothing," added Lim

"I don't know what you two think," continued Alex. "But this wire looks like it's been here for a while, no tracks and it's slightly embedded in the dirt, look. And even if Evans was stealing it, which I doubt, even a big man like him couldn't lift or roll something of this size and weight."

"Agreed," said Shuen.

Alex continued his train of thought out loud. "And why would a man earning three to four thousand quid a month steal a measly roll of copper in the first place? It doesn't add up."

"So the question is, why was he here in the first place and what drove Kwan, or whoever, to murder him?"

"Maybe it was a drugs deal gone wrong, or gambling debt," suggested Heidi Lim.

"Possibly, Senior Constable, possibly," said Shuen. "I think that's more plausible than the theft idea, but I think we need to ascertain if they actually knew each other prior to this, find a link, find a realistic motive, find out the real facts."

"Next stop the divers bunk-house? Maybe they have some info," Alex suggested.

"OK," said DI Shuen, already heading off.

*

As they approached the hut with the Union Jack flying above it, they could hear men's muffled voices coming from inside. Shuen knocked on the door and someone shouted mockingly from inside in a high-pitched voice. "Pizza must be here...we're home...do come in!"

The three officers entered the hut. Alex immediately thought of the eighties TV program 'Auf Wiedersehen Pet', where a group of British builders worked in Germany. The hut looked sparse with six single beds, numerous posters of topless women, and very few home luxuries, just like the TV show. There was a musty, damp smell, mixed in with alcohol and tobacco.

Four caucasian men sat around a table in the middle of the hut playing cards. Alex took the lead. "Sorry to interrupt, gents. I'm Detective Inspector Wu Torrence and this is DI Shuen and Senior Constable Lim. We've been over at the crime scene and wondered if you could spare five minutes?"

A large man with long hair and a goatee beard spoke first. "No problem, officers, what can we do you for?"

Alex noticed an Australian twang. The man put his cards flat on the table next to his can of San Miguel beer and continued. "I've took enough money off these pommie bastards for one day!"

"Lost enough, more like it," one of his friends retorted.

There was an atmosphere of testosterone and camaraderie around the hut and the men were obviously comfortable in each other's company.

"Did any of you know Darren Meakin, the man who got killed?" Alex asked.

The Australian replied, "I think we all knew Big Darren a bit, they drafted him in for a day or two to show us some welding techniques top-side..."

"Top-side?" Alex enquired as Heidi Lim took notes next to him.

"Yeah, 'top-side', on top. Not in the water. There are miles of piping under the runway; sewerage, tidal pipes, drainage, that kind of shit. Anyway, when the fuckwits laid down the pipes, they didn't secure them well enough, so after they dropped a few thousand tons of rubble on top of them they started to pull apart, which is where we came in." The man took a swig of his beer. "We've been securing them for the last few months using copper links. We did a few dry runs with Big Darren topside around November time. He showed us how to weld the links before we started on them underwater."

"And what was Darren like?" Alex asked.

"Top man," one of the other men replied. "Bit quiet, a family man. I think he went home at Christmas to see his missus and kid. He was sending all he could home, I think."

His Australian friend nodded in agreement. "He'd have a few beers after work with the other welders and whatever, but he was saving money. I reckon that's why he would've come back early on Saturday."

Shuen spoke for the first time. "Do you know where he had been drinking on Saturday?"

One of the other card-players replied. "I heard he'd been in Tsim Sha Tsui in the Watering Hole but left about eight-ish. Man United aren't playing until today so he wouldn't have been arsed about any of the other games."

"And he lived in one of these huts as well then?" Alex asked.

"Yeah, the last one on the left. Some of his mates are around today but they're pretty choked up about the whole thing. Good job you caught the little Chinese bastard, they would've fuckin' killed him if they'd got to him first," added the Australian.

"Regarding the copper wire," Alex wanted to tread carefully, "would Darren Meakin have any reason to steal it?"

The men around the table laughed in unison. One of the Brits replied. "Why would he want to steal copper? There's tons of the stuff around here. Welders are on a good whack, and anyway, who would he sell it to? Of course he wouldn't, that doesn't make any sense."

"Did any of you know Kwan Yo Hang?" Shuen asked.

"Eh? That Chinese scrotum that killed him?" replied the Australian; the other men shook their heads. "Look it's like this, we all know the constructors pay their bungs and let the fuckers on-site but none of the gweilos have anything to do with them."

"No, Wayne," his friend interrupted him. "Some of the younger ones buy dope off them and stuff."

"Yeah, fair do's mate, but none of the divers would smoke that shit," he replied as he took another large swallow of his beer.

Outside they saw the pizza delivery-man pull up as the sun started to set over the South China Sea.

"Just before we leave you to your dinner guys," said Alex. "Do any of you have the key for the dive container?"

The man whom they now knew as Wayne stood up. "No worries, I know where it's hidden. I'll walk over with you. I could do with a piss anyway."

One of his English companions piped up. "He's just trying to get out of paying for the pizza, as bloody usual, tight-wad Aussie wanker!"

The big man winked. "Save us a bit, Sheilas!"

He then led the three officers out of the door. As they walked past the furthest hut Wayne remarked. "That's Big Darren's hut...well that was Big Darren's hut, looks like nobody's home... can't say as I blame them. I wouldn't want to sleep in there tonight unless I was absolutely rooted; they must be in the pub", the big commercial diver shivered.

"Tell me, Wayne, is it?" Alex asked.

"Yeah, Wayne Harris. Tell me what, mate?"

"Would Darren have had any reason to be near the dive container or water's edge on a Saturday night?"

The big Australian had lost a bit of his earlier bravado now they were outside in the early evening light. "Maybe he was just taking a piss or having a ciggie...who knows? I never come down here myself at night. Once I've clocked off that's me done for the day."

The police driver was leaning against one of the two police cars whilst talking and sharing a cigarette with the on-duty officer, as the group approached. They both stood to attention.'

"Sir," said the driver, addressing Shuen.

"At ease, Constable, it's been a long day. I think we've earned a cigarette, don't you?" Shuen said in Cantonese.

The other constable took the hint and passed the senior officer his pack of Lucky Strikes.

"Thank you, Constable. Are you on duty all night?"

"Yes, Sir," answered the young officer.

Shuen inhaled on his cigarette. "I don't want anybody near this crime scene, understood? And be vigilant, anything out of the ordinary, however small, call me." Shuen passed the officer his business card two handed, the polite way of doing so.

"Yes Sir," said the constable as he raised the police 'do not cross' tape for the group to pass under.

Wayne Harris knelt down outside the container and lifted up a breeze block. "Shit! The key; it's not here! I locked up Friday and I'm sure I put the key in the normal place."

"Do you have a spare?" Alex asked.

"Andy, Andy Goff the supervisor, he's got the other one, but he lives out at Kam Tin near the yard."

"Have you got his phone number?" asked Shuen.

"Yeah, it's in the fuckin' container! He'll be here in the morning about eight, if that's any good?"

Alex turned to face Shuen and Lim. "I'd like forensics to have a look inside there, personally. I don't know what you think, Jackie?"

"Yes, agreed. Look, it's getting dark, I'll get forensics to come back out first thing, there's no point breaking the door this time of night. I want to get back and arrange for Kwan to be interviewed again, also."

Alex addressed Wayne. "We'll be back out again in the morning, thanks for all your help."

"No worries, mate. Do you think we'll be able to work tomorrow?"

"I don't think so. And thanks again," replied Alex.

CHAPTER FOUR
Black Christmas

Dec 7th 1941. New Territories, Hong Kong.

At the lookout on Gin Drinkers Lane, Jock was pouring two cups of tea into his and Billy's steel mugs whilst Billy tuned the transistor. He could hear the familiar tones of the BBC world service:

"We interrupt this broadcast to bring you a special news bulletin; the Japanese have attacked Pearl Harbour, Hawaii, by air, President Roosevelt has just announced. The attack was carried out on all naval and military activities in the American territory. The Prime Minister Winston Churchill has pledged to support our American allies and has confirmed that, should The United States of America declare war on Japan, the British declaration will follow within the hour...."

The two friends looked at each other without speaking. Jock sipped his tea and said simply, "I suppose that's that then."

Before he went to sleep that night, in addition to his normal prayers Jock asked the Lord above to watch over him and his friend Billy.

At 08:00 the following morning the bombardment of Hong Kong started.

*

Monday 8th December 1941. Kowloon

Lily Wu was sitting at the breakfast table in her crisp white uniform eating her breakfast of eggs and toast, whilst feeling slightly aggrieved that there hadn't been any bacon for over a month now, when Chan, the family driver, entered the dining-room. Lily had never seen Chan in the main house before and he looked oddly out of place in his loose-fitting uniform, twisting his hands together.

He addressed the girls' mother. "Madam, the Japanese are bombing the New Territories, it is on the radio. You can hear the bombing also. What would Madam wish to do?"

All of the colour drained out of the mother's face as Lin Lin entered the room. She appeared to be just about to scold Chan when indeed they all heard the distant crash of artillery. On a normal day, they would have assumed this was thunder, but on this crisp, sunny, December morning there was no mistaking the noise of weaponry coming from behind the famous Lion Rock Hill.

Mother seemed to regain some of her composure, she dabbed the corner of her mouth with a napkin and said, "We will wait for Father. In the meantime, Lin Lin, pack some bags just in case. Chan, go and see Mr Lee at the office and see what the situation is."

"Yes madam," they replied in unison.

Lily and Ah-Lam asked to be excused from the table and headed for the garden. Looking up at the Lion Rock there was nothing to see other than the familiar outline of the proud lion's head watching over Kowloon.

*

By mid-morning, Jock, Billy and the other soldiers of the 2nd Battalion Royal Scots had all heard a lot of artillery but not actually seen anything from their look-out bunker on Gin Drinkers Lane. The fighting appeared to be two or three miles closer to the border and the Sham Chun River, where the Canadian battalions were stationed. Their commanding officer had told them to be alert, as the Canadians were under orders to fall back to the stronghold of Gin Drinkers Lane, should the fighting become too intense.

Jock had actually been on the latrine when the first sound of artillery had been heard earlier in the morning, nearly making him lose his balance. As he pulled his trousers up and adjusted his tin hat he couldn't help but think that this never happened to Gary Cooper in the movies.

At mid-day, they fired their Vickers machine gun for the first time in anger, as around ten Japanese planes flew overhead in a triangular formation. Their dated weapon seemed hopelessly inadequate as the planes flew in the direction of Kai Tak airport. An order was shouted from somewhere further down the line not to waste ammunition. They all knew they would need this sooner rather than later.

*

Lily and Ah-Lam were still in the garden when the war planes flew over Lion Rock Hill. Lin Lin beckoned the girls in.

"Li Lai, Ah-Sun! Come inside this minute!"

Lily stood looking up at the sky, momentarily mesmerised, until her big sister pulled her out of her stupor.

"Lily! Let's go!"

Lily took one last look at the airplanes, they looked strangely beautiful.

Hong Kong had only five aircraft and two old naval boats in the territory that day. They were destroyed within hours.

*

Dec 13th 1941. Kowloon Bay

Other than his mother in her open casket, Jock had never seen a dead body. Within the space of forty-eight hours he had seen dozens. One poor soul had the top of his head blown off by a Japanese mortar on the second evening of the attack. The top half of his skull stayed in the helmet. Jock thought it reminded him of a boiled egg with the top cut off. He could see the Canadian boy's brain inside the bottom half of his skull. He didn't even know his name. Jock knew that if he had been one foot to his right it would have been him. He thanked God Almighty.

Those that remained of the Royal Scots and the Canadian infantry were sitting at the water's edge in Kowloon Bay after losing Gin Drinkers Lane two days earlier. They were waiting for evacuation to Hong Kong Island itself. Numb, dirty and exhausted; every time the young Scotsman closed his eyes he could see the Canadian's face, it didn't look calm like his mother's, it looked grisly, twisted and scared. Jock opened his eyes suddenly; he knew then and there that he didn't want to die, it wasn't his time.

After the Canadians fell back in to the line on the first day, the plan was for all the soldiers to dig in and hold the line for at least a hundred and thirty days; in the end, they managed just three. They were out-gunned and outnumbered by the battle-hardened Japanese, with absolutely no air cover. On the second night of fighting the Japanese sprang a surprise attack from a high peak called Smugglers Ridge at the Shing Mun area of Gin Drinkers Lane. The Scots and the Canadians did their best for another forty or so hours, until it was obvious defeat was unavoidable, and they were ordered further down the line after the sun had set. Jock had fired round after round towards the Japanese lines but he couldn't say in all honesty if he had killed or even injured any of the enemy or not. It certainly wasn't like the cowboy movies where the baddies held their chests and fell over. It was hell on earth as the Japanese just kept coming in waves and waves and had totally overwhelmed them. Earlier in the day through his binoculars, Jock had seen Japanese soldiers hurdling over rolls of barbed wire by the first soldier lying on the coil and his comrades running over his back, quick, efficient and ruthless. The Jap on the wire must have been in agony.

One bunker after another had fallen, until eventually, with the cover of darkness, they were ordered by the Canadian officers to walk overnight towards Kowloon Bay and Victoria Harbour. The sheer terror on the faces of the Chinese they passed on the way shamed Jock; he knew that they were leaving the civilians completely to the mercy of the Japanese. The people were carrying all they possibly could, babies were swaddled to their mothers, and he had seen old people pushed in simple wooden carts. Chaos reigned supreme with some civilians heading south toward the harbour and some heading north to the New Territories and the Chinese border. Some of the soldiers remonstrated with them not to head north but their cold, expressionless faces didn't respond. Jock had felt numb.

As the sun rose he shared a cigarette with Billy. Billy's hands were shaking uncontrollably. They were now waiting for the Star Ferry to take them to Hong Kong Island, the last point of the colony still in British hands.

*

Lin Lin pleaded, "Madam, we need to go!"

"We shall wait for Father or Mr Lee's call," replied the girls' mother.

Lily could hear gunfire and explosions outside.

"Madam we have to go, now!" Lin Lin repeated.

Lily's mother slapped Lin Lin across the face. They both looked momentarily stunned. Another explosion this time closer broke the silence. It seemed suddenly to shake her into action. Mother spoke first without apologising, addressing the girls. "Get in the car. Now!"

Outside, Chan had already started the motor, before the girls, their mother, and Lin Lin crouched down in the back of the Mercedes-Benz. As the car cautiously pulled out of the entrance of 2a Dunbar Road, almost immediately there was a loud crash and the front side-window shattered. Chan then put his foot on the accelerator and rammed into the wall opposite, he was slumped over the steering wheel with the accelerator still racing.

"Chan! Chan!"

From the rear Lily noticed a small trickle of blood running out of a hole in the old man's temple.

Lin Lin took control, "Back to the house, keep down!"

Noises and bangs crashed overhead as everybody half ran and half crawled back into the house as people were running in all directions. It was impossible to tell which way the shooting was coming from. They were trapped.

"We need to hide, everybody hide under the veranda quickly!" ordered Lin Lin.

Mother looked in shock and seemed to obey her servant in a trance-like fashion. Lily and Ah-Lam gathered up tins, rice, and anything else they could hold as they ran through the kitchen and back door to the rear steps and to their familiar childhood hiding place.

*

Monday 20th December 1941. Hong Kong Island

Within hours of their landing on Hong Kong Island, the bombardment from the Japanese had started. The allied troops had dug in and Billy and Jock had been stationed in a pill-box with six other men overlooking Wong Nai Chung Gap, one of the highest points on the island.

Most communications had been destroyed by the Japanese and instructions were hit and miss at best, with a runner normally bringing written instructions, the last order being to hold this point at all costs.

The constant noise of the artillery had taken its toll on the two friends, with Billy suffering badly from shell shock. In a brief lull in the fighting, the two young men knelt down in a corner of the pill-box and said what could be their last prayers. They also made a pact.

Jock began. "Billy, this is me' last letter to my Da' and my sisters. If I don't make it, go and see them in Govan. Tell em' I was brave and I did my duty, Pal."

Billy replied. "Aye, tell him yersel, Jock." A tear rolled down his dirty face making a line of white. "Here's mine to my Rita. If the Japs do anything horrible to mae' body, tell her I was shot, died straight away, you know. Tell her I went peacefully, Pal."

Jock nodded, they had both seen corpses with their hands tied behind their backs, both soldiers and civilians, who had been bayoneted, time and time again. They'd also seen other bodies; old people, women and children, mutilated, eyes gauged out, genitals dismembered, stomachs and intestines pulled out: unspeakable horrors that only those who had witnessed them could truly believe.

The two chums then each gave the other a single bullet, and an unspoken pact not to let the other one suffer.

*

Wednesday 22nd December 1941

The four females had been hiding under the house for nine days already. Lin Lin had been sneaking into the house at night and finding food which they were now rationing. They had been going to the toilet in a big bowl that Lin Lin had once used for making cakes, they then buried the mess in the middle of the night. They slept in the day and rarely spoke, even then only in a whisper.

On the third night, the Japanese soldiers came and kicked the door of the house open and ran about shouting incomprehensible words but the girls knew that they were well hidden; scared, hungry and tired, but well hidden. The Japanese had left shortly afterwards with a bottle of Father's brandy and leaving the garden gate ajar. Lily could see, now that the gate was open, that the Mercedes-Benz had also gone.

Before he had been shot, Chan had told mother that Mr Lee in Father's office had said they might be able to get a boat to Macau or even Singapore, but probably not until the fighting had died down. They were under instructions to wait for a call or message.

Lily was dozing with *Pride and Prejudice* on her chest when a piercing ring broke the mid-morning silence.

Lily pushed her Mother's shoulder and said as loudly as she dared, "The telephone! Mother, the telephone!"

Her mother immediately crawled across the floor and exited the hideout to climb the rear stairs to the house.

She reached the phone in the lobby and answered, "Wu residence!" Moments later she dropped the receiver and froze. A Japanese soldier was standing in the door-way.

The girls and Lin Lin had heard the soldier's boots above them on the steps before they heard mother's screams. Lin Lin covered both Lily and Ah-Lam's mouths with her old, calloused hands, Lily could taste Lin Lin's blood in her mouth as she bit down. None of them made a sound whilst mother screamed for mercy above them.

The last clear words she ever heard her mother shout were, "Go to Mr Lee, he has a boat!"

More and more heavy boots could be heard overhead for what seemed like hours and hours of shouts, screams and even laughter, a foreign cold laughter. When it eventually came, the sudden quiet was a strange relief.

Lin Lin buried the girls' faces into her bony chest, one noise from any of them and the same fate would befall both young girls. Lin Lin tried unsuccessfully to shield the two girls' eyes as the soldiers dragged her former employer's corpse by the ankles though the beautiful gardens. Still laughing, they dumped her body into the chaotic street beyond, like a piece of rubbish. A human piece of trash that had been systematically raped, tortured and finally killed; human rubbish with both breasts sliced off.

*

25th December 1941. Stanley Village, Hong Kong Island

The Japanese were in control of most of Hong Kong Island by Christmas Day morning. The Royal Scots, the Hong Kong Rifles and the Canadians had fought valiantly but it was becoming more and more apparent that they were fighting a losing battle.

Jock, Billy and four other men were hiding in some woodland above Saint Stephen's hospital. They were well hidden, had slept in shifts, and had even managed to find some food in a nearby deserted bungalow. The last officer they had seen had told them the day before to head south to Stanley village where they were to surrender.

After everything that they had seen and heard, the men had decided overnight that there was no way they were going to hand over their weapons until they had seen with their own eyes that the Japs would indeed take prisoners.

From their vantage point they could see numerous western people, both civilians and military, milling around outside the building, and the red-cross flag could clearly be seen on the roof of a green ambulance.

Earlier the men had each drawn straws and worked out a plan. When the Japs arrived, if they were letting the military surrender they were to walk slowly down the hill, unarmed and with a white flag. One of them was to remain hidden however, and if the Japs started to bayonet or torture any of the other five, the remaining man in the bush was to shoot his friends cleanly and as quickly as possible – Jock had drawn the short straw.

Around 11.30am Jock felt Billy jab him in the ribs. "Look, Jock!" he whispered,

Two cars pulled up with mostly Japanese officers but also two senior British officers; salutes were made and a discussion was in place, and the situation seemed cold but calm.

A Canadian called Jim said, "Well, it's now or never, I guess?"

The chums shook hands and five of the six walked towards the hospital. To his immense relief, Jock followed them twenty minutes later.

Hong Kong had officially been surrendered; the first British colony to surrender in over 150 years. The day became known as Black Christmas and heralded in three years and eight months of brutal Japanese rule.

CHAPTER FIVE

January 1997

The huge neon advertising lights reflected in the back window of the police car as Alex Wu Torrence checked his watch – seven pm Hong Kong time. Having previously asked to be dropped in Tsim Sha Tsui on Kowloon side, Alex removed his jacket and tie and then sprayed another splash of deodorant both under and over his shirt.

En route he made another quick call from the back of the police car, this time to an old friend of his Dad's. "Uncle Taff?"

"Who's this?"

"Uncle Taff, its Alex. I'm in town. Listen, is the Watering Hole still one of your haunts?"

"Alex! It can be, my boy; it can be. How the devil are you?!"

"I'm fine thanks...."

"I thought you'd be over when I saw that gweilo had been murdered, rum job that."

"Yes, listen, what time can you get to the bar?" Alex interrupted the old man.

"I can be there in a jiffy. Twenty minutes OK?"

"Perfect, see you then. Bye." Alex stifled a yawn.

"You tired, Inspector Wu Torrence?" Heidi Lim asked.

"I'm getting that way. And it's Alex, please."

Lim smiled coyly and returned to her notes.

Shuen looked in the rear-view mirror as the car entered the neon-lit Tsim Sha Tsui district and asked, "Any particular reason you are going to the Watering Hole, Alex?"

"Just meeting an old friend, Jackie. I thought I could get a feel for the place also. Is that OK?"

"Sure. But just remember that you are only *liaising*," half joked Shuen.

Alex had previously made a conscious decision not to bring along his colleagues to the Watering Hole bar for two reasons – firstly, he knew that the two Chinese detectives would stand out as police straight away in a mostly western bar, and secondly, he felt he needed to fly solo for a while and have a sniff around.

"Absolutely, Detective Inspector, absolutely," Alex mock-saluted and smiled.

The car came to a halt and the driver asked, "Is Nathan Road OK for you, Sir?"

"Perfect. Thanks." And with that Detective Wu Torrence headed out into the humid, crazy atmosphere that is Tsim Sha Tsui.

Within five minutes of walking up Nathan Road from the Peninsula Hotel, he had been offered everything from a copy-watch to a new suit, ecstasy, or a woman for the night. Tsim Sha Tsui at night, one of the larger tourist areas of Hong Kong, both exhilarated and annoyed Alex; so much so that the dimly-lit stairs down into the Watering Hole basement bar came as a welcome relief, and the blast of air-conditioning as he opened the door even more so.

He spotted Taff Williams at the far end of the bar engaged in what appeared to be a heated discussion with the barman. Taff looked like something from a bygone era in his khaki safari suit, slip-on leather boots and knee-length woollen socks. Alex wondered if you could even buy clothes like that anymore. He also noticed that Taff had added a walking-stick to his attire since he last saw him well over a year ago.

"Alex, my boy!"

Taff Williams greeted Alex with a warm two-handed handshake. No hugs from Taff's generation, that was for sure.

"I'm just sorting out this bloody ruffian here," he said, nodding to the overweight, blonde-haired, smiling barman.

"And I'm bloody telling him that I'm not bloody serving him after what he did last time he was in here," said the barman good-naturedly, pulling a pint of San Miguel which appeared to be for Taff.

"Do you know what he did?" The barman didn't wait for a response. "I've got a table of German tourists in here last week having a meal, spending good money, when Hong Kong's tightest wallet here starts bloody goose-stepping up and down the bar singin' 'Hitler has only got one ball!'"

The barman paused.

"Coke please," asked Alex.

"Coke my arse, get him a pint!" said Taff.

The barman dutifully obliged and continued his story. "Anyway, one of them stands up, looks like a seven foot Boris Becker, says he's not being insulted like that and wants an apology off this soppy old sod."

"So," interrupted Taff, "I said quite reasonably that I would apologise for my actions if the man would kindly apologise for being German."

"Forty dollars please gents," laughed the barman. "Nearly had to bloody separate the two of them, I tell you."

Alex handed him the equivalent of about five pounds and nodded to one of the vacant booths. "Still doing your bit for international relations then, Taff?"

"Gotta 'ave a laugh Boyo. It's either that or shrivel up and die, I tell you. How's your mam?"

"She's fine. I've not seen her yet but she sounds fine."

"Good, good. So, I'm presuming this isn't a social visit then. What d'you want?"

Taff's intuition was right. Taff had been in Hong Kong for over thirty years and had been close friend and colleague of Superintendent Jock Torrence when they both served in the Royal Hong Kong Police Force.

Alex spent the next ten minutes telling the ex-copper about the Darren Meakin murder, with Taff listening intently.

Taff asked after a while, "So, you smell a rat, is it?"

"Basically, yes. This Kwan boy might be involved to some extent, but he is taking the full rap for whatever reason. The powers-that-be are happy for him to be doing this. They just want Jackie Shuen to join the dots and make it all fit whilst I comply like a little nodding dog or something."

"I heard on the grapevine that that big poof Hayton is looking at a Knighthood or an OBE, you know. Prince Charles will be handing out awards at Government House on Handover day. I'm sure this murder must be inconveniencing Chief Inspector Mark Hayton *terribly!*"

Alex knew well that even though Taff was retired he still had contacts inside the force and an ear to the ground. He wasn't a hundred percent sure exactly why he was sitting opposite the old man, but he knew it certainly couldn't do him any harm.

"What's the word in here, Taff? Some commercial divers told me earlier that Darren Meakin had been drinking in here that day?"

"Divers you say? See a lot of them about, noisy drunk buggers. That Meakin fella wasn't one though, was he? Quiet man by all accounts, few pints and the football, that's it. Not like some of them airport workers here though, they spend all week grafting in 95% humidity, working their balls off and then blow the lot in Tsim Sha Tsui and Wanchai every weekend on booze and girls. I've not heard anybody say a bad word about this Meakin fellow though."

"Exactly, I get the feeling he was just in the wrong place at the wrong time."

"Saturday night. On a building site, when nobody else was there or expected to be there, right?" Taff asked. "So, something was going on that maybe he interrupted? Maybe the Kwan boy was stealing or getting up to no good?"

"Maybe, but I don't think he'd have the physical strength or the will to do it on his own," said Alex.

"I know, but put him with a bunch of his triad mates and they are like a pack of rabid dogs. They'd never lose face in front of another brother."

"I know," agreed Alex

"Which leads us to one of two conclusions," Taff continued. "He had somebody else with him."

"Or?" asked Alex.

"Or, somebody else committed this murder."

*

Alex said goodbye to Taff, who had promised to keep him informed of anything he found out, either at the Watering Hole or through his old boys' police network. Alex then hailed the nearest red taxi and instructed the driver to take him to Sai Kung town centre.

Alex's phone started to vibrate in his pocket. His display said "Mum" and the time 20:37.

"Hi Mum!"

"Alex, have you eaten?!"

"Not yet, Mum, I've got one more visit to make, and then I will come home, OK?"

"OK? How you going to do your job if you're not eating? And when did you sleep last?!"

Alex laughed inwardly. After his Dad had died seven years earlier in England, his mum had decided to move back to Hong Kong to be near her sister Auntie Ah-lam in Sai Kung. She'd wanted Alex and his sister May to come with her, but Alex had his career and May had her English husband, Tom.

"Mum..." Alex laughed. "I won't be long."

"Better not be, or dinner in dog!"

"What dog?"

"Dog that I'm going out to buy if my thirty-three-year-old very important detective son doesn't come home soon for his noodles! Bye-bye."

There had always been a directness about his mum ever since he could remember. Black and white, no questions asked; both he and his sister knew, growing up, that you did your homework, ate what was in front of you, didn't answer back and went to bed on time. They also knew that they were secure and loved. His dad was working long hours in the Royal Hong Kong Police Force, so Lily became the disciplinarian as well as the home-maker. Then all that changed in the mid-seventies when Jock, Alex's dad, suddenly resigned and within a month they were all in cold and dreary Britain. Dreary Morecambe in dreary England to be exact.

The reasons behind Jock Torrence's resignation were never fully explained to the kids and it came as a massive culture-shock going from a private Hong Kong school for civil servants to a British Comprehensive in the Northwest of England. Alex went from being the tallest, quickest boy in his class to merely a 'Chinky' or 'Slanty-eyed git'. Playground fights ensued and Alex undertook a steep learning curve until he found the right bunch of friends, an improved talent for football, and a tasty right hook.

The taxi went around the last roundabout coming in to Sai Kung without changing gears or slowing down. Sai Kung had a mixed population of local Chinese, expatriates and British-born Chinese, or BBCs as they were sometimes referred to. Some of the local Chinese could trace back their clans hundreds of years and still lived in the same cluster of villages surrounding Sai Kung, which at one time was a sleepy fishing village; feuds or co-operation between clans could go on for generations. The clean air and un-hurried atmosphere attracted other Chinese in the seventies, eighties and nineties as well as expats who tended to be linked to Kai Tak airport by occupation. The last couple of decades had also brought a lot of BBCs back to Hong Kong. Initially their parents had emigrated to make a better life in the UK, but as Indigenous New Territories law stated that every male heir had a birthright to land (which in the nineties was at a premium) a lot of BBCs were heading back to Hong Kong where they could make serious money and also claim their birthright. Alex, having a Scottish father, wasn't entitled to this, which infuriated Lily. He'd heard her say on more than one occasion, "Thirty years your father was here, fighting the Japanese in the army during the war, being good policeman, helping everybody, stopping blasted communists at the border, but did you get land rights? Did you, no?! It makes me mad!"

Alex asked the driver to pull up near the Newcastle pub. On exiting the cab, he saw a scruffy-looking teenager, hassling the owners of a shiny new Mercedes E-class.

"I'll watch your car for you, uncle, HK$50," said the youth with an outstretched hand.

The parking scam had been operated for years by local triads. In this case, judging by the youth's dragon on his scrawny arm, he was a 49er for the 14k triad, a large triad group that was represented all over the colony.

The man searched inside his wallet uncomfortably as Alex approached.

"Thirty dollars," said Alex in Cantonese.

The young triad looked confused. "Eh?"

"The going rate is HK$30," said Alex figuring the youth was skimming some off the top for himself.

"What's it to do with you, *Jaap Yung*?"

"Jaap Yung" is a derogatory term used for Eurasians by Chinese people. Alex had not heard the phrase for a long time and instinctively grabbed the youth by the throat before twisting his arm up behind his back. He then frogmarched him down the nearest alley causing the youth to lose both his cigarette and a flip flop in the process.

He pushed his head against a brick wall. "Do you know Curly?"

The youth nodded in the affirmative.

"Well go and tell Curly that I can smell his whore of a mother from here. Do you understand?"

"Yes, yes."

Alex threw the young triad to the floor. "I'll be over there," he nodded in the direction of the bar. Alex always thought Chinese swearing to be a lot more imaginative and liberating than English bad language.

As he passed the couple with the Mercedes he nodded courteously and spoke in polite Chinese. "Your car will be fine, Sir. Don't worry."

He pushed open the big oak door to the pub and for the second time that evening received a blast of air-conditioning and beer fumes. The bar was quiet.

"Two pints please, I'm expecting somebody," he said to the barman.

Alex sat facing the door when bang on cue the door burst open with two mean-looking triads entering with the scrawny youth in tow behind. He pointed at Alex.

"That's him, Boss," he pointed nervously at Alex.

The curly-haired boss-man paused menacingly, the barman suddenly decided he needed to be elsewhere and the scruffy youth looked like he might soil himself.

"I'm surprised a dog's fart like you could smell anything with your head up your own arse."

The man took a step forward. Alex stood up. There was a pause.

"Alex!" The man broke into English. "Why the fuck didn't you tell me you were home!"

The two men embraced warmly.

Curly turned to the scrawny youth and switched back to Cantonese. "What the fuck are you looking at, chicken? Go out and make some money, arsehole!"

Curly's two accomplices turned around and left their boss, with the younger one looking completely bemused.

Alex's cousin, Ah-Yun Wu, or Curly as he was known, sat down and took a large gulp of the pint in front of him. "Alex, lah! Good to see you, brother."

"Likewise," said Alex, smiling.

Ah-Yun Wu was Alex's slightly older cousin, loveable rogue and mid-ranking 14k member, much to Auntie Ah-Lam's frustration. As children, Alex and Ah-Yun had been inseparable and more like brothers than cousins, but after Alex left Hong Kong, Ah-Yun tended to drift in with the wrong crowds as an adolescent, mainly due to his sense of mischief rather than a lack of guidance from his mother. Alex came back to Hong Kong every summer for long holidays and the two remained friends but ironically chose completely opposite paths.

"Tell me," said Alex. "That boy out there; would he do anything you told him to?"

"He better do, the little chicken-shit. Smoking, and spitting whilst he's working, probably trying to skim off the top too. Needs to learn some respect, that one."

"Would he take the rap for something you had done?" Alex asked.

Ah-Sun looked at Alex. "What's this? Turtle questions or cousin questions?"

"Cousin questions," laughed Alex. "How much flak would a 49er take for an elder brother?"

"Depends on what it is and how far the brother is up the mountain; if he gets pulled over for something small, he has to follow the code, stay quiet, do the few months, no problem."

Ah-Sun had got the nickname Curly ironically and knew all about doing a few months. When prisoners arrived at jail in Hong Kong then, inmates automatically got their heads shaved, and when Ah-Sun was younger he had been in and out so many times, the moniker "Curly" had stuck.

"What about something bigger like murder?"

Ah-Sun shifted awkwardly in his seat. "Ayah Alex, why do you ask me this? You know it's difficult for me to say anything. Is this about the gweilo killed at the airport?"

"I know it's difficult, I appreciate that, but it's not all about the gweilo. This boy whom they have is only eighteen and he's looking at twenty plus years. Would he really have to take the rap for a murder?"

"OK, OK, I don't know so much about Sun Yee On, but if one of our brothers was asked, it would have to come from the top."

"Mountain master, top?" asked Alex.

Almost like military rankings, a triad had ranks and titles with the lowest foot-soldier being a 49er and the highest being a mountain master. Alex guessed but didn't know for certain that his cousin was a "straw sandal", a kind of go-between or lieutenant.

"Yes, or deputy.... Alex, why you asking me these questions? Let's talk about football or how fucking ugly you've become!" Ah-Sun took another swallow of beer.

"Just one thing more, cousin," Alex laughed. "Are Sun Yee On in control of the airport?"

"Alex, lah! I have a vow to my brothers, keep quiet, take parking money, go home, make jiggy-jiggy, that's it. I don't know about the airport."

"So, the Sun Yee On *are* in control then?"

"Don't try the reverse psychology crap on me, ugly man! Listen, I'll tell you, it's no big secret, everybody knows anyway, but then you stop talking turtle, OK? Agreed?"

"Agreed," replied Alex.

"Look, the airport is big, big money, it's running late. Gweilos going to lose face; even worse, China is going to lose face if it doesn't open in time for the Handover. Nobody wants trouble; Government, construction companies and triads, nobody wants trouble, pay the money, get the job done, no problem. There are three brotherhoods involved, 14k took half of the site, Sun Yee On took the other half, and they both pay the small triad from Tsing Yi Island – Fei Fu Tong. It's near their territory, so they get some money. That's it, that's all I know."

Alex suspected his cousin knew more than he was letting on, but decided not to press him further. He also knew what Curly was telling him was correct, as back in Manchester they had received counter intelligence briefings along these lines stating that it was believed that the heads of all three groups had held a meeting and worked out an agreement. The 14k triad was traditionally based on Tung Chung, one of the islands that the new airport was being built on, and Sun Yee On in Tuen Mun, the nearest town on the mainland. They needed the co-operation of Fei Fu Tong as they were based on Tsing Yi, an island nearby, and controlled the main shipping port for Hong Kong which processed nearly all the shipping supplies for the construction work. Fei Fu Tong triad was pretty localised and made nearly all of its money from the port, but both Sun Yee On and 14k had grown and diversified in and outside the colony. The police weren't a hundred percent sure who was currently mountain master for Sun Yee On after the last head had been arrested five years earlier and the organisation had closed ranks and become more secretive to avoid further arrests. 14k was set up differently with separate cells operating independently and with more than one boss. If there was a big turf war the gangs would call on other 14k gangs from different towns to help, but essentially they worked independently which made things harder for the police and police intelligence. It was rumoured that the 14k did actually have a yearly summit and that there were constant power struggles.

Alex knew that his cousin would talk in general terms up to a point, but would never disclose anything regarding the 14k or his *brothers*. In a strange sort of way this suited Alex also; he didn't specifically want to know what his cousin got up to and he certainly didn't want to think any less of the cousin he had looked up to as a boy. The two men paused and sipped their beer.

For the next hour or so the cousins reminisced about old times, playing football, and about getting up to no good as children, until a combination of jet lag and alcohol made Alex call it a night.

On leaving the bar, Ah-Sun walked with Alex towards the taxi rank passing the young triad from earlier in the evening, who was now making a show of polishing the Mercedes.

"Goodnight Curly, good night Sir," said the youth nodding politely.

"Goodnight," said the cousins in unison, as Alex slipped a few dollars in the boy's pocket.

*

Alex got out of his third taxi of the day five minutes later outside of his mum's place. The three-storey village houses were sometimes used as a whole house but generally split into three separate flats: in this case Lily was on the ground floor, Auntie Ah-Lam (and occasionally Ah-Sun) was on the middle floor, and the two sisters rented the top floor out to supplement their pensions.

His mum, Li Lai Wu Torrence, or Lily to her friends, was waiting on the doorstop as soon as she heard the taxi's engine. Lily ran to her only son and Alex scooped his tiny mother up easily. Shows of affection can be frowned on in some aspects of Chinese culture but Lily had always doted on both of her children, and kisses and cuddles were always on tap.

"You've got flabby, Alex! English food is no good for you. Ah yah! Fish and chips rubbish no good, come in, come in!"

Alex put his head through the taxi window and paid the driver and told him to keep the change. From the middle floor balcony, he heard an almost identical voice to his mother's.

Auntie Ah-Lam shouted, "Alex la, Alex la! I'm coming down!"

The two old ladies seemed to be both shrinking and morphing into each other with age, and even before Alex had reached the sofa he had been subjected to a barrage of questions from, "Why wasn't he eating?" to, "Why hadn't he got a girlfriend yet?" and, "What happened to the nice blonde English girl?"

He reached into his bag and produced identical bottles of duty-free perfume for the sisters.

"Alex! Alex la! Too expensive, ayah," said Auntie Ah-Lam dabbing some behind her ears and kissing her nephew on the forehead.

"It's too expensive, even on your salary," said Lily, never missing the opportunity to get 'one up' on her sibling.

Auntie Ah-Lam seemed oblivious to the slight as they both headed in to the kitchenette seemingly without pausing for breath and totally in sync with each other. Alex decided not to tell them he had seen Ah-Sun earlier as it might cause upset.

A bowl of noodles miraculously appeared on his lap with delicious *char sui* pork and *pak choy,* a kind of Chinese cabbage. The food was truly excellent and Alex was on his third helping before his hunger began to abate.

The questions continued at length, and Alex wondered not for the first time if he got his inquisitive nature not just from his policeman father but from his mother also. His mum must have noticed his drooping eyelids and ordered Auntie Ah-Lam out of the apartment with very little fanfare.

"Alex has a very, very important job to do tomorrow, goodnight elder sister."

"Goodnight, Auntie Ah-Lam," said Alex with a kiss.

By the time Lily had bolted the two locks and chained the door and dried the dishes, Alex was fast asleep on the sofa.

Lily slipped her son's shoes off and covered the sleeping detective with a blanket. Smiling she ran her fingers lovingly through her beautiful boy's hair as a tear escaped onto Alex's shoulder. She quietly wished her son goodnight, and as she did every night, she picked up an old framed black and white photo of her husband, her Jock, looking splendid in his Royal Hong Kong police uniform. She kissed the glass.

"Goodnight, my handsome man."

CHAPTER SIX

Christmas Day 1943, Kai Tak Aerodrome

Two years had passed since the British surrender. Jock knew it was Christmas Day, but other than extra prayers at roll-call that morning, this day merged in with all of the others; work, sweat and toil, mingled in with shouting and the occasional outburst of random violence dished out by their Japanese captors.

Jock liked the end of the working day before sunset and darkness. He was left alone for as much as a whole hour some days as he accounted for all the machinery under his care. And he then had to measure the number of feet and inches (or *kanejaku*) reclaimed that day. By now he was able to decipher and write the Japanese numbers, which afforded him a bit more autonomy than some of the other prisoners. By rights, Billy should have been making the rounds with him, but whenever possible Jock let him stay in the shed and pretend to make simple repairs on a bit of machinery, giving him more of a rest because of his dysentery and the recent beating.

The beating had come at the hands of that nasty wee bastard, Keije, after Billy couldn't fix the piston on one of the compressors quickly enough, the reason being that one of the supposed "Resistance Gang" had walked off with a valve in his pocket and Billy wouldn't have been able to fix it even if he *had* known how to do so. If truth be told Jock had been carrying him, sometimes literally, for the last two years. When they had arrived for hard labour duty twenty months earlier and three stone heavier, Jock had re-attached a cultivator blade one day after bowing deeply to one of the guards and asking permission to do so. The guard had grunted *hai* in Japanese, waited until he fixed it, and then slapped him across the face for insubordination. After this, however, Jock was given more and more mechanical tasks and always insisted that he really needed Billy's help, until eventually, little by little, they were both doing hardly any menial work at all. Tempers were raised in the dormitory one night when it was suggested that what they were doing was tantamount to fraternising with the enemy, but common sense prevailed, and Jock's rational argument that the more the enemy needed them the more indispensable all of them became. Inwardly he hated the Japs as much as any of them, but he wanted to see the war out, and if that meant bowing a little bit deeper, fixing a few machines and learning a few Japanese phrases, that was a price he was willing to pay.

Originally when they came on site their job was to clear the old grass runway of debris and fill in the bomb holes that the Royal Engineers had made before the ill-fated retreat to Hong Kong Island two years earlier. Then they were to concrete the whole site and increase the area from about 180 square yards to 380 square yards by reclaiming outwards into Victoria Harbour (or whatever the Japs called it nowadays) and making the old aerodrome into an airport, with two runways instead of one.

It was slow, back-breaking work, undertaken by both Chinese forced labour and British and Canadian prisoners-of-war. They were half-starved, beaten and dehydrated; deaths were commonplace and the corpses were buried then and there under the runways with little or no ceremony.

Jock, being one of the few POWs with access to a pencil and paper, had always written down the deaths and mistreatment in the margins of his work sheets or his little black book, as he liked to call it: he had worked out an abbreviated system in which codes and numbers; undecipherable to the Japanese guards, were a record for Jock of the atrocities he witnessed daily.

The pebbles had started appearing about six months ago. Whilst walking around the water's edge, he saw three pebbles one on top of the other near the wooden pontoon that the junks and sampans were moored to.

"Pssst."

Jock was sure he'd heard something.

"Psssst...down here, Tommy soldier!"

Through the loose slats of the rickety pontoon, he could see the top of a traditional straw Hakka hat.

"Don't look, Tommy Soldier!" said the Chinese man in broken English.

Jock pretended to write something on his clip-board.

"Listen, look for three pebbles, I help you, give you presents la...OK?"

Jock didn't turn away from his notes but coughed twice in affirmation.

"Good, good. Listen very carefully, Tommy Soldier. Yankees won a big bang-bang in the ocean. Japanese getting scared! Uncle Sam got some big boats. Things are changing, Tommy Soldier. Stay strong."

With that, the mystery man handed Jock a Chinese apple-pear. Jock couldn't remember the last time he'd seen fruit, never mind actually eaten any.

"What's your name?" whispered Jock.

Jock briefly saw the glint of a gold tooth beneath the large hat before the figure below him bared his right arm, revealing a tattoo of a ship's anchor similar to the ones he'd seen on British sailors.

"You call me Popeye the Sailor Man. Toot-toot! Look for the three pebbles, Tommy Soldier."

With that Popeye slipped out of sight and under the jetty.

The news of the Americans winning the "big bang-bang" lifted Jock's spirits immeasurably and the Chinese apple-pear that he and Billy secretly shared after dark, core and all, tasted like the best thing either of them had ever eaten.

The following day he whispered the news about the "big bang-bang" to his commanding officer; an amiable Canadian called Captain Campbell, who had then decided to pass the good news on to the rest of the POWs, whilst wisely withholding his source, thus protecting Jock in uncertain times. Jock didn't tell him about the fruit.

In the following six months Jock saw Popeye the Sailor Man only twice under the jetty but received numerous notes, a small newspaper clipping, and on one occasion, a tin of sardines! Through the notes he learned that Popeye was a member of the East River Guerrillas and his job was to keep the POWs informed and their spirits up. Each note did exactly that; but had they been found in Jock's possession, he would have been killed without hesitation.

That Christmas Day evening, for whatever reason, Jock wasn't really expecting to see the three pebbles but was pleasantly surprised as always as he reached under the jetty. No Popeye this time but a note pinned down by some small hazelnuts.

'ENGLUND BOMMING BERLIN HAPPY CHIRMAS.'

Happy Christmas indeed, thought Jock, as he thanked the Lord for getting him through another day.

*

Sai Kung, New Territories, Hong Kong

Lily had enjoyed that morning's service even though she still didn't understand some of the Hakka dialect used by Pastor Lai, but the little chapel was a haven and she felt close to God and both her late mother and father, although even after two years she still refused to believe that her father was dead; a part of her just couldn't bring herself to do this. Not now, not ever.

On this Christmas evening, a 16-year-old Lily and 18-year-old Ah-Lam were shelling ginko nuts that were going to be cooked later on the open fire with some garlic and sea weed. Lin Lin was cleaning the seaweed outside on the doorstep and the girls could hear her gossiping to their elderly neighbour Grandma, or *Por Por* in Cantonese, as they called her, as a sign of respect.

The villagers had from day one treated them with kindness, maybe due to their shocked state on arrival or the obvious respect the sampan handlers had for the girls' father. On the night after Mother's death they finally fled. They had expected the sampan to take them south to Macau, but the boat driver had explained it was too dangerous and Mr Lee had arranged passage and a safe-house in Sai Kung for as long as they needed. Lin Lin had cut their hair like a boy's and muddied their faces, and bound Ah-Lam's breasts (Lily had nothing to bind at the time), before they set off to catch the boat. They were under strict instructions that if they were stopped by Japanese soldiers, they were to slobber, act crazy and even piss and shit themselves if need be. Lily was taken aback as she had never heard words like that before in any language, but Lin Lin had to make a point she guessed. They'd taken as many possessions as they had dared and Lin Lin even put some of Mother's jewellery in their tuppences. Lily had cried, but Lin Lin told her it was nothing she hadn't seen before and would only hurt a bit; she said Lily would be glad of it one day. The ring and the broach had itched like crazy for the whole journey.

In the two years that followed, Lin Lin took on the role of mother, father and provider for the two sisters. Other than the secret whispers at night to Ah-Lam, Lily had barely spoken for the first six months in Sai Kung, choosing instead to read *Pride and Prejudice* over and over, somehow trying to immerse herself in this fantasy world where a charming Mr Darcy or possibly her father would sweep her away from the dirt floor and hunger.

Lin Lin had taught the girls what roots and plants they could and couldn't eat from the woods, and how to forage for seaweed, mussels, crabs and winkles when the tide went out. The first time they ate frog, Lin Lin laughed hysterically at the girls' reactions.

They had a small amount of money for rice but spent as little as possible. Lin Lin had buried the rest with the jewellery under the dirt floor of their one-room house that the village elder Mr Tsui said they could have for as long as they needed. The old man was obviously indebted to Father, possibly for sampan work or trade, but in true Chinese clan tradition he honoured the favour; which, as convention dictated, was for life. *If one man does you a favour you are honour-bound to return the favour.*

Few Japanese soldiers came to Sai Kung due to its geographical nature. And as it had no roads from Kowloon, invariably when they did come it was by boat, so the villagers had advance notice and Lin Lin always sent the girls up into the woods smeared in mud with chests bound (Lily included), until they had left. The Japanese who did come seemed older and calmer than the animals that had killed their mother. They usually came to ensure that the Japanese Yen was in use and that none of the East River Column resistance movement were hiding out there or had been seen. Lin Lin had heard they sometimes hid in the hills above Pak Kong, and she said that she would give these brave boys her last penny if she had to. She prayed in the local temple that the translators the Japanese brought with them and the collaborators would die a thousand painful deaths.

Some days, when there were no Japanese in Sai Kung, Lily helped out in the local Christian ministry school. The village children usually only went in the mornings as they had chores to do in the afternoon and normally stopped schooling altogether at around fourteen-years old. Lily helped Miss Wong teach English and Maths using western symbols rather than Chinese. Miss Wong in return helped Lily after school with her written Chinese.

When food was scarce, which was often, and Lily and Ah-Lam's tummies started to rumble, Lin Lin had taught them to drink lots of water and chew on mint stalks like she had to do when she was a little girl on the mainland. She also told them not to be spoiled and be grateful for what they had and *not to complain about what they didn't have*. She scolded them often and occasionally slapped them also, but on that Christmas night as with every night, as they slept on their pallets on the dirt floor, the little old woman held them tightly.

CHAPTER SEVEN

Sai Kung, Hong Kong, January 1997

Detective Alex Wu Torrence could hear his mobile phone ringing and vibrating simultaneously and instinctively reached to his right where his bedside table back home in Manchester would be, instead his hand found the back of his mother's ancient settee. Gaining his senses, he looked to his left, and saw the little blue light of his Nokia phone. 06.23 read the display, with an unlisted phone number below it.

"Wu Torrence," he answered groggily, rubbing his eyes.

A female voice replied. "Detective Inspector, this is Senior Constable Heidi Lim."

"Morning, Heidi, what's up?"

A cup of tea miraculously appeared from out of nowhere, delivered by his mother, who was now opening the living-room curtains.

"There has been an incident at the crime scene overnight. An Englishman has been arrested for assaulting a police officer."

"Who is it?" Alex asked, taking a sip of his tea – strong "English tea" with half a sugar and a splash of milk. Perfect.

Heidi Lim paused and Alex heard paper rustling. "His name is Andy William Goff, aged thirty-one, from Kam Tin, near Yuen Long in the New Territories. He is the supervisor at Coniston Marine, the dive company."

"The supervisor that Wayne Harris was talking about, I assume?" Alex asked.

"I think so. I've spoken to the arresting officer, the young constable from last night. His English is not so great but he thinks the Englishman told him he was the boss before this happened. The Constable also sounded a bit shook up when I spoke to him on the phone earlier, so he might be mistaken."

Alex asked, "So, what was the incident exactly?"

"Well, it seems that this Andy Goff man turned up at the site just before 5am this morning in an aggravated state and smelling of alcohol; he told the Constable that he wanted to go into the dive container. The officer told him that no-one was entering the crime scene. Anyway, an altercation took place and the drunk man pushed the officer out of the way and tried to unlock the container, the officer then drew his service revolver, but the accused pushed him again causing him an injury to his head, I believe."

Alex was momentarily distracted by the smell of bacon coming from the kitchenette, but he immediately refocused his attention on the phone-call.

"The constable is now in the hospital receiving treatment, I believe it is a minor injury."

"He must have been pretty drunk to take on a police officer with a gun," Alex said as a bacon sandwich appeared in front of him.

"Very drunk, very aggressive, and also very large, according to the constable. Apparently even when he was handcuffed he still put up a fight."

"Where is he now?"

"He's in the...what do you call that in English? Oh yes, he's in the drunk tank at Tsuen Wan police station. That is the closest station to the airport with holding-cells," Lin replied.

"Has anybody spoken to him yet?"

"Other than the arresting officer and the desk sergeant, no. He's sleeping off the alcohol apparently. Inspector Jackie Shuen is on his way over to Tsuen Wan now, he will meet you there as soon as possible. A police car is on its way to pick you up from your mother's home shortly."

"OK, I'll just shower and I'll be there soon. Bye."

"Goodbye."

Even before Alex could wolf down the sandwich, a police car had pulled up outside. He heard his mother telling the uniformed officer in Cantonese that the "Detective Inspector" would be outside in ten minutes and would the officer like breakfast?

"Good morning, Son," Lily said as she walked back inside briskly and kissed him on the forehead.

"Morning, Mum, gotta' run unfortunately"

"I'm used to it, remember! Your clothes are ready in the spare room," said Lily, whilst briefly looking at the photo of Jock on the mantelpiece.

Alex headed into the spare room with half a bacon sandwich still in his mouth. His clothes were ironed and freshly laid out on the single bed. Alex wondered if the woman ever slept.

"Just one thing, Mum. Do you still have Dad's toolbox?"

*

Ten minutes later Alex was in the back of the squad car in his freshly-ironed clothes, showered, with a packed lunch in his shoulder-bag along with a small hacksaw from his father's toolbox. There was a tell-tale smell of bacon in the air as the driver set off whilst looking in the rear-view mirror sheepishly.

He placed a long-distance call to CID Manchester to check in with the UK office and run the name Andrew William Goff through the UK database. CID said they would call him back as soon as they had run the checks.

The Tsuen Wan station was the exact opposite of the elegant colonial Central headquarters. Tsuen Wan, like a lot of towns in the New Territories, was a new town built to accommodate Hong Kong's expanding population and Chinese refugees fleeing Chairman Mao's "Cultural Revolution" in the sixties and seventies. The Tsuen Wan station mirrored the drab concrete architecture of the town itself and wouldn't have looked out of place in Milton Keynes or Luton.

Jackie Shuen was waiting on the station steps smoking a cigarette. He acknowledged Alex by stubbing it out and nodding in the direction of the station.

"Did Senior Constable Lim fill you in?" Shuen asked.

"Pretty much; has Goff woken up yet?"

"If he hasn't, he will by the time we get in there. The Constable from last night will need stitches over his eye. Sounds like he got off lucky," Shuen said.

"Jackie, remember I'm only here to observe."
DI Shuen replied sombrely. "Well you can observe me waking this lousy shit up then. I don't know how it works in England nowadays but we tend to frown upon the attacking of policemen."

"I know, Jackie, but the Chief Inspector..."
Inspector Shuen stopped as they approached the station doors. "I don't see Mark Hayton here, do you, Alex?"

Shuen had almost spat the Chief Inspector's name out, the first-time Alex had ever seen his colleague's façade slip, even if it was only momentarily.

Two minutes later they were approaching the middle-aged, slightly overweight desk sergeant who was positioned at the head of four sterile-looking holding-cells.

"Good morning, Sergeant Chan." Shuen obviously knew the officer.

"Good morning, Detective Inspector Shuen, and er..."
Jackie Shuen touched the man's forearm. "It's about time for your coffee break, is it not, Sergeant?"

The desk sergeant didn't miss a beat and nonchalantly started to walk off. "Yes, Detective Inspector, I normally take *ten minutes only* around this time of day. There appears to be only cell number four occupied anyway."

The Sergeant walked around the corner and Jackie Shuen leant over and picked key number four off the hook. He also picked up the desk sergeant's cup of green tea.

Shuen checked the porthole, placed the key in the lock and gestured to Alex to follow him.

The room smelt of stale wine, vomit and piss. The drunken, snoring man had half a well-built arm hanging out of bed.

Shuen threw the cup of tea over him.

"Wakey wakey, hands off snakey," Shuen said, in a surprisingly good cockney accent.

The big man grumbled, shook his head and tumbled off the bed.

"What...er...what...?" Andy Goff mumbled, still slurring his words.

"Good morning, Mr Goff, been having fun?" Shuen said.

Andy Goff started to sit upright on the floor. He was well-built and had a sharp crew-cut. He also had blood-shot eyes and stank of alcohol. Obviously ex-military, thought Alex.

"I said, have you been having fun? Did you have a good night last night, Mr Goff?"

"Eh...fuck knows. I need a piss."

With that, the large man stood over the stainless-steel toilet, seemingly oblivious to the two detectives. He still seemed unsteady on his feet. The big man shivered and grunted on completion. He then sat on the edge of the bed rubbing his temples and looking at his shoes.

"What happened last night, Andy?" Alex asked.

"Name, rank and number only," laughed the drunken man.

"I suggest you answer the question, Andy. What happened last night?" Alex repeated.

The drunken man spat on the floor hitting Shuen's shoe. He slurred. "Andrew William Goff, Sergeant 9234871, Sir!"

Jackie Shuen delivered a perfectly timed kick straight into his groin, felling the man who was nearly twice his size. Andy Goff lay prone on the floor holding his genitals; his head beside a splattering of dried vomit.

"You chinky bastard, I've got rights you know. I'll..."

Quick as a flash Jackie Shuen crossed the room and put his foot on the prone man's throat. Alex instinctively covered the door.

"My officers have rights too, Mr Goff. They have the right not to be attacked whilst doing their duties, don't you think?"

The Englishman was holding the Chinese inspector's ankle with both hands. He croaked, "I just wanted to open up the container, honest."

"At five o'clock in the morning?" Shuen replied.

"I was drunk, I wanted to sleep off the drink."

Alex spoke. "You do realise it was a crime scene, don't you?"

"I was drunk, I just wanted to kip, and the chink...ahhhhh"

Shuen had pressed down on his throat.

"The officer, the officer...he...he...didn't speak English. I just pushed him, honest."

Alex spoke again. "Where were you Saturday night, Andy?"

"I want a lawyer, I have rights...ahhhh..."

Shuen appeared to increase the pressure.

"I can't remember, the pub, home, I don't know...ahhhh...I honestly don't know."

"What do you know about Darren Meakin, Goff?" Alex asked.

"I didn't know him, the Chi...the triad kid killed him, didn't he?"

Alex heard whistling outside in the corridor. He presumed it was the desk sergeant returning.

Shuen took his cue and leaned closer to the prisoner. "Just one more thing: we are going to be coming back shortly to interview you formally and you are going to sober up and tell us exactly what we need to know, agreed?"

"OK, OK!" Goff nodded whilst rubbing his neck.

Alex unlocked the door, Jackie Shuen started to walk away but Andy Goff made a grab for him. Instinctively, Alex stepped in and kicked the man in the balls, making the big Englishman keel over once more.

Alex leaned in and whispered in the big man's ear. "And another thing, don't ever call my colleague a chinky."

Back at the desk, the sergeant didn't react as Alex placed the key on the table.

Jackie commented, "Terrible things, those slippery floors, Sergeant."

"Certainly are, Sir," said the Sergeant, lighting a cigarette. "They certainly are."

Alex hardly had time to compute what had just happened in the station before they were back in a police car.

Jackie Shuen breathed deeply and interrupted the silence. "Forensics should be at the airport already and I've asked one of the police divers to come back if we need any technical help in the container."

"You OK, Jackie?"

"Yes, fine, thank you," replied Shuen, looking out of the window. "They charged Kwan Yo Hang last night."

The statement hung in the air a moment.

"On whose orders?" Alex asked

"Senior Inspector Karl Roberts; they pulled Kwan out of the cells around 9pm which meant we couldn't get the undercover in there. He's in Pik Uk Prison at this moment, amongst his triad friends. We've got no chance of a covert plan now."

Shuen's frustration was visible. He had obviously been undermined by people further up the command chain and had seriously lost a lot of face.

"Jackie, don't take this the wrong way, but were you taking your frustrations out on Andy Goff back there?" Alex asked respectfully.

"If I was, he deserved it anyway," replied Shuen, calmly. "I understand it is different in England, but if you attack an officer in Hong Kong you should expect to pay the consequences."

Alex nodded as DI Shuen continued. "Plus, we need to know exactly what Mr Goff back there knows about the Darren Meakin murder, and as soon as he sobers up properly, I want a statement. I think we've just got time to do one more trip to the airport and get back around mid-day for another little chat with a sober Andy Goff and his lawyer."

"Why do you think they transferred Kwan?" Alex asked.

Shuen paused once more. "I think a lot of people want this to go away; the airport authorities, the Governor of Hong Kong, the Chinese, the British. This has happened at a very politically sensitive time and the last thing these people want are stories about foreigners being murdered, just before the world's press arrive to report on the Handover. Don't worry about the truth, just get it done and dusted."

Alex nodded. "So, what do we do?"

"How many cases have we worked on together previously Alex? Ten? Twenty? I've seen how you work and I think you are a police officer like me. Not a politician. What do you think we do?"

Alex replied. "I think we solve this case."

*

The crime scene, although familiar, looked slightly different with the early morning sun reflecting off the South China Sea. Alex noticed what he presumed to be Andy Goff's Coniston Marine pick-up truck parked askew. A police constable held the tape at shoulder height for the two detectives to walk under. As they approached the container, they could see the forensics team dusting for fingerprints on the outside of the unit.

"Now how do we get access to the container with no key?"

Alex opened his jacket to reveal his dad's old hacksaw.

"I think I might be able to help there, Jackie."

Alex crouched down in the dust and was just about to start sawing when something caught his eye in the dirt under the container.

"One minute," he said

He had spotted a key and a key-ring with the Coniston Marine logo on it, lying in the dust. He took a pen from out of his pocket and hooked the ring.

Alex carefully opened the padlock using the edge of the key, and beckoned a forensics officer over.

"Can you see if we can lift a print off this, please? And any chance we can do it on-site?"

The man behind the mask nodded in the affirmative and placed the key and key-ring in a sealed bag. He also handed the two detectives blue plastic gloves.

Shuen asked, "Didn't the big Australian diver say there was definitely no key here when we asked yesterday?"

"Yes," agreed Alex. "We better go and have a chat with him later, whilst we are still here."

With his gloves in place, Alex opened the stiff container double-door to what appeared to be some kind of control centre with dial and intercoms. On the floor also stood a set of dive equipment.

"Kirby Morgan's," a voice from behind them said.

The police diver from the previous day had arrived; he entered the container and pointed at the kit. "It's a Kirby Morgan helmet, it's American kit, very expensive, and shouldn't be lying around like that, that's for sure."

The yellow diver's helmet was perched on top of a scuba cylinder and a kind of harness. There were numerous hoses and a gauge attached to the kit.

"I'd be annoyed if any of my team left gear hanging around like that. It hasn't even been washed."

"How do you know? Erm, sorry I didn't catch your name?" Alex asked.

"Eric, Eric Tsang, senior police diver. Look, there is salt residue all over the harness. It should be cleaned with fresh water and dismantled like the set over there."

He pointed to an almost identical set that was in separate parts and hung up on a rack at the rear of the container. There was also a space for the kit that was now laid on the floor.

Alex, who had taken a PADI Discover Scuba course on holiday in Greece a few years previously, asked, "So, they breathe off the bottle, right?"

"No, not in this instance. That's what they call a 'bail out bottle'. It's backup if the air from the compressor fails for any reason. The breathing air comes through the umbilicals which are the large hoses hanging up outside, and you also have communications cables so the supervisor can talk to the diver."

"The diver is on his own? Why are there two sets of kit then?"

The police diver laughed. "Been diving in Thailand have you, Detective? Recreational divers always dive in buddy pairs but commercial divers generally dive solo with a safety diver on the surface in full equipment in case of an emergency."

Alex nodded. "But why would only one set of kit be set up? Could one person dive on his own, using this kind of set-up?"

The police diver scratched his head. "In theory yes, but they would have to be experienced and physically strong to carry all the kit and the umbilicals. Normally they have a guy called a tender on the surface just for the hoses alone. And why would anybody want to dive without surface support?"

Why indeed, thought Alex. Why indeed?

*

Alex could hear a commotion going on outside the container. A fat European man was talking loudly to the police constable. He had just got out of a black BMW.

"Who's in charge here, Mush?" said the man with a southern twang.

Portsmouth or Southampton, thought Alex, as he followed behind Detective Shuen towards the obviously agitated man.

The man barked, "You in charge?"

Shuen showed him his badge. "DI Jackie Shuen, can I help you?"

"Yes, I'm Chris Slater, boss at Coniston Marine. When can I get my unit back? Ten fuckin' grand a day I'm losing out!"

Shuen replied politely. "Sir, investigations are ongoing, we might need some more time..."

"More time? You'd pull yer' fuckin' finger out if it was costing you ten grand a day!"

Alex spoke to the man for the first time. "Mr Slater, you do realise a man was murdered here at the weekend?"

"'Course I do, but what's that got to do with my dive kit? I've got divers lying in their bunks and a fuckin' supervisor gone AWOL and not answering his phone..."

"Andy Goff?"

"Yeah, where is he?"

"We have Mr Goff in custody at Tsuen Wan police station, he attacked a police officer here at around 5am this morning."

"Fuck, fuckedy fuck! What a prick!" Slater shouted whilst lighting up a cigarette and visibly shaking with anger.

Overweight, smoking and stressed, thought Alex, as Chris Slater sucked on his Marlboro. This man is a walking heart attack.

Alex continued. "Who has keys to the container, Mr Slater?"

"Andy Goff, and there is one hidden under the unit usually, probably under a brick or something?"

"And was anybody here Saturday night, Mr Slater?" Alex asked.

"No, we sometimes work Saturday mornings, but we were waiting on materials so they clocked off on Friday."

"And who locked up on Friday?" Alex continued

"Dunno, probably the Australian what's his name, Wayne, Crocodile fuckin' Dundee or whatever he's called. Andy was up at the yard in Kam Tin."

"Do they always dismantle the equipment before they leave?"

"They better fuckin' do. Those helmets alone cost me ten thousand fuckin' quid! Have they left it in a mess? I'll string them up if they have!"

Alex didn't address the question directly. "And you're sure you didn't have divers in the water on Saturday?"

"Positive. What's this, Question Time or something? When can I get my unit back?"

"As soon as possible, Mr Slater," Shuen answered calmly

"One final question, Mr Slater," asked Alex. "Did you know Darren Meakin?"

"The geezer what got murdered? I never met him. We paid him to do some welding training but Andy Goff set that up."

"So, Andy Goff knew him, then?"

"Yeah, when can I get my container back?"

*

The two detectives approached the hut with the Union Jack ten minutes later and knocked. Muffled noises came from inside until a skinny caucasian man opened the door in only his underpants. Alex could see the pizza boxes from the previous day and assorted other takeaway wrappers and beer cans.

"Mornin'," grunted the man.

"Is Wayne there?"

The man turned around. "Wayne, its Demi Moore, she's had enough of Bruce Willis and wants an Australian with a small cock."

Alex stifled a laugh. The big, hairy Australian walked up behind his friend whilst pulling a yellow and green t-shirt over his head.

"Good morning fellas, can we work yet?"

Alex noticed he had blood-shot eyes which were not dissimilar to Andy Goff's.

"Afraid not, Wayne," answered Alex. "Maybe tomorrow. You got a minute?"

Alex heard a collective groan from the assorted bunks and a call to close the bloody door.

Wayne Harris replied, "Sure, what's up? You haven't got a mint, have you?"

Alex handed him a stick of gum instead. "Where were you all last night, Wayne?"

"Oh, mate, we went on a right bender, mostly at the Watering Hole, we figured we wouldn't be working so we got totally blotto!"

Shuen asked, "Was Andy Goff with you?"

"Yeah, mate, front and centre, he's a crazy bastard when he's pissed, that one, I tell you."

"In what way?" Alex quizzed.

"Oh, you know.... It's a bit difficult with him being my boss and all," said Wayne, rubbing the back of his neck.

Alex paused momentarily and replied, "Anything you tell us here goes no further, Wayne; you've got my word on that."

The men walked a bit further away from the huts.

"Well it's no big secret, any of the boys will tell you, he's a prick at the best of times, but put a few beers in him and he's a complete prick."

"Did he get up to anything in particular last night?"

"Oh, you know, the usual. You see, the thing about commercial divers is that most of them are ex-military and they can't leave it behind. Me, you see, I wasn't in the forces, plus I'm Aussie obviously, so I'm considered a bit of an outsider." The Australian paused. "Fuck, I could do with a coffee, my mouths as dry as a nun's cunt."

Alex prodded him further as they continued walking. "So, was he misbehaving last night?"

"Well, no more than usual, it's just I try and keep out of his way when he starts talking all this commando bollocks. He reckons he was some sort of big-shot Marine or SAS kind of shit. Dave in the bunkhouse reckons it's a crock of shit and he was a postman in Birmingham."

As if a thought dawned on him, Wayne Harris stopped once more. "Why are we talking about Andy Goff, by the way? Did he bring the key this morning?"

Shuen spoke. "Andy Goff assaulted one of my officers early this morning near the diving container."

Wayne Harris looked impassive. "Doesn't surprise me, to be honest, mate, he can be a nasty fucker when he's pissed. Was this when he opened up this morning?"

"What time would he open up normally?" Alex replied.

"Normally about eight. He said he'd knock us up if we could work today. I figured, when he didn't come around then, that we weren't working and I rolled back over to sleep."

Alex continued. "This was around five in the morning. Did you come back here with him?"

"Five in the morning; what was he doing at that time? No, mate, like I said, he's a nightmare when he's pissed, so me and the lads sneaked off about one or two-ish. Grabbed a kebab and got a taxi back here. When we left him, he was talking to some old duffer at the bar in a safari suit, looked like David fuckin' Attenborough!"

Alex didn't react but made a note to call Taff as soon as possible, as the three men approached the dive container.

Wayne pointed at the abandoned Coniston Marine vehicle which was parked at an angle of 45 degrees from the police cordon. "Jesus, I know they're a bit slack on the drink-driving here but he must have been absolutely slaughtered when he got in the ute."

"Ute?" Shuen asked.

"Ute, pommies call it a pick-up, I think."

Alex nodded. "Wayne, yesterday, when you went to open up the unit for us, are you absolutely sure the key wasn't there?"

"Yeah 100 per cent; you saw me. It should have been under the breeze block, but it wasn't there."

"What about under the unit, did you look there?" Alex pointed at the spot where he had found the key earlier.

"Yeah, I think so. If it was just there under the door, I would have seen it, wouldn't I?"

"And what does it look like exactly?" asked Shuen.

"It's a jagged metal thing that fits in a lock!" Wayne answered sharply.

"He means, is it on a key-ring, for example?" Alex explained.

"Sorry blokes, my hangover is just starting to kick in. It's got a white key-ring with a Coniston Marine logo on it," answered Wayne.

"And is Andy Goff's key the same?"

"No, his is on a chain. Have you checked the ignition in the ute?"

All three men walked towards the pick-up and could clearly see Andy Goff's keys plus key-chain still in the ignition under the steering-wheel of the works vehicle.

Shuen whispered to Alex out of earshot of the Australian, "I'm going to get forensics to check the pick-up also."

Alex nodded and guided Wayne back towards the unit.

"And you locked up on Friday; you were the last one out, correct? Was it tidy when you left?"

"Yeah, me and the team left at roughly the same time but I locked up. We tidied it up as usual and I put the key in the normal place."

Alex paused for effect, focused his attention on the diver and opened the container door once more.

"Jesus Christ! We didn't leave it like that! I'd lose my job if the bosses saw this!"

Alex answered, "You're sure? You didn't leave in a hurry and forget to dismantle it for example?"

"No, mate. Listen! The other blokes were with me and it was cleaned, dismantled, and put away. Our lives depend on this gear, we look after it. And another thing..." The big Australian pointed at the dive kit. "The dive-knife is missing."

*

Alex put on his poker face as Shuen joined them once more. "Wayne thinks the dive-knife is missing, DI Shuen."

"I *know* its missing, look..."

Wayne went to touch the kit but Alex stopped him calmly and said, "Careful big fella...fingerprints!"

"Oh, yeah, right you are, but look there, you see the curly thing that looks like a telephone wire; a lanyard we call it. It's been cut. There should be a Green River attached to that."

"What's a Green River?" Alex asked.

"It's the best diving-knife in the world, mate, will cut through anything. Proper commercial divers won't use anything else, it's the only knife that's sharp enough to cut through the umbilical if you really got in the shit, trapped or something." Wayne Harris paused. "There's one on the safety diver's kit, look!"

Sure enough, there was a large, yellow-handled knife clipped to the harness on the rack. Alex put his latex glove back on and slowly removed the knife from its sheath. He was immediately drawn to the serrated edge and thought back to Darren Meakin's cut throat in the morgue.

Alex put his other hand on the big Australian's shoulder as he gave him his mobile number. "Listen, Wayne. Thanks for your assistance, you've been a big help. Here's my personal mobile. You can call me directly, day or night, if you can think of anything else. OK?"

"OK," replied the diver as he slipped the card into his wallet.

CHAPTER EIGHT

Mau Tau Chung Internment Camp, August 10th 1945

Jock thought that Billy's shakes seemed to have been getting worse and worse of late. Most prisoners' uniforms had pretty much disintegrated over the last few years and the general attire was now shorts and a bare chest, especially in the stifling heat of August in Hong Kong. Billy's ribs were protruding from his chest, his breathing was shallow and the shakes were accompanied by the night terrors that he and many other men, including Jock, experienced during the dark, mosquito-ridden nights. But the most worrying thing that morning, as Billy lay in the so-called "medical dormitory", was the smell of his breath; they had all smelt beriberi before but none of the chums in the barracks wanted to acknowledge it as they headed out for reclamation work near the airport that morning.

Jock spoke. "Hang in there, Billy, we'll be back at sundown, Pal."

Other men patted his bony shoulders and offered words of encouragement as they headed out of the hut.

Spirits had been lifted considerably in the last few months, especially since the note back in May from Popeye telling them, "HITLER DEAD, RUSANS IN BERLEN." Red Cross parcels and even letters from home had also been arriving every three or four months, and the fact that Jock knew his family were well and healthy made the daily grind much more bearable. The letters were heavily censored and any mention of the war was strictly forbidden. Corporal Hamasaki had been born in Canada, spoke perfect English, and had an intense hatred of the Canadians, in particular, which was probably due to childhood bullying. He seemed to take a twisted delight in tearing up letters in front of the POWs.

Jock's father always passed on the local news; the shipyard, the church, his sisters, whilst Jock in turn had played down the horrors of internship and written to his family about the comradeship and camp humour. He didn't mention the beatings, malnourishment and disease. Govan seemed a million miles away.

In the Pacific, the Japs were still hanging in, stubbornly clinging on to the Imperial Empire, but the mood in the camp was gradually changing and everybody in the camp knew that it was only a matter of time until they were liberated. For a few like Billy however, it was just a case of hanging on for dear life and trying to survive.

Every morning at roll-call after the prisoners had been accounted for and bowed deeply to the Japanese officers and the Japanese flag, Hinomaru, Major Koizumi would give his morning speeches usually including phrases such as, "Recent victories for the glorious Imperial Japanese Empire against western colonialists" and "More and more Chinese territory liberated by the Emperor's brave soldiers."

Even with the hunger pangs, lack of medicine, mosquitoes and dysentery, the mood in the camp had lifted immeasurably. On his better days, Billy could do a fantastic impression of General Koizumi. "His glorious Emperor Hirohito has today successfully boiled an egg marking a major victory for glorious Japanese chickens in Tokyo!"

The roll-call that morning was more subdued with Major Koizumi absent and First Lieutenant Saito simply giving the day's work orders to the POWs with Jock's group heading to Kai Tak for maintenance work. Jock smiled inwardly as there would be a good chance of seeing the three pebbles or maybe even Popeye himself. He also knew that he wouldn't be adding Billy's name to his little book in the tool-shed, for today at least.

*

Sai Kung, New Territories, August 10th 1945

Seventeen-year old Lily and her elder sister Ah-Lam were out in the sand-banks ankle deep in sludge searching for whelks, as the tide was out. The tide would turn shortly and they would maybe try and barter for a fish or two at Pak Sha Wan pier with one of the fishermen for half of their whelks.

Both girls had started wearing traditional Hakka attire of all black robes and large rimmed-hats whilst they were out during the day. Their worn dresses and tatty shoes were simply for Sunday best and in Lily's case when she helped out at school. Even then the girls still wore their Hakka clothes over their female clothes until they were safely inside and the doors were locked.

On the beach, they could see a man with a white shirt waving his arms frantically in the distance. They recognised him as George Leung from the marine office. A nice boy, who, since seeing Ah-Lam eighteen months earlier, seemed to have miraculously found religion and now accompanied them to church every Sunday. Or more accurately, accompanied Ah-Lam, with Lily tagging on behind.

Ah-Lam had told Lily, in strictest confidence, that George had been monitoring English radio transmissions and translating broadcasts for the resistance. Ah-Lam had puffed her chest out when she told Lily, but made her swear on Mother's memory not to say anything to anybody. If he were to be found out he could be killed.

"Sisters, sisters!" George started to run over the mud-flats in his full office clothes.

Lily scratched her temple. "What's the crazy boy doing now?!"

"The Americans, the Americans!" George stopped in front of the girls, out of breath and covered in mud. "The Americans, they've dropped an atom bomb on Japan; Japan will have to surrender!"

Ah-Lam spoke. "What's an atom bomb? Whe...when...."

George Leung interrupted Ah-Lam by giving her a big kiss full on the lips. He then paused momentarily as if he realised the magnitude of what he had just done. Before she had the chance to object, he removed her hat and kissed her once again.

Lily took the opportunity to deposit a large lump of mud on both their heads and before long all three were covered in mud, laughing and crying like they hadn't done in a long time.

*

"Psssst, psssst! Tommy Soldier, down here."

Jock could hear the familiar voice of Popeye the Sailor man under the pontoon.

"Tommy soldier, it's nearly over. Japanese going to surrender. Yankees dropped big bombs...boom...boom!"

Jock momentarily looked over his shoulder. He'd never heard Popeye this loud or brazen before.

Jock asked, "Are you sure?"

"Hundred percent, Tommy soldier. Japanese doing 'harry carry' in China. Few more days then surrender. Be careful, Tommy soldier. Japanese crazy, crazy."

On returning to camp he went to see Captain Campbell straight away. The Captain had obviously heard similar news.

"Now listen, Jock," the way he pronounced it, it sounded like York. "We don't know how the Japs are going to take this; they might take revenge on us. Get your men in your hut prepared over the next few days: rocks, sticks, tools, anything you can lay your hands on."

That night Jock hardly slept a wink, the more able-bodied men had sharpened the wooden supports from under their beds and they all had large pebbles in their pockets, only rocks and wood against rifles and bullets, but Jock for one had no intention of going out without a fight. In the distance, they could hear the guards drinking and shouting incomprehensible Japanese, and outside the barbed wire fences Hong Kong seemed strangely quiet as if bracing itself for the next few days of uncertainty.

*

Mau Tau Chung Internment Camp, August 11th 1945
During the night Private William McCray of the 2nd Battalion Royal Scots passed away. He was twenty-four years old.

CHAPTER NINE

Tsuen Wan Police Station, 1997
Andy Goff rolled over on the grubby bunk, his head was spinning, but he felt that just half an hour's more kip would sort him out. The pain in his balls was numb and the bile was starting to retch up again. "Fucking Chinese twat," he muttered to himself. "Lucky for them that there were two of em', else I would have battered the little cunt."

He felt his belly rumble and momentarily thought he should have eaten at some point the previous evening. His head was pounding, and at that moment he just needed sleep, a greasy breakfast, a couple of paracetamols and a cup of tea and then he'd be right as rain, as his old nan back in Solihull used to say.

Thoughts raced through his drink-sodden skull; "What a fuckin' week; what a fuckin week! Everything had just been going fuckin' great up to now until some daft twat decided to start to let every Tom, Dick and Harry start kipping on site six months ago, gettin' in the way and generally fuckin' everything up for everybody. Honestly, twelve more months and I'd have been able to fuck off to Thailand and live like a King."

He heard footsteps in the corridor, sounding like a hospital wing or something. He braced himself and thought, "I'll be ready for the little cunt this time, with his little kung fu kicks, the slanty-eyed little bastard." He braced himself. The footsteps stopped and he saw the eye-hole cover momentarily move.

"Come on, you bastards, let's be avin' yer!" he shouted. His speech still slurred.

The eye-hole closed and the footsteps began getting quieter and quieter. He put the flimsy pillow over his head and tried to cut out the daylight whilst piecing together the previous evening. He had flashbacks of "his" boys in the Watering Hole. He'd bought them a few drinks as every good leader should, without them taking the piss that is, show em' you can be one of the boys but then they need to know who's boss – when it's their round, you just have to tell em' like it is, being top of the tree has its perks. He hadn't liked the look on that Australian cunt's face that's for sure, but a few extra hours underwater in the shit-pipes under the runway will sort that kangaroo fuckin' convict out, that's for sure. Staring at *him, the boss, the gaffer, top boy*; who the fuck did he think he was?! The other ones knew how it was; do your job, keep your head down, no back chat and stand your round at the bar. That's what the forces taught you; they should make it a rule that all divers should come through the forces – even better, the British forces – then yer wouldn't get any fuckin' didgeridoo, sheep shaggin' bastards givin' yer the eyeball, putting you in a bad mood, clocking a chinky copper and getting a night in the drink tank. I'll give the bastard a two-hour shift underwater he thought, maybe even sack him."

Just then the hatch at the bottom of the metal cell door slipped open and a metal tray appeared with a clunk. Andy Goff opened one eye and focussed on his jail breakfast of noodles, bread and water. Could be worse, he thought, he'd heard of internees back in Baghdad having Iraqi turds pushed under the door.

He started to eat his breakfast sparingly. Think, Andy, think! All he had needed to do was give the kit a bit of a wash or even just put it on the rack, put the key back and Bob's your Uncle. Two-minutes tops, but the fuckin' chinky copper had to get in the way, didn't he? Job's-worth little yellow bastard. I'd told him two minutes, just two minutes. Probably didn't speak English, in a British colony, can you believe it? Two minutes and I would've been sorted. Granted, the whiskey the old Welsh fella had been pouring down his neck in the Watering Hole might not have helped, but for fuck's sake.

He drank some water from his breakfast tray, giving him a bit of clarity. "Now think, Soldier," he said out loud.

Keep schtum, name, rank and number. He thought they'd have to give him a lawyer soon, it was the law, wasn't it? And if the two coppers came back, he'd be ready this time.

And what about a phone-call? Wasn't he allowed a phone-call like on the telly? But who would he call? His boss? Slater? The missus? or Number Six? Fuck, fuck, fuck! Slater and the missus would both be livid.... fuck, fuck! And Number Six was still mightily pissed off about the welder, shit! He thought if he could only think straight he could sort this out. They probably couldn't link the welder and the chinky copper, no way. He barely touched the copper and if he hadn't turned his back just at that moment he could've never got one on him and cuffed him, no way, even if he was a bit pissed. He must have hit him with his truncheon when he was bent over, or something.

He stood up and felt his head momentarily spin before steadying himself. He banged on the door. "I want a phone-call! I want a lawyer!"

"Be quiet!" came the reply from down the corridor.

He sat back on the bunk. He massaged his temples and tried to think once more. The copper thing, now that wasn't so bad, drunk and disorderly, maybe ABH? Christ, he'd barely touched him. No, keep quiet, take the rap and get the slap on the wrist. That'll be a piece of cake.

But the welder?! Fuck! Why did he have to be there in the first place?! He still didn't like thinking about it. Jesus, he'd killed a few rag-heads in Iraq but this wasn't the same, was it? He'd just gone into the container to turn the air off; thirty-seconds tops. Then Big Darren was looking through the dry box. Shit, shit. Probably more money than he'd ever seen in his whole life, the dippy Mancunian cunt. Christ, if only he'd have just got knocked out when he hit him with the dive weight that would've been the last of it. It's not like Big Darren had even seen him or anything as he'd hit him from behind. He'd just misjudged it...too bloody hard. He thought to himself that Big Darren could've even been dead before he hit the ground the way he went down. He'd checked for a pulse, wishing he was just knocked-out, but he wasn't, the stupid big bastard! He was obviously dead, and that's when Andy Goff had panicked. He rang Number Six who was spewing, he was under strict instructions never to call him. They'd only ever sent and received texts since they first started two years back, after he was first approached. Two numbers, that was all. Number Six sent a text with two numbers; which inlet to pick up the box from and which inlet to drop it off at. Simple. All under-water, out of sight, dead easy. But then two things happened; they started to house the site workers actually on the airport, meaning that he had to do it later and later at night whilst being more cautious, and secondly, Andy had got curious, he'd started to wonder what was in the boxes. At first he just skimmed a bit of cash, the odd Rolex watch or jewellery. He'd left any drugs or shit like that alone but had just skimmed enough stuff off the top to make it a bit more worthwhile for himself. For fuck's sake it was just like a little tax, wasn't it? He was the one with all the skills and the diving know-how; he was the one taking all the risk. Fuck em'. But he'd been scared, scared of getting found out, scared of Number Six.

Andy Goff lay back on his bunk and thought of the night with the welder. Number Six had eventually calmed down and told him to chop him on the arm like a triad thing, then throw away the mobile and the weapon. Number Six would send the cleaners in. Andy had then heard a taxi pulling up near the huts, he had to act quick, he chopped the welder twice on the arm and did his throat too just to make sure. He thought he heard people nearby and didn't have time to dismantle the gear so he put the spare key in his pocket so his boys couldn't get in to the container, then he'd dismantle it before work on Monday. Number Six had said to leave the body; he might just have been able to throw the big welder over the wall and into the water, but Number Six said he had the cleaners on the way (whoever they were). He'd take care of everything.

Andy obviously hadn't told Number Six that he'd opened the box. He'd thrown it down another inlet and remembered the location number as he was driving off-site, he'd sort that out later. On the airport bridge, he threw the Green River dive-knife and the mobile into the sea.

Meanwhile, back in the present and the brightly-lit cell in Tsuen Wan, Andy Goff picked at a bit of processed ham in the noodles, it was pink and pallid. He then retched at the thought of slitting Darren Meakin's throat, which had felt like cold, raw meat.

Regaining his composure, he thought to himself once more; that's it... keep quiet, get a good lawyer, take the rap for the assault on the copper. Let the chinky triad boy take the rap for the murder and get out of Hong Kong as soon as possible. He then closed his eyes.

Thirty minutes later as Andy Goff had entered deep sleep once more, the cell door opened and a uniformed officer stood in the doorway. The officer said in broken English, "Mr Goff get ready, you have been bailed."

*

While still at the new airport, Alex decided to give Taff's mobile a call. A Chinese lady answered in English. "The United Serviceman's Recreational Club, how may I help you?"

Alex was momentarily confused, then he realised Taff must have forwarded his phone to the USRC, one of Alex Wu Torrence's old childhood haunts.

Alex answered, "Er, is erm...Mr Williams there, please?"

The receptionist responded curtly. "I believe Inspector Williams is indisposed at present, Sir. May I take a message?"

Alex managed to stifle a laugh. His guess was that either the Inspector was indisposed sleeping off last night in the drawing room, or around the pool. "Would you be so kind as to inform the Inspector when he is less indisposed that Detective Inspector Wu Torrence will be joining him for lunch?"

"Yes Sir, very well."

Alex smiled and turned back to the crime scene, where DI Jackie Shuen was briefing some junior detectives including Heidi Lim. He heard him say, "So, we want all the divers and work colleagues of Darren Meakin interviewed independently again today, we want to know where they were, and who they were with at the time of the murder. We also want to know if they knew or previously had any contact with the accused, Kwan Yo Hang. OK, any questions?"

With no answer forthcoming, the junior officers dispersed and Shuen headed towards Alex. "OK, we've got the junior officers tying up a few loose ends with statements and the forensics going over the container and Andy Goff's truck. This should take two or three hours, then we'll head back and see Mr Goff, who hopefully will have sobered up a bit by then."

"What about Kwan Yo Hang?" Alex asked.

"We'll schedule another interview for later but he's had a night with his 'brothers', so he'll be well drilled by now. He's going to be more scared of them than anything we can throw at him. I'd be very surprised if he says a single word to us now, to be honest."

Alex nodded. "Any news from the Chief Inspector?"

"He seems to have calmed down a bit from yesterday. I think the press-briefing appeased Government House somewhat and the press are now off chasing a Canto-pop star who got caught on film snorting cocaine. Darren Meakin's murder is yesterday's news by the looks of it. Either way, it gives us a bit of breathing space."

"By the way, I'm meeting an old friend for lunch, if you can manage without me for an hour or two?" Alex asked.

"Sure, take a staff car, one of the uniforms can drive you," Shuen replied. "I've got plenty to be going on with here."

As he drove off ten minutes later, he noticed the big Australian diver talking to Heidi Lin whilst she took notes.

*

On the way out of the construction site, on a hunch, Alex asked the police driver to pull over at the main office. He entered the temporary building and asked to speak to the site manager.

"Mr Barnett is very busy," answered the receptionist dismissively.

Alex flashed his UK warrant card, fully aware that this carried no jurisdiction in Hong Kong should she choose to inspect it more closely.

"One minute, Sir," she responded without looking in his direction.

While he waited, Alex looked at the miniature model of the new airport. The sheer scale of the construction, even in a glass case, was impressive.

"Mr Barnett will see you now, he has ten minutes exactly," the receptionist said as she led Alex to the site-manager's door. The gold-embossed name of "Raymond Barnett MBE" was embedded on the door.

Raymond Barnett MBE had his back turned to Alex as the receptionist left the room; his striped shirt, red braces and general demeanour oozed power as he spoke into the telephone, "Just make sure it is done, on time, on budget; no questions. Thank you."

Raymond Barnett turned to face Alex for the first time as he put the phone on the cradle. He firmly shook hands with the detective and offered him a seat whilst keeping eye-contact at all times.

"I spoke at length with some of your colleagues yesterday, officer...erm?"

"Detective Inspector Wu Torrence, Sir," Alex said.

The large bald-headed man opposite him pointedly removed his watch, a gold Breitling, and rested it on the leather-bound desk. He was obviously giving Alex a clear indication that his time was at a premium.

"Terrible business, we'll be sending condolences to his family of course. What's the latest?"

"Investigations are on-going, we have a suspect in custody," Alex replied sticking to the standard police line.

"And what can I do for you today exactly, Detective Inspector?"

"I was just wondering if you could explain to me about the diving works going on where the murder actually happened?"

"Sometimes I wonder myself, to be honest," he rubbed his temples. "It's almost like they make half the bloody work up because it's out of sight, underwater so to speak."

The site manager paused and took a sip from his tea without offering Alex a cup. "Basically, they are here with two remits, when we do landfill they check that the plastic sheeting is in place before we drop the rubble, it's like a massive lasagne under there, if we dropped rubble on rubble that would be a waste of materials as it would sink too much. Secondly, there are the tunnels. The expat divers do maintenance, inspections, repairs, that sort of thing. Problem is I reckon the buggers make half of the jobs up on purpose. If there is something broken underwater they just take a photo and we sign the chit for them to fix it. It's money for old rope, really."

"And is everything going to be finished on time?" Alex asked.

"No worse than anything else. Look, the deadline is Handover day and it's my job to make sure it is finished by then."

"And will it be?"

The large man paused and rubbed his temples once more. "Officially, yes. But between you and me and the closed doors…not a hope in hell. We'll be lucky if we're a year late. At least red China will be able to take the plaudits once we are part of the motherland when it's finished though. That goes no further, Inspector, obviously."

"Obviously," nodded Alex. "And would you happen to have a map of the tunnels by any chance, Mr Barnett?"

Raymond Barnet glanced at his watch as he pulled an A4 sheet out of his top drawer. The tunnel plan looked like a small London Underground map. "There are several types of tunnel: dry, wet, drainage, utilities, lighting, all sorts."

Alex looked at the map. "It looks in theory like you could get from one end of the site to the other completely under the runways?"

"Yes, that's the idea, personnel, equipment etc. can all go from one end to the other without obstructing the aircraft."

"I notice some of the pipes are off-shore from the reclaimed land, why is that?"

"Well basically, you know old Kai Tak? Stinks to buggery, doesn't it? It's stagnant water, and we didn't want to make the same mistake here. Water can run right through the underground tunnels any direction we decide and the water goes or comes from these inlets way off site." Barnett paused. "You know quite a bit of old Kai Tak was built by the Japs in the war, don't you? Meant to be loads of allied prisoner-of-war corpses under the runway, they buried them as they went, you know?"

Alex certainly had heard that said, but he needed to focus on the here and now.

Barnett continued. "The problem at the moment however, is that some of the flooded tunnels should be dry, which is where the divers come in."

Alex coughed and chose his words carefully. "The accused Chinese boy, Kwan Yo Hang. We have reason to believe he has triad affiliations. Do you know why he was on-site on Saturday night?"

Raymond Barnett MBE looked briefly irritated by the question, but masked his annoyance by putting his Breitling back on his wrist. "I heard he was a security guard with all the correct papers. I'm sure your colleagues would have checked these already, Inspector."

"Yes, that's correct," Alex figured his time was nearly up. "Finally, would you happen to know why anybody would be diving on Saturday, Mr Barnett?"

"Haven't the foggiest, maybe they were looking for fishes?" he shrugged. "Is that all, Inspector Wu...?"

"Wu Torrence, Sir."

"Wu Torrence, eh? I'll be sailing with Chief Inspector Mark Hayton on the weekend, I'll mention you dropped by. Feel free to take the map."

Shit! thought Alex, and very much hoped he would be on a plane to dreary Manchester long before then.

CHAPTER TEN

Mau Tau Chung Internment Camp, August 1945

The men stood to attention for the morning roll-call. All of the prisoners had heard the commotion in the guards' barracks overnight as it became apparent that Japan had surrendered. The whisper amongst the POWs was that one of the younger guards had committed hari-kari that morning with his traditional samurai sword. Jock sincerely hoped it was nasty wee bastard Keije, but was disappointed as he appeared on the platform to coldly introduce the camp commander, Major Koizumi.

The men bowed hesitantly, and with Billy's death on his mind Jock could feel the salt water in his eyes and the sharpened stones in his tatty pockets rub against his skinny hips. The other whisper that had gone around the camp the previous evening was that the Japs were going to go out with a bang and take all the POWs with them. Each prisoner had come to roll-call with some sort of improvised hidden weapon. Major Koizumi cleared his throat and simply said, "Glorious Emperor Hirohito, commander of the Japanese forces, surrendered yesterday."

You could hear a pin drop as the Major took out his sword. He then walked down the wooden platform steps towards Captain Campbell. Jock gripped his stones so hard that he drew blood. The Major walked towards the Captain, bowed, and formally and simply handed him the sword.

A wave of emotion and relief ripped through Jock and the other prisoners as the Japanese soldiers turned around and marched back to their barracks. Jock dropped to his knees and clasped his bloodied hands together and thanked God that he had made it!

Someone at the rear of the ranks shouted, "Bonzai! You bastards!"

Later that day a strange calm had come over the camp. The Japanese had stayed in their barracks and the interns had been roaming around the camp freely. Red-cross medicines and bandages had been found in the storerooms which had obviously been held back by the Japanese guards and were being distributed amongst the sick and needy, and the local Hong Kongers were now approaching the fences with confidence. Rice balls and fish were being passed through the unlocked gates to the skinny gweilos.

*

Hung Hom, Kowloon, August 1945

Mr Lee had certainly done well out of the occupation. As Lily, Ah-Lam and George Leung sat opposite him in their father's old office, Lily couldn't help but notice the cut of his suit, the gold watch, and the greased side-parting like the Shanghai movie stars had worn before the outbreak of war. It had been an emotional day and Lily was drifting in and out of the conversation.

"We have never heard a single word from your father."

In the days after the surrender the girls had begged Lin Lin to allow them to return to Kowloon, as this was the first time they had felt safe enough. Maybe there had been a miracle and there had been contact from their father, either at the old house or at his office. Lin Lin had at first refused, but relented if George were to chaperone them on the trip. Lin Lin, who by now was beginning to look frail, also refused to accompany them as she didn't want to encounter any ghosts.

"We have to assume the worst, I'm afraid."

Earlier in the day, Lily had felt to be floating out of her body as they turned the corner of Dunbar Road. Their old house was in tatters; a makeshift road had taken the wall and destroyed Mr Chan's beautiful garden.

"Of course, I tried for a short while to continue the original company."

Neither Lily nor Ah-Lam could physically or emotionally enter the building after the trauma of three years earlier. So it was left to poor George to enter the dilapidated house to search for any clues to their father's whereabouts.

"Given the nature of the circumstances I would obviously generously compensate you two girls for the business."

Having entered the house, George had found nothing but a shell of a building, opium pipes, dried blood, rats and human faeces. There was nothing at all to say that their father had ever even been there.

"And the house..."

On her good nights, Lily used to see her father on the veranda with a crisp white shirt on and the sun shining behind him with the red roses in full bloom making a frame as he beckoned her towards him with open arms.

"We can get my lawyers to draft something up quickly."

On her bad nights, it was her mother on the same veranda in a white Chinese dress of mourning. Her mother also beckoned her towards her but she had black holes where her eyes should have been, and two bright circles of blood where her breasts had been cut off.

Lily suddenly snapped out of her stupor. "We need to leave, Mr Lee. Our sampan will be leaving soon."

Mau Tau Chung Internment Camp, August 1945
By mid-afternoon, as the sun was beating down, a Japanese military car came through the gates driven by a European in

military fatigues and with a British officer in the rear. The soldier opened the rear door, Captain Penham-Smythe stepped out calmly, placed his riding crop under his arm, and formally saluted his Canadian counterpart Captain Campbell. Like all of the interns Penham-Smythe looked skinny, but in contrast his uniform looked neat and tidy compared to what the Hung Hom prisoners were wearing.

Skinny and with protruding ribs, a bare-chested Jock was playing cards in the drill area as Captain Campbell beckoned him over to the officer's quarters. "Watch the door please, Torrence."

Captain Penham-Smythe stiffly saluted the smattering of seated Canadian officers and spoke with an air that only the British upper-classes seem to possess. "My name is Captain Penham-Smythe of the Hong Kong Volunteer Defence Corps, and I will be coordinating the transition period before his Majesty's forces arrive from Singapore. We are told they are bringing much-needed food and medical supplies both for internees and the local Hong Kong population."

"When will they arrive?" Captain Campbell asked.

Jock could see through the bamboo door that the British commander seemed affronted that he had been interrupted.

"Er, yes, er…that could be anywhere between one to three weeks."

"And in the meantime?"

The Englishman again seemed to be put off his stride and slightly flicked his riding-crop as he twiddled his moustache.

"Hopefully the Yanks will be making air-drops of emergency supplies in the New Territories and the local volunteer forces are co-ordinating whatever rations the Japanese have stored until the boat arrives."

Captain Campbell nodded before the pompous Penham-Smythe continued condescendingly.

"Of course, it goes without saying that the British armed forces will be taking over from now on, etcetera, etcetera. But there have been rumours that the Kuomintang might be coming over the border from the mainland, nothing to worry about, according to our sources, as they believe the local populace are willing to embrace British rule once more, assuming that their little bellies are full."

The conversation continued, about logistics and British rule, with Captain Penham-Smythe asserting his authority with his ever-present riding-crop, until finally he began his goodbyes.

"Right, must toodle-pip as one has a thousand and one things to do before nightfall, please make sure there is no retribution with the nips over the next few days, Captain Campbell, however tempting it may be, it's just not cricket, eh?"

Jock stood to attention as the English Captain walked through the rickety door.

The Captain breezed past Jock and asked rhetorically, "For goodness sake, soldier, where is your shirt?!"

Momentarily shocked, Jock muttered under his breath "The same place as your fuckin' horse, pal!"

Hung Hom, August 1945

After the shock of what they saw at the family home, the two sisters and George became somewhat unresponsive to what they saw of the horrors of three and a half years of Japanese occupation; beggars, amputees, and ruins were common sights on the Kowloon streets that day, but as they walked past the internment camp for the foreign soldiers, they were truly shocked by the tall, straggly, ghost-like men behind the fence.

"Hurry up, let's get to the ferry pier," said George, "I don't want to be in Kowloon after dark."

On the other side of the fence, Jock was asking his commanding officer, Captain Campbell, if he could get to the supplies store and collect his little black book.

"I'm sorry, Corporal, I don't want anybody off barracks until the dust has settled and we know it is safe to do so."

"Sir, I need to get that record of everything they did, and I want to record Private McCray's death in it also," Jock replied.

The Captain looked up from his papers and removed his glasses. "Listen, Jock, we know how upset you are about Billy's death. We all are. Just be assured the Japanese will get what is coming to them through a court of law. In a week or so we will have supplies, transport and assistance and so on. And then we can retrieve your book, OK? Dismissed."

Jock saluted and left the commanding officer's hut, but he felt a deep longing to get that book. He'd put his life on the line writing down every abuse, every death, every abusive guard's name in detail, in that book. He had a need to put his best pal's name in the book, not in short hand or code but in large print English letters. "Private William McCray died at the hands of the Japanese, through mistreatment and malnutrition."

Jock had never disobeyed a single command from the Captain in the previous three and a half years, but in this instance, either through grief, stubbornness or both, he needed to do what he felt was right. He made a decision to slip out at sunset in local clothes and get his book.

Meanwhile, over at the ferry pier, a queue had formed and the girls and George were looking at the notices pinned to a wall, seeking information; hundreds of names, where the people were last seen, rewards offered. Hundreds and hundreds of names. For the first time, Lily felt deep down that she would never see her father again.

Jock quickly slipped past the unmanned gates in a black Chinese-style tunic and hat that he had taken from the guards' kitchen. With his stature and weight, he could easily pass for Chinese as long as his face was out of sight. He almost started to march out of habit on the ten-minute walk to the tool shed but quickly shortened his stride and lowered his head, until he reached the water's edge near the runway. Out of habit he looked for the three stones from Popeye. There were none.

When he reached the shed he was surprised to see the padlock undone. As he gingerly opened the door, he didn't hear a sound, and even with day-light fading, he knew exactly where his treasured book would be; at the very back, near the tools, hanging on a nail with a piece of string.

Jock took small, quiet steps. The room where he had spent so many hours fixing machines seemed strangely eerie. He slowly lifted the book off the nail.

"Yameru!"

Jock instinctively stood to attention as he knew full well the Japanese word for stop. More Japanese words followed as Jock slowly turned around.

The prison guard, Keiji, was standing facing him. He was stripped to the waist, with a white bandana with the rising sun emblazoned on it. He had his sword on a belt. Jock raised his head and made eye-contact with the guard. Looking slightly confused, the Japanese shouted in English, "Prisoners shall bow!"

Jack could tell from the smell and the slurring of the words that Keiji was drunk. He paused before bowing.

"Why do you have that book, Prisoner?!"

Jock paused, "Er, I wanted a souvenir."

Even as he said the words, he knew they sounded lame. Keiji stepped forward and snatched the book, he then spat in Jock's face.

"Don't lie! Don't lie to me!"

With this, he hit Jock with the back of his hand and sent the malnourished man across the floor. He then began to leaf through the pages whilst drinking from a bottle of sake with the other hand. Jock managed to pull himself up on one knee, he could taste the blood on his tongue.

"What do the numbers mean!?"

Whack! Another blow. Jock barely had the strength to lift his arms, never mind defend himself.

Whack! Another blow. Jock had been on the recieving end of numerous beatings from Keiji, but this was on a different level. More intense, more cruel.

"What do the numbers mean?!" Keiji shouted, as he breathed heavily.

Jock tried to talk but blood just bubbled from his mouth as he lay prone and motionless on his back. The kicks and fists rained down as Jock drifted in and out of consciousness. Jock could see his former captor drink once more from the bottle before walking towards him with his hand now on his sword

"I ask you one more time...what do the numbers mean?!"

As he raised the sword, Jock tried to say a prayer, but no words came. The sword was above his head, then suddenly Keiji fell to his knees. Standing behind him was Popeye, with a bloodied rock in his two hands.

Calmly and quietly Popeye took the Japanese man's sword and stabbed the former guard cleanly through the heart.

"Popeye..." Jock managed to whisper.

"Toot-toot, Tommy soldier. Toot-toot."

Jock saw the familiar glint of Popeye's gold tooth before the blackness came.

*

Sai Kung, September 1945
Jock had no idea where he was or how long he had been there as he gradually focussed on the white ceiling, as a beautiful angel appeared above him.

"Am I dead?" he said.

"You have a worm coming out of your bottom," answered Lily.

CHAPTER ELEVEN

1997 United Services Recreational Club, Kowloon

The police car pulled up through the tight gates of the USRC opposite the Queen Elizabeth II Hospital, where both Alex and his older sister May had been brought kicking and screaming into the world.

The police car pulled up in the car-park opposite the bowling-green where an assortment of elderly men and women in uniformed whites slowly slogged it out before lunch, gin and tonics, and a snooze on the veranda overlooking the pool. The club had been a regular haunt of Alex Wu Torrence's father and many an ex-serviceman, as well as "civvies" including civil servants, policemen, lawyers, barristers, doctors, and by the 1970s more and more wealthy Chinese.

The club had been a favourite haunt of Alex and May during their formative years, with lazy Sundays around the pool, tennis and ping pong, before their father would wobble rather unsteadily back to their Vauxhall Viva and the Wu Torrences would head over Hiram's Highway back home to Sai Kung. The trip was nearly always accompanied by Dad's explanation that Hiram's Highway was named after the Hiram's tinned sausages that the chief engineer John "Hiram" Potts loved so much whilst building the road. His father never mentioned that it was his former enemies, the Japanese guards, now prisoners-of-war, who had done most of the manual labour.

His mother had also taken considerable pride in the fact that the people of Sai Kung were given the road as a reward for their resistance during the occupation.

At first glance the club looked exactly the same as it used to, with the exception of more Chinese faces on the bowling-green. In the distance, he could hear a British Army battalion being put through their paces in the adjoining Kowloon barracks. Within six months there would be Mandarin Chinese in the air and not English, as the Red Army were due to be stationed there.

A few eyebrows were raised as the police-car parked and Alex checked that his attire was suitable enough for the club: sleeveless shirt, chinos and shoes. "Should be OK," he thought.

He told the constable not to wait for him, but the officer insisted that he was under orders to wait. Alex wondered fleetingly if Chief Inspector Mark Hayton was keeping tabs on him.

As he entered the beautiful colonial building a smiling receptionist asked if she could help.

"I'm here for lunch with *Inspector* Williams," said Alex.

"And who shall I say is here, Sir?"

"Detective Inspector Wu Torrence..." said Alex, before he was interrupted by the booming voice of his Uncle Taff walking down the arched staircase.

"Alex, my boy! Do you remember the old place?" Taff enquired.

Alex smiled, "How could I forget!"

Taff addressed the receptionist. "Let me sign him in, will you. This young man's father was Inspector Jock Torrence, a local legend you know, my dear!"

The receptionist nodded and smiled but looked decidedly unimpressed as she pushed the ledger towards the old man.

Alex asked, "And would you be so kind as to take the officer waiting outside a club sandwich and an iced tea, please?"

"Hayton keeping an eye on you, is it?!" winked Taff, not missing a trick.

"Certainly, Sir, and could I remind you to turn all mobile phones and pagers off, please," she said courteously with a nod.

In the dining-room overlooking the clear blue pool, Taff was just beginning to tell Alex about the club's fantastic garden salads before Alex reminded him that he was on expenses. The old man then began to explain the merits of a chilled Bordeaux when washing down a fillet steak.

"So, what's the latest, young man?"

"Well, I've been trying to get hold of you all day. The big diver you were drinking with last night was arrested for assault in the early hours of this morning."

Taff whistled quietly and leaned closer. "Rum job that one. Drunk as a skunk and like a powder keg waiting to go off, I can tell you."

Alex asked, "Did he say anything in particular about the murder?"

"Nothing specifically, but he was mumbling a whole load of nonsense, that's for sure."

Alex lowered the menu. "Such as?"

"Well, I was at the bar when all those noisy bugger divers arrived, and I sat near them so as I could listen in a bit, isn't it. The thing is you see, when you get to my age you become invisible. Well, they start talking about the murder and how they should have a whip round for his widow and this kind of stuff. They should hang the triad boy, that kind of thing. Anyways, this fella, what's his name?"

"Andy Goff."

Taff continued. "Right, Goff is it? Well he looks like he's had a few too many even before he'd even got there. He starts angling for a fight with the other big brute, the Australian one with the long hair and a beard. Every time the Australian says anything whatsoever, he's contradicting him. Saying he's going to fire him, yadder, yadder, yadder! Looked to me like none of the crew could stand this Goff fella, by the way they're looking at their shoes and the like."

"Then what happened?" Alex asked.

"Anyway, this is going on for ages, mind. The Aussie would say black and Goff would say white just to get the ride out of him, I reckon. Anyways, sometime after midnight, Goff goes to the toilet and all the others bugger off while he's in there. Sensible decision if you ask me."

"And you spoke to him after this?"

"Yes, but it was like getting blood out of a stone, Boyo. I'm asking him things like, did he think the triad boy did it and the like? But he starts going off at tangents, he started telling me about Iraq, Desert Storm. How he'd killed Iraqis or *rag-heads* as he so eloquently put it. Then he's almost crying into his whiskey and I'm wondering if he's upset about the man who was murdered at Chek Lap Kok or about the Iraq war. A true nut-case, in my humble opinion."

The main courses arrived and Taff collected his thoughts before continuing. "The thing is, he was all over the place, one minute he's angry, then the next almost crying. I couldn't put my finger on it. One thing though, he kept mentioning Number Six."

Alex asked. "The number six?"

"No, Number Six like it was a nickname or something? I don't know. Bearing in mind it's the early hours by this point, and whiskey has been taken by both parties. But he was saying things like, 'Number Six will get what's coming to him' or he's got to 'sort something out before Number Six finds out,' something like that. I don't think he was on about the Aussie bloke, he was calling him Warren or something."

"Wayne." Alex corrected.

"Wayne, that's it." Taff clicked his fingers as he took another bite of steak. "Do you know him?"

"Yes, we interviewed him on-site, and he's got a cast-iron alibi for the night of the murder. He was with all the other divers all night."

Taff continued, "And you've got this Goff chap in custody, is it?"

"Yes, we saw him briefly this morning but he was still drunk. They're interviewing him again this afternoon." Alex looked at his watch; half past one.

"Any chance you could get me behind the glass when you do it, boyo?"

Alex replied, "I doubt it, to be honest, Uncle Taff. Chief Inspector Hayton is keeping a close eye on this one and he's made it quite clear that I'm here in liaison capacity only."

"That sounds like Hayton all over boyo. He'll want it all done and dusted so he can bugger off sailing."

Alex laughed as he pushed back his plate. "I'll try and get a transcript and get Jackie Shuen to throw in 'Number Six' when he interviews him."

"Jackie Shuen? Good young copper that one. Hong Kong will need detectives like him after the Handover."

Alex nodded in agreement. "Listen, Uncle Taff, I'm gonna' give the uniformed the slip and go out the side entrance, can you give me a thirty-minute head-start and then tell him I've gone sight-seeing or something?"

Taff tapped his nose as Alex left plenty of Hong Kong dollars to cover the meals, and a desert for the old man.

Taff spoke. "Just be careful with that Goff chap, Alex. I've seen blokes like him come back from wars and the like, sends them a bit funny in the head."

Alex stood to leave but paused momentarily. "Uncle Taff. My dad, did he ever explain to you why we left Hong Kong when we did?"

The old man rubbed his chin and looked up at Alex. "I knew your dad for years, boyo. Thick as thieves we were, would have done anything for each other. But...." He paused and collected his thoughts. "Old Jock you see, he could be a closed book at times. He had a rough time with the Japanese in the war but never uttered a word about it. Never. He could be the same with policing; if he had a contact or an informer he'd never in a million years divulge anything that would harm the case or an individual." Taff paused and took a sip of his wine. "What do you know about the ICAC?"

"The Independent Commission Against Corruption, Hong Kong's agency against bribery, corruption that kind of stuff? I don't understand what that would have to do with my dad?"

Taff shifted awkwardly in his seat. "Well, there was talk you see, idle gossip; after Jock and your mum left so quickly. The ICAC was formed in the early seventies to root out corruption in politics and the police and such like. Career policemen like that idiot Hayton were coming over from Britain and stirring up all sorts of problems for local policemen, both gweilo and Chinese. Dozens of police officers were getting fired every month, we all had our bank accounts checked, assets audited; cars, houses that kind of thing. There were bloody sergeants with Mercedes Benzs and three or four mistresses, that kind of stuff!"

The old man laughed and coughed. Alex remained quiet as Taff continued. "You see Jock was whiter than white; a church-goer, family-man, well respected by the locals on his patch in the New Territories. He would never have taken a bung, not in a million years, but idiots in here were coming up with all sorts of conspiracy theories after he left, that they would have never have dared say to his face."

"And what do you think?"

Taff paused. "I honestly don't know for sure, but I've always wondered...."

"Go on," said Alex

"I've always wondered if he was protecting somebody."

CHAPTER TWELVE

September 1968, Fei Ngo Shan

"Another, another errplane, look Daddy," three-year-old Alex looked out at the horizon as the Pan Am aircraft banked right in the distance.

"Aye, that's right. That's a shiny one, isn't it?"

Jock was sitting with little Alex on his knee enjoying the cool autumn breeze on the hill-top. Originally the plan had been to fly a kite with the little un' for an hour or two whilst his sister May was at dance class, but Alex had quickly got bored and now they were plane-spotting, and father and son were enjoying their Saturday morning together.

Jock would be fifty next year and his bones were beginning to creak a little, but he still felt that he had enough energy to run around with the kids or kick a ball with little Alex. Lily falling pregnant with Alex had been a complete surprise at their time of life, but they had both taken it as a blessing. Initially they thought they could never have kids after about the third or fourth miscarriage, but first came along May and then four years later another happy surprise.

"And the big lion, Daddy!" Alex pointed.

Jock had told him on the last visit how the big lion watched over Hong Kong.

"That's right. The big lion, grrrr!" He tickled the little boy who was now sitting on his lap.

"And that down there is where your mummy grew up," said Jock pointing at Dunbar Road.

Jock always wondered how Lily and Ah-Lam would have turned out if their father had returned or their father's manager hadn't swindled them out of most of their inheritance.

"The big tower, Daddy?"

"Well it's a big tower nowadays, but there was a house there, before your Mummy was a little boy."

"A little girl, don't be silly!" Alex yawned.

"Oh, aye that's right, a little girl. And that down there is where the runway used to be. The one which I helped to build."

Alex yawned again and Jock could sense the boy dropping off to sleep in the mid-afternoon sun. He carried on regardless.

"And that's where me and Billy used to live while we were building the runway. That's why we called you Alex William. Alex after *my* daddy. And William after my best pal."

"Alex William Wu Torrence," said the little boy as his head dropped.

"Aye, he was a fine man. Too young to go, but a fine man all the same. You know we used to deliberately mess up all the time with the runway, making holes, making the cement mixes up wrong, all kinds of things. It was probably the worst thing the Royal Engineers ever built."

The little boy snuggled into his father's chest as Jock continued.

"There was another man, a Chinese man who saved my life. But I guess I couldn't call you Popeye, could I? I never saw the man after the day everything happened in the tool-shed. I asked your Uncle George if he knew him but he said they didnae' know most of each other's names and the likes. I guess it was safer that way I suppose. I wouldnae' be here today if it wasn't for him, that's for sure."

Jock could feel the little boy's breathing as he brushed his son's fringe from his little face.

"And neither would you be, little man."

*

October 1968, Sai Kung Police Station

Desk-sergeant Taff Williams hurriedly slipped the *Racing Post* under the counter as Superintendent Jock Torrence entered the lobby of the station and looked at the police bulletin intensely.

"Good morning, Williams."

"Good morning, Sir. Good weekend?"

Both men knew the boundaries at work; "Sir" and "Williams", which tended to blur into Jock and Taff after a few whiskeys at the club out of work, however.

"Fine thanks, Williams." Jock nodded towards the chalk board. "Anything interesting happening, Sergeant?"

"Not much, Sir. We've got one cell occupied by Tang, the local stationer. He gambled away a good part of his kid's inheritance last night playing mah-jong which didn't go down too well with Mrs Tang apparently. There was a bit of a disturbance and uniform thought he'd be better off in here until it cooled off a bit."

Jock chuckled.

"Anything else?"

"Not really, Sir. The Shing and Cheung clans are at each others' throats again out towards Pak Kong. It has something to do with access to each other's fields and the like. Constable Chan told them to cut out the threats or they'd be in trouble."

Jock could remember this going on even when he was on the beat twenty years earlier. Clan disputes could last generations and the general feeling was to leave it to the village elders to mediate.

"I suppose they'll work something out eventually," Jock mused; then added, "Anything in the bulletin?"

"A new Deputy Chief of Police is in place apparently, a chap called Mark Hayton. Fresh off the boat from Scotland Yard I believe. He'll be making the rounds of the districts in the next month or so, according to this."

It had been a fairly open secret that if Jock Torrence had applied for the Deputy Chief of Police's job, it would have been as good as his. Jock, however, had no intention of moving his young family over to the hustle and bustle of

Hong Kong island and much preferred the sedate life that Sai Kung and the New Territories offered them.

Jock put his cap on a hook. "It might do some good to have some fresh blood. You never know."

"Maybe, Sir. Maybe"

*

December 1968, Royal Hong Kong Yacht Club, Senior Policemen's Ball

Deputy Chief Inspector Mark Hayton beckoned Jock over to him with his index finger from the other side of the room. Jock made his excuses and passed his champagne flute to Lily who was wearing a beautiful beige and lilac gown.

Jock saluted.

"Ah, Torrence, isn't it? Sai Kung, yes?"

"Yes, Sir," replied Jock.

Slightly unusually, the senior offered his hand to Jock. Immediately Jock felt the tell-tale sign of a masonic handshake which was not returned by Jock, on account of the Scotsman not being a mason himself. In his line of work, Jock had been offered a shoe-in to more than one of the masonic grand lodges dotted around the colony, and it was rumoured that the Governor was a *worshipful* member also. Jock however had always politely turned down the requests, partly due to his working-class background, partly due to the personalities of the people asking him and partly due to the conflict of interest that Jock felt existed. He would never put himself in a position to get a fellow mason out of anything, even something minor such a traffic fine for example.

Hayton coughed. "Yes, well er, apologies for not getting out to the sticks sooner, Torrence. One has had a million and one things to do since arriving, obviously."

Jock could hear a slight slurring of Hayton's words as the man continued.

"So, any problems? How are the natives out there?"

Jock could see his beautiful young wife at the far end of the room talking effortlessly to a small group of officers' wives. He bit his lip.

"We have a few clan issues Sir, which are normally long-running territorial disputes, but nothing too out of hand."

"And problems with the lefties?"

"Well, nothing like on Hong Kong Island, Sir. There are a few communist sympathisers dotted about, Sir, but on the whole most Sai Kung families have been there for generations and have full bellies."

"I hear they put up a good show against the Japs, what?" Hayton sniffed as he took another gulp of champagne.

Jock had no intention of going down that particular conversation route with the drunken *superior* standing in front of him, instead taking a small hors d'oeuvre from a passing waiter.

"Now Jock, may I call you Jock," he asked rhetorically without waiting for an answer. "I see that you've come up through the ranks, so to speak."

Because of the man's accent and champagne-induced-slurring, Jock really couldn't tell if this was an insult or a compliment as Hayton continued and placed an arm around the Scotsman.

"Now I've been told on good authority that you run a tight ship out in Sai Kung, what. Now strictly in confidence," he tapped his nose, nearly missing. "London and the governor's office here in Honkers are growing concerned about corruption in the force."

Jock nodded and felt increasingly more uncomfortable as his shoulder was squeezed a little too tight.

"Now, what's my point? Er…yes? The point is we're going to need more chaps like you, Torrence. There has been talk of a commission of sorts against corruption and they'll be needing a few whiter than white chaps, like yourself, to help out and the like."

Jock took a bite on the hors d'oeuvre and listened further as Hayton continued.

"At present, every Tom, Dick and Harry is on the take, including men in the forces. Do you know the fire brigade went to a factory fire in Mong Kong last month and wouldn't turn the hoses on until the owner had given them a bribe? Truly scandalous!"

"Yes Sir, I read about that incident."

"Well the thing is we have no power at present to check bank accounts or seize property and the like, so the independent commission, which will be named the ICAC, apparently will have independent powers and hopefully clean the old place up, so to speak."

Jock had long been advocating some sort of police action on corruption in the force and welcomed the news, however he certainly wasn't sure how the inebriated, chinless wonder in front of him could be involved or interested.

Just then the Deputy Inspector spied somebody obviously more important than Jock and knocked the Scotsman's shoulder as he trailed off across the room.

"Lady Cawshore, how delightful to see you again," he said.

Jock scratched his head and walked back to his wife.

"How is the new Deputy Chief Inspector?" Lily asked as she handed him his glass back.

Jock shook his head and laughed. "God help us, Angel."

CHAPTER THIRTEEN

1997 United Services Recreational Club, Kowloon
Alex stepped out of the side entrance and was immediately hit by the mid-afternoon heat and humidity. He glanced sideways over at the police car in the car-park before stepping out quickly through the side gate and turning left onto Jordan Road.

After switching his mobile phone back on, Alex could see he had eight missed calls. Five from Jackie Shuen and two from Heidi Lim, plus one from headquarters back in Manchester. He was just about to call back Jackie Shuen when the phone rang with Heidi Lim's caller ID displayed.

"Detective Torrence, we have been trying to get hold of you!"

Alex could sense the urgency in her voice. "I'm sorry, I was in a private club..."

She cut him off. "Please hold, Detective Inspector Shuen wants to talk to you." Alex could hear the sound of driving in the background.

"Alex, where are you?" asked Jackie Shuen.

"I'm in Jordan, why?"

"Good, get in a taxi quickly and get to Kam Tin as soon as possible, I'll get Heidi to text you the address."

"What's happening, Jackie?"

"They've released Andy Goff, charged him with drunk and disorderly only and let him go!"

Alex immediately flagged down a passing taxi and gave the driver instructions before continuing the phone-call. "Who authorised that, Jackie?"

"Officially the Chief Inspector at Tsuen Wan station, but it must have come from higher up. I only found out because the desk-sergeant is an old friend of mine."

Alex asked, "So what do you want me to do?"

"We're just leaving Hong Kong island headquarters now. You get to the dive place in Kam Tin as quick as possible and re-arrest him. We'll be twenty-thirty minutes behind you."

"Jackie, I'm a British police officer. I have no jurisdiction in Hong Kong!"

"I know that, you know that..." He paused. "But Andy Goff doesn't know that! Hurry!"

*

Kam Tin was once a walled village belonging to the Tang clan, and Alex could vaguely remember doing a school project on the village gates which were stolen by the colonial rulers but eventually returned by the British. Nowadays, however, as the taxi-driver asked a local Hakka man for directions, Alex noted that the small historic village looked more like a scrap-metal merchant's, with shipping containers, old cars and scrap metal adorning the insides of numerous industrial yards.

As instructed, the driver took a right at a zebra crossing and Alex immediately recognised the now familiar Coniston Marine logo on the side of yet another dive container.

"Here, please," said Alex as he handed over the fare without waiting for change.

Alex moved towards the unit with caution and then pushed the meshed gate open and walked gingerly into the untidy yard. Almost immediately he was approached by a large black Labrador type dog. The animal was wagging its tail and barking whilst doing circles on the spot.

"Not much of a guard dog are you, mate..." said Alex patting the dog's head. He thumbed the name tag on the dog's collar. "...Tyson."

The dog seemed friendly enough but was obviously either aggravated or excited. Alex paused, realising he was about to apprehend a violent knuckle-head, with no back-up, no weapon, no handcuffs and no authority or warrant. He wondered momentarily if it would be wiser to wait for Shuen and Lim.

He then spoke quietly to the dog. "Come on Tyson, we're going to have some fun and games with that prick of an owner of yours."

Warily turning the corner, Alex could see a container similar to the one used by the divers at the new airport, but this one had a side window, and on inspection, he could see it was doubled up as some sort of office. He could hear English-language radio coming from the inside but could not see anybody around. Opposite the container and across the yard stood a contraption that looked like a small white submarine. The unit had a small oval-shaped door with a circular handle like something out of a World War II movie. Moving closer, Alex could now read a small plaque which read, *Recompression Chamber*. The door was ajar and banging slightly on the breeze as the dog started to bark once more while facing the oval door.

"Ssssh," said Alex as he slowly opened the door. He could see an Adidas sports shoe near the entrance.

"Andy, this is Detective Inspector Wu Torrence," he could hear the hesitancy in his own voice.

No answer.

"Andy, are you in there?" Alex mentally and physically braced himself as his eyes adjusted to the dimly lit chamber.

The sports-shoe was attached to the foot of Andy Goff, whose brains were now splattered against the far wall. He had been shot in the face.

Instinctively Alex turned around to see if anybody else was in the vicinity. Nothing, just him, a whimpering dog and the corpse of a thug whose cerebral fluid was partly covering an assortment of tacky pornography on the inside of the chamber. Alex took a step inside the chamber, and without wanting to disturb the crime scene, he felt Andy Goff's dead hand which was not yet cold.

At the victim's feet was a black revolver, "a smoking gun", thought Alex to himself. Just then, Alex heard a vehicle pulling up outside and turned around, facing the harsh mid-day sun-light to see Jackie Shuen's Honda Civic pulling up at the gates. Within seconds Shuen was striding purposefully towards him with Heidi Lim following in his wake.

"Did you apprehend him?" Shuen asked.

Alex Wu Torrence nodded towards the chamber. "Not exactly...."

*

Within the hour, a uniformed unit and forensics were working on the scene with typical Hong Kong efficiency. All three detectives understood time was of the essence in these situations, and standing outside in the yard they were keen to exchange information.

"Anything new?" Jackie Shuen asked Heidi Lim whilst drawing on a cigarette.

She shook her head. "No, Sir, nothing."

"And has he any next-of-kin?" he continued.

"One of the neighbours in the adjoining yards says he has a wife nearby; headquarters are searching the address. And he didn't see or hear anything this afternoon," she added, pre-empting her boss's next question.

Alex, who had already given his version of events to his two colleagues earlier, thought outloud. "The neighbour wouldn't have heard anything if it was inside a locked recompression chamber, it's airtight."

"But you're sure the door wasn't closed when you arrived, yes?" asked Shuen.

"The door was definitely ajar. Maybe the dog could have dislodged it, or if Andy Goff did shoot himself, the kickback from the weapon could possibly have opened it," answered Alex.

Just then Alex's mobile rang. Chief Inspector McGregor's familiar voice boomed out at him from Manchester CID. "Wu Torrence. Been trying to get hold of you all day. I've got a bit of info. on that Goff bloke of yours."

"Yes, Sir." Alex massaged his temple.

"It looks like there is an outstanding UK warrant out on him from six years ago, racially aggravated GBH by all accounts."

"He's dead, Sir."

"Seems that he and a couple of his ex-squaddie mates used a young Pakistani lad's head as a football late one night in a fast-food shop. Andy Goff fled the country whilst on bail, seems like his mates did two to four at her Majesty's...."

"He's dead, Sir."

"Yes, I heard you the first time....at her Majesty's pleasure, but he went to Australia and then to Hong Kong by the looks of it. It could have been attempted murder, if this coloured boy hadn't pulled through."

Alex looked at the phone wondering if McGregor had stopped or if he was just catching his breath. "We found him dead with a shot to the head earlier today, Sir."

"Top himself, did he? Well at least that'll save on the paperwork, I guess. Looks like you'll be bringing two bodies back then, Wu Torrence. Better bugger off, it's late here."

Clunk.

At exactly the same moment and out of the corner of his eye, Alex could see a commotion by the yard gates.

"You'd better 'ave a fuckin' warrant, you bastards. Police victimisation this is. My Andy's done nothing wrong," shouted a peroxide-blonde woman, raising her finger at a young Chinese PC.

Alex was on the scene quickly and said calmly, "Mrs Goff?"

The angry woman focused on Alex. "I'm his fiancée, as it so happens!"

Alex noticed the woman still had her slippers on, as he beckoned her towards the office. "Please sit down, Miss?"

"Speed, Melanie Speed." She momentarily seemed to calm down. "What are you all doing here?"

Heidi Lim walked over from the doorway and placed a hand the woman's shoulder. "I'm afraid we have some rather bad news..."

*

Thirty minutes later, in Andy Goff and Melanie Speed's cramped apartment, Senior Constable Heidi Lim was busy in the kitchen making a cup of tea as Inspector Jackie Shuen spoke softly to Melanie Speed, who had already gone through half a box of tissues.

"Has your husband been depressed lately?" he asked.

"Fiancée actually," she corrected once more before continuing. "Andy doesn't get depressed, he gets pissed off, drunk, or both."

Alex, who was standing behind the woman's sofa with his back to her, noted the elongated "e" in fiancée – West Midlands, Brummie, the same as her recently-deceased boyfriend. He was looking at an assortment of photos on a wicker book-shelf devoid of books. Military photos, diving photos and one portrait picture in particular of the couple with two small girls. He noted the cheap floral dress – Primark or C&A he guessed – and the equally cheap permed hair style, long since absent from the sobbing Melanie Speed sitting in front of them now. He also noted the crew-cut that Andy Goff seemed to have sported since he left the military. He sensed that, like a lot of ex-squaddies, Andy Goff had never really left the forces. Looking over the back of the sofa, Alex Wu Torrence could see the raggedy bitten fingernails and a cheap tattoo of a non-descript bird on her forearm. Alex wondered how many times she had been on the receiving end of her drunk, crew-cut, "pissed or angry", fiancé?

"Did your fiancé mention the murder at the airport?" asked Shuen, calmly.

She scowled at the officer. "Only that you bastards were sniffing about the place and would be causing trouble as usual!"

Heidi Lim placed a cup of tea on the coffee table in front of the visibly distraught woman. "Melanie, any information you could give us will help us find out what happened to Andy."

From behind the sofa Alex could see seamless teamwork at play from the officers as the penny seemed to drop for Melanie Speed that there was no fiancé to protect anymore. She pulled another tissue from the box. "I can't believe that he would top himself if that's what you mean." She paused. "It's just not in his nature. He went all through Iraq and all. He never has none of that post-trauma stuff of whatever."

Alex noted the use of the present tense as if he was still alive.

"Did he have any enemies?" Shuen asked.

She paused and chewed one of her fingers. "Look. If Andy didn't like you he'd tell you to your face. Some people didn't like that, but I knew the real him." She inspected her tatty finger but didn't elaborate on what the real him was exactly.

"Did he mention the murder at the airport at all?" Heidi Lim asked calmly.

"Why are you asking that?!" snapped the woman.

Lim kept her calm and explained. "We have two incidents, both involving English men from the construction site and we need to find out if they are connected."

"But it won't bring my Andy back, will it?!" cried the distraught woman.

Alex could see that that she was going to be of little or no help. She seemed to be one of those women who ran a parallel life to their partners without knowing much about her man at all. He did have one final question however. "Did Andy ever mention Number Six, Melanie?"

The woman looked confused. "Number Six? What are you talking about?"

*

Detectives Wu Torrence and Shuen were walking the short distance from the apartment to the crime scene as a uniformed officer beckoned them into the office.

He addressed Shuen. "Sir, we found this." He pointed to a sheet of A4 typed paper which was placed on the computer keyboard,

It read, "I have decided to end it all. I killed the welder after a drunken fight and I'm not going to prison for it. I killed him with a diver's weight and then slit his throat and arm with a diver's knife. I am sorry. Tell Melanie and the kids I love them. ANDY."

Detective Shuen nodded and thanked the officer.

Alex could see the forensics were working in the dive chamber. He also saw the now familiar figure of Dr Rufus Chan come out of the chamber and remove his mask. Alex walked over to the pathologist.

"Suicide, Dr Chan?" Alex asked.

"Probably," he replied.

"Probably or possibly?" he prodded further.

"You've found a note, I gather, Inspector?"

Alex nodded in the affirmative, as the doctor continued. "Well, in my experience, a dead body, a weapon and a suicide note normally means *probably* inspector."

Alex wasn't sure if he was being patronised or if this was the doctor's normal manner. Either way he was curious. "Are you familiar with the weapon, Dr Chan?"

The pathologist appeared slightly irritated but replied anyway. "It is a standard-issue British army revolver, no serial number – it's been filed off – quite common..."

DI Shuen interrupted them. "Good afternoon, Rufus."

The pair exchanged greetings and Alex noted that the pathologist seemed slightly more relaxed with Shuen than with himself.

"Do we have a time of death?" asked Shuen.

"Recent, bordering on the very recent I would say," Rufus Chan replied. "At what time was the first officer on the scene? And who would that be?"

Alex's heart momentarily sank as it suddenly dawned on him that he was at a murder scene both unauthorised and with no witness.

Jackie Shuen didn't miss a beat and lit a cigarette. "That would be me, Rufus, around 14:20."

Alex's heart resumed its normal pace as Shuen's reply seemed to pacify the pathologist.

"I'd say that you were extremely close in terms of time. The weapon and the body were still warm and many of the bodily fluids had not run very far down the wall when we arrived at 15.30. I would put the time of death between 12:00pm and 15:20."

Shuen drew on his cigarette. "And it was suicide?"

"As I was saying to your colleague, we have a body, a weapon and a note. These indicate suicide," he said.

Alex could sense a, "but..."

Rufus Chan straightened slightly and rubbed his chin. "Listen, Jackie, we go back a long way. I've been under intense scrutiny over the Meakin murder and my autopsy report."

Shuen placed a hand on the doctor's arm. "You can speak off the record Rufus, and I can vouch for Alex here also."

Chan nodded. "There are just a couple of anomalies. Normally with a suicide involving a firearm the victim would put the weapon to their temple, forehead, or in the mouth. In this case, it appears that the gun was fired about a foot away, so he would be looking down the barrel at the gun. Not an appealing thing for anybody, even for somebody contemplating suicide."

"Anything else?" asked Alex.

The doctor looked uneasy. "It is likely that this is suicide and that is what my report will say, Detectives. And this is totally off the record...."

"Of course," said Shuen.

"The print on the trigger is from Mr Goff's right index finger. He would have had to have held the gun at least twelve inches away from his face and twisted his hand almost 180 degrees. I would have thought the thumb would be a more probable digit, wouldn't you?"

Both detectives nodded as Tyson the dog walked by. If only dogs could talk, thought Alex.

CHAPTER FOURTEEN

September 1973, Sai Kung Police Station
The fresh-faced constable was standing to attention in front of his commanding officer and Jock Torrance was in no mood for leniency towards his subordinate as he looked up from his desk at the young man.

"How long have you been at this station, Kwok?"

"Six months, Sir," answered the PC.

"And in those six months has it not become apparent that I do not tolerate any kind of corruption on my watch?"

"Yes Sir."

"So why have I received a complaint that one of my officers has been asking for tea-money in the old town, Kwok?!"

The young man looked slightly ruffled, but didn't respond.

Old man Tung had approached Jock the previous Sunday after church and, when prodded by his wife, had told him that a new *luk ji* (or *green clothes,* after the colour of the uniforms) had asked for money in return for not looking at his hygiene certificate for his little tea-house.

"Do you have any idea how long the Tungs have been living in Sai Kung, constable Kwok?"

"No, Sir."

"I'll tell yee…generations, Kwok, gen-er-ra-tions laddie! And an old man, probably in his eighties by now, who we are meant to be protectin' as it so happens, comes to me wi' tears wellin' in his eyes tellin' me that some young upstart is asking for tea-money!"

Jock could feel the blood rising in his face and his Glaswegian accent getting stronger to the point where the young Constable might not be understanding him anymore. He closed his eyes momentarily and reached for his Lucky 7 cigarettes.

"Listen, Kwok," he lit the cigarette. "I don't know how things operate in Mong Kok division or wherever you've come from, but I simply will not tolerate this kind of behaviour in Sai Kung division. Do you understand, young man?"

"Yes, Sir," said the ashen-faced man.

This was not the first-time Jock had come across this type of problem with lower-ranking officers. The main problem, other than moral fibre, was that they simply weren't paid enough, and the lure of easy black money was too much for some younger officers like the one standing to attention in front of him.

"Here is what is going to happen now, Kwok, you're going to go to the Tung tea-house immediately and pay back everything you took, and apologise on your knees if you have to."

"Yes, Sir."

Whilst understanding that the lack of money was the root cause of the problem, Jock could not and would not tolerate any kind of insubordination on his watch.

"Believe me, there isn't a family in this town that I don't know or that doesn't know me, laddie. We are here to do our duty. Now, if I ever – and I mean ever – hear of anything like this again, Kwok, you will be off the force and charged with theft, before you know it."

The Constable looked like he was about to say something but thought better of it.

"Dismissed."

Kwok saluted and turned one hundred and eighty degrees. As he passed the desk sergeant in the lobby, Taff Williams could not help but stifle a grin as he stirred his morning coffee.

Taff chuckled quietly. "Gen-er-ra-tions laddie, gen-er-ra-tions..."

*

Sai Kung sports field, October 1973

"Go on, Son! Go on!" Jock shouted.

Lily gently tapped the back of Jock's hand to subtly remind him to calm down, as young Alex burst through on goal to complete his hat-trick. Jock turned to his wife who was seated beside him on the tartan picnic-rug with Aunty Ah-Lam and Alex's uninterested looking teenage sister May, occupying the other corners of the rug.

Uncle George, who was referee for the day, blew his whistle and pointed to the centre circle as Alex's cousin Ah-Yun (or "George junior," as only his mother insisted on calling him) ran from his right-wing position to congratulate and ruffle his cousin's hair.

Jock returned the gesture and tapped the back of Lily's hand as she unscrewed the flask of coffee.

"Ah, sorry Angel. I jest get carried away with the wee lad when he's on fire like today. He's some player, isn't he?"

Lily smiled. "Yes, but the whole town doesn't need to hear it, do they?!"

Auntie Ah-Lam spoke also. "Don't forget little George junior passing it to him, Jock."

"Oh, aye of course not, Sister. That was some pass from the boy."

Jock had lost count of the score and the opposition were beginning to look a bit dishevelled even before half-time. In previous weeks, Uncle George (who was also Sai Kung Baptists FC's coach, kit-man and physio), had to tell young Alex to ease off a bit and had even put him in goal on occasion just to keep the score line looking reasonable. Opposition coaches had been complaining that he was too old for this league when in fact he was just a bit taller than the local boys, on account of him being Eurasian.

On the opposite side of the pitch in the small stand, Jock could see the familiar figure of Wan Li Yong (or "Black Tooth," as he was more commonly known) standing and applauding also. Black Tooth had a fairly long criminal record, and Jock had been briefed that Black Tooth recently become the head of 14k Triad for Sai Kung and district. It was known that he was probably a Deputy Mountain Master answering to a full Mountain Master in

Kowloon or Tsim Sha Tsui. There had been a bit of a power vacuum after the natural death of Big Brother Tam a few months earlier, and judging by the subservient behaviour of the young men around him in the stand, Jock's briefing had been correct. One young man had passed Black Tooth a cigarette and another subordinate was lighting it for their boss. Wan didn't appear to acknowledge either youth but did nod in Jock's direction, a gesture which Jock returned.

Jock had had a pragmatic approach to the triads in his fiefdom; firstly, as a beat copper and for the last ten or so years as District Superintendent. In many a late-night conversation with Taff Williams, Jock had likened them to rats; if you stamped one out there would be another one in its place within days. The Sun Yee On and Black Tooth's 14k had been operating in the New Territories since the British had arrived in Hong Kong, and the Hong Kong Government and the Royal Hong Kong Police Force had neither the manpower nor the resources to rid Hong Kong of the triad problem completely, especially with the more pressing matter of the influx of mainland Chinese refugees engulfing the colony, trying to escape Chairman Mao's red China.

Jock, like most of his colleagues, had tried to manage the problem rather than wipe it out. The triad groups all had a code of ethics, membership and rituals that all members had to adhere to; and vandalism, petty theft and attacks on non-triads, especially women, were frowned upon and punished by more senior triads, and subsequently Hong Kong was a relatively safe place to live in or to visit.

One event sprang to mind that had happened a couple of years previously. A ten-year-old girl had been grabbed and sexually assaulted on her way home from school, an extremely rare crime for a tranquil place like Sai Kung. This had sent shockwaves through the small town and the police had to act quickly.

From the description that she gave of a distinctive dragon's-head-in-a-circle tattoo on a fat, scruffy young man, the Sai Kung constabulary had strongly suspected a well-known 49er belonging to the 14k triad. Jock had taken it on himself to go straight to the gang's snooker-hall hangout and respectfully ask to speak to Big Brother Tam. Within the hour, the fat 49er was sitting on the station steps with blood splattered down his shirt and Black Tooth and his cronies sitting nearby in a car. Initially, the suspect had protested his innocence, until Taff Williams suggested they return him to Black Tooth and his friends. With that the disgraced young man confessed to everything and was still in jail, ostracised by his *brothers* for life and serving a long, lonely sentence.

"And another one!" Lily shouted, whilst applauding as young Alex scored his fourth.

The boys crowded around Alex once more as his Uncle George motioned him to slow down a bit. Two of the team-mates were sons of Black Tooth, but Jock and George also had no problem with this as they felt that sport (like discipline) was good for all boys whatever their background.

Jock wondered momentarily if Black Tooth wanted a different life for his own children from the one he had chosen. Jock knew that Alex, because of his mixed parentage and his father's occupation, would be safe from the clutches of the triads, and as long as Uncle George was around, so would young Ah-Yun.

CHAPTER FIFTEEN

January 1997, Sai Kung Waterfront
"And so the first words I ever said to his father were, 'You have a worm coming out of your bottom!' Can you imagine! Ay yah!" Lily clasped her hands together and smiled, as she told them all the story that they had all heard a dozen times before.

A waiter placed another delicious steamed dish in front of them. Alex smiled at his mother as he wolfed down another bite-sized *Dim Sum*. They were seated around the circular breakfast table, outside of the two sisters' favourite Dim-Sum restaurant. His mother, Auntie Ah-Lam, and even his cousin Curly had managed to make an early morning appearance. His fresh black eye had not been mentioned.

Maybe it was the sampans in the harbour or another wedding anniversary without Jock that had started the family stories, but Alex was content to sit back and listen as his mother held court.

"Of course, he was in a terrible mess when they put him on the same sampan that we were travelling on. After that it was a good week or so before he regained consciousness. Your father would never talk about the Japanese or the prison camp, but he used to scream terrible things in his sleep. She paused for effect, "but when he did wake up that first time, here in Sai Kung, do you know what he said?"

"Are you an angel!?," the three others replied in unison.

Alex was enjoying the early morning company and an excuse to be away from the crime scene for a short while. After a good night's sleep, part of him was now telling him that maybe, after yesterday's goings on, it could be best simply to back away and do the job he had been sent to do; collect the body (or maybe bodies), fill in the paperwork, nod in the right places and go home to Manchester.

"The Japanese soldiers had already left Sai Kung so we didn't have to hide him really, but the resistance decided that somebody who spoke English should be with him for when he woke up, so Ah-Lam, Uncle George and I took turns..."

Ah-Lam interrupted. "Guess who did the longest shifts!?"

Lily continued. "It wasn't just the injuries, however. Dr Wong said that it was the biggest tapeworm he had ever seen! He put it in a jar in his office!"

Both Alex and Curly put their food back on their plates.

"He was in such a mess. We had to feed him like a baby with congee or rice milk. His system couldn't take anything solid. But slowly, slowly we built up his strength, and we talked and talked about Scotland, about his friends, about my family..."

"And no more shifts for anybody else!" Auntie Ah-Lam interrupted once more.

Alex had noticed that the two widowed sisters had started, not just to finish each other's sentences, but to rely on each other more and more as old age beckoned.

"When he was well enough, they decided to send him on a medical ship to Singapore and then on to Britain. We exchanged addresses and became pen-pals but I never expected him to return! Aiyah!"

Lily continued, "He just couldn't settle back in Scotland. I think everyone just expected him to be normal even after everything he had been through. Alex's grandfather told me once that Jock used to hide food around the house and he couldn't even eat in the same room as his sisters. So, when he got the offer to return to help prosecute the Japanese he came straight back, I think it was only four months or so later that he returned. And the rest, as they say, is history!"

As expected, Detective Inspector Jackie Shuen pulled up in his Honda Civic in front of the restaurant at exactly 10:00am. Curly quickly made his excuses and slipped away before the officer had walked towards the group.

Alex made introductions and Shuen was offered tea, which was kindly accepted. After the chaos of the last few days, Shuen, like Alex, seemed to have visibly relaxed as he fended off more and more suggestions of Dim-Sum from the sisters.

"We were talking about Alex's late father, Inspector." Auntie Ah-Lam said.

"Jackie, please."

"Well, Jackie, Alex's father was very well known in the Royal Hong Kong Police force, you know."

The Royal part of the title seemed to hang in the air. Six months from now it would change to the rather less grand Hong Kong Police Force.

Jackie Shuen wiped his mouth with a napkin and smiled. "Yes, I have been told he was a bit of a Hong Kong legend. Alex has a lot to live up to."

As his mother loaded yet more food onto Shuen's plate, Alex couldn't tell if Jackie had actually heard that about his father or if he was just being polite to the old ladies. In truth Jackie Shuen was a bit of a closed book, a poker-face both in and out of work. Alex didn't even know if the man had a family. One thing was for sure however, if DI Shuen hadn't stepped in and said that he was the first person on the crime scene the previous day, Alex would have had some serious explaining to do to his superiors, both in Hong Kong and in Manchester.

"Was he based in Sai Kung, Mrs Wu Torrence?" he asked.

"Lily, please. Yes, he was the head of Sai Kung and adjoining villages. Although it didn't look like this way, back then."

"In what way?"

"Well for one thing, this is all land-fill. We'd be sitting in the water today if this was old Sai Kung!"

*

A little while later the two detectives were leaning on the bonnet of DI Shuen's Honda Civic at the top of Fei Ngo Shan hill, overlooking the old Kai Tak airport. By night it was a lovers' lane, but by day it was a lookout point for the plane enthusiast, who could see giant 747s bank, right before just missing the skyscrapers of Kowloon City.

"I just wanted to get some fresh air before we went to the station," said Shuen as he inhaled deeply on a cigarette.

Alex thought there was probably more to it than that, but decided to keep quiet as a United Airlines 747 skipped down the runway below them.

Alex finally broke the silence. "Jackie, do you mind if I ask you a question?"

"Sure."

"Yesterday, when you realised that Andy Goff had been released, why did you ask me to go to Kam Tin?"

Shuen paused and took another drag on his smoke. "Two reasons. I knew that you would probably be closer than me as I was on Hong Kong Island."

"And secondly?"

This is where it gets complicated." He paused. "Look, Alex, the last thing I had in mind was for you to get into any trouble. I certainly wasn't expecting a murder victim. I just had a feeling that he might try to abscond."

"And?"

"I can't put my finger on it exactly, but things aren't right here at the moment. I feel like we are working...how do you say it in English? Yes, working with one hand tied behind our backs."

"And what has that got to do with me?" Alex asked.

"Listen, British police officers like Karl Roberts, the Chief and others, they probably won't be around long or even at all after the Handover, whereas myself and other local police officers see this place as home, and there is a lot of unrest at the moment. From the Governor down, it's almost like they don't want any trouble or hassle before the 30th of June. Then it will be somebody else's problem."

Shuen stubbed his cigarette out on the floor and thought momentarily. "Look, I'm telling you this in confidence, Alex, OK?"

"Of course."

"Rufus Chan, I've known him twenty plus years. He's a model professional who takes pride in his work."

"And?"

"Well, let's go back to the murder at the new airport. Rufus told me that after he'd given us his opinion about the murder weapon, time of death etc., well, before he sat down to write his formal report, he got a visit from his boss, some Australian man I don't even know. According to Felix he's hardly seen his boss for the last two years and you're more likely to find him on the golf course than in a lab. Anyway, he got Felix in the office and grilled him over every little aspect of the murder. Chan was left in no doubt that if he didn't play ball, he could be in trouble career-wise."

Shuen's words hung in the air for a minute before Alex spoke. "I suppose that's why he was a bit sharp with me yesterday at the container."

"Possibly. He hardly knows you, that's all, I wouldn't take it personally, which brings us on to yesterday and the Andy Goff death. Take the angle at which he was shot in the face for example. Imagine it, he would have had to twist his wrist by 180 degrees and then he would have been looking straight down the barrel of the gun. Now I know Goff was supposedly a tough guy but surely even he would have put the gun in his mouth or to his temple?"

"He didn't look so tough when you kicked him in the balls, Jackie!" Alex joked.

Shuen laughed briefly before lighting another cigarette.

"Now, Chan has raised a few questions about Goff's death to you and me, but he won't put them on the record because he's scared about his job. This is not right, Alex, it's not right."

"I know, Jackie, it isn't, you're right. But you've still not explained the second reason exactly."

"The second reason is that I believe I can trust you, Alex. And in today's environment that is important. I'm genuinely sorry if you feel you've taken too much on, Alex, but you being here has given me an extra pair of hands, someone who isn't tainted. Other than you and Heidi Lim I don't know who I can trust."

With that Shuen stubbed out his half-smoked cigarette and looked at Alex.

"Are you in?"

"I'm in!"

The pair then shook hands.

*

As the two detectives entered the station room, Senior Constable Heidi Lim beckoned them into an adjoining cubicle.

"Good morning, DI Shuen, DI Wu Torrence."

Alex grinned once more at her formality.

"We've had some interesting information about the Goff death. OK, so as far as we can tell he was wanted in the UK for a Grievous Bodily Harm offence from…" She checked her notes. "…from 1991. Then he skipped the country and went to Australia for about two years. Prior to this, his military records show quite a few disciplinary problems over the years, mainly involving alcohol and violence."

She paused momentarily and checked her notes.

"Now, I was wondering how he actually got to Hong Kong if there was a warrant out for his arrest. Here's where it gets interesting, he's been using his brother's passport for the last few years. His name is Patrick Goff and he is – or was – two years older than his brother. On his visa, ID card pay-slips etc., he's been using his brother's identity all this time. He told people at work that Patrick was his father's name and he's always been known as Andy. Plus, the photo on the passport is pretty similar."

"And how did you find this out, Heidi?" asked Alex

"Well that's the other interesting thing. I saw Melanie Speed here in the station yesterday. She was here to do some formalities but fortunately for her not to identify the body. Anyway she looked terrible so I took her to the canteen for a drink and she just basically opened up to me. The story of the passport spilled out. Do you remember at the flat when I called her Mrs. Goff and she corrected me?"

They both nodded.

"Well, she always wanted to marry him but couldn't because he was on the run, which was obviously an issue between them especially as they have kids etc. Their birth certificates say father unknown, apparently. She knew all about the passport, the assault in the UK, but stood by him anyway. She also told me that on the day after the airport murder, he'd told her that if anybody asked, they'd been at home watching TV all night."

"So, he knew he would have been in serious trouble if we'd made the connections," Shuen interjected.

She continued, "Exactly. Because he had been arrested for the assault on the constable at the worksite, he would have known that we would probably find out about the UK assault, and of course now we have the suicide note saying he committed the Meakin murder also."

"But would that be enough for a man like Andy Goff to be suicidal?" mused Shuen.

Alex rubbed his temples. "Who knows, but one thing's for sure, I don't think I can ever recall a situation where two people have claimed to have committed the same murder. What's the latest with Kwan Yo Hang, by the way?"

"He's coming in later to be interviewed. He doesn't know about the Goff confession," she said.

"Or maybe he does?" Alex shrugged.

CHAPTER SIXTEEN

1973 Canton Road Government Offices, Kowloon
Jock and the other twelve men were sitting facing the smart-suited man who had just introduced himself as Quinton Charmers, QC. He was standing in front of a blackboard and had written in large letters: INDEPENDENT COMMISSION AGAINST CORRUPTION (ICAC).

"Greed is a human instinct," Chalmers said. "When people are greedy, you have corruption."

Jock looked about the room, a standard colonial setup with minimal furniture and the obligatory ceiling-fan.

"Gentlemen, you are seated here for what is going to be an auspicious day for Hong Kong. As you may know, Government House and London have made graft and corruption their number one target over the next few years. Our job, here in this room, is to sit down and deliver a blueprint and timeframe to offer the government." He sipped his tea before continuing. "What you probably don't know, however, is that we have been monitoring your movements for the past few years and come to the conclusion that you are some of the finest and whiter-than-white public servants that Hong Kong has to offer."

Jock stifled a smile as he knew full well that his movements had been monitored, because Mr Chan, the manager from the Hong Kong and Shanghai Bank in Sai Kung, had told him discreetly that the Royal Hong Kong Police Force had been authorised to check his bank accounts. Jock had thanked Mr Chan but had not been unduly worried, since every penny could be accounted for, including Lily's small inheritance.

The man continued. "Everything that is said in this room is top-secret and you will be asked to sign the official secrets act and speak to no-one about what goes on behind closed doors."

Jock knew only three of the other men; Smith from Sha Tin police, Wilson from Repulse Bay division, and Edwards, a fellow parishioner at Sai Kung Baptist church, who was high up in customs and immigration. Of the others, Jock knew one or two of them by sight but had yet to be introduced. However just by their demeanour and attire, he could tell that they were all fellow civil-service expatriates.

Charmers carried on. "Gentlemen, every aspect of Hong Kong government from top to bottom will be transformed by the work we do here. From policing to hygiene, from customs to hospitals, every part of Hong Kong administration will be cleaned up. Based roughly on the model of Singapore, the ICAC will have powers and independence that will transform the colony for the better. Does anybody have any questions?"

A man at the back raised his hand. "What powers will we have exactly?"

"Well, like I said earlier, it's very much at the drawing-board stage. But at present policemen, firemen, and even doctors are not accountable for the money and assets they have. Once the ICAC is formed, a Hong Kong government employee will have to justify where his or her huge bank balance and new car came from. Gentlemen, we will give both you and the ICAC the tools to delve into and clean up the civil service for good; believe me when I say that after next year, if you are corrupt, you would have to be either extremely stupid, extremely weak or extremely greedy!"

For the next few months Jock was to spend at least two days a week locked in the dusty room with his new colleagues, under the supervision of Quinton Charmers, QC. They looked at every aspect of the Hong Kong civil service before the unveiling of the ICAC. For corrupt officials, this meant that the net was closing in.

*

Harvest Festival, Sai Kung Baptist Church, 1973

Lily looked to her right at her family as she smiled and passed the collection plate to the pew behind her. Thirteen-year-old May was becoming increasing bored with church recently, and virtually had to be dragged out of bed that very morning. Next to her was little Alex, who at that specific instant was scratching the collar of his new cotton white shirt and almost certainly daydreaming about football. But it was the intensity in her husband's face that caught her eye. The sunlight was coming through the stained-glass window and through his greying red hair; nowadays you could see his scalp as his hair was also thinning.

Jock had been under pressure with his new tasks at work recently, but today at church, when he was at his most calm, she could see the same intensity in those clear blue eyes, as he listened to the Reverend, as he first had all those years ago, when he woke from his coma after suffering at the hands of the Japanese. Those same eyes that Aunty Lin Lin, God rest her soul, had said looked ghostly. The same eyes that Lily had fallen deeply in love with, and still was, to this very day.

Reverend Smith asked them all to rise and join him in song. Lily Wu Torrence felt in her heart that she had so much to be truly grateful for.

*

1973 Canton Road Government Offices, Kowloon

After eight or so hours, the four men in the stuffy room were beginning to wilt. It was getting late and the intensity of the work was, at times, beginning to show. Jock rubbed his eyes and loosened his tie as he once more listened to Chalmers. Also seated around the table were his police colleagues, Smith and Wilson.

Chalmers cleared his throat. "As we've discussed previously, these latest developments regarding Chief Inspector Peter MacFarland are extremely serious and have to be dealt with. I cannot stress enough that this is to be kept in-house and treated with the utmost importance. It's come to light that MacFarland's wife left the colony this week and he has been making moves about early retirement or ill-health, this type of thing. I am absolutely sure that he has been on the take for years. We just have to prove it, and make sure he doesn't abscond."

Superintendent Brian Smith spoke as he fingered a copy of MacFarland's bank statement. "Even on a Chief Inspector's salary there is no way he could have amassed this amount of money."

Jock nodded in agreement. "I don't believe for one minute that he's done this on his own so I think the important thing is that when we do act we do it quickly and raid his house *and* the houses of people close to him at exactly the same time. This way there can be no tip-offs or people slipping through the net."

Philip Wilson from Repulse Bay division shook his head. "We can't just go accusing people with no proof, Jock, plus we could be looking at anywhere between fifteen to twenty people."

"Aye, I know, but if they have nothing te' hide they have nothing te' worry about do they?"

Chalmers placed his hands on the table. "Look chaps, it's been a long day. I'm in agreement with Jock, I think we need to arrange a date, possibly even as early as next week, and hit MacFarland, his deputies, close allies and family, at exactly the same time. It has to be done in a quick, coordinated manner with hopefully not too many innocent people inconvenienced. It is getting late however, and I feel we should finalise details tomorrow when we are somewhat fresher."

It was already dark as the men said their brief goodbyes on the steps outside the government building and the old Chinese security guard locked the doors behind them. Superintendent Philip Wilson turned the opposite way to his colleagues and put his umbrella up against the light rain that was beginning to fall. He rounded the corner onto Tung Kun Street, and at the first payphone he could find, he looked both ways and dialled.

"Hello." Deputy Inspector Mark Hayton sat up in bed.

"Brother Hayton, listen. It's me, Brother Wilson. Jock Torrence will be coordinating a raid on your house in the next few days."

"Thank you, Wilson. That's good to know. Of course, I have nothing to hide, but appreciate your call all the same."

The rain started to come down heavier. "Well, Goodbye Hayton."

"Goodbye Wilson, this won't be forgotten, thank you."

In his comfortable Mid-Levels apartment, Deputy Inspector Mark Hayton rubbed his eyes and tapped the naked young Filipino man, who was sleeping beside him on the bed, on the shoulder.

He buried his head in the pillow. "No more, I'm tired...."

"Listen to me, Angelo. We have a slight problem, I'll need you and Pancho to sail *The Chief* down to the Philippines tomorrow. You'll be taking a few boxes with you."

"Whatever, just let me sleep won't you," he replied.

Mark Hayton was briefly distracted by the contours of Angelo's toned brown back but then pulled himself together. Maybe this is the wake-up call I need thought Hayton, "a kick up the jacksy", as his late father would say. Short-term, he could move a few incriminating things down to the Philippines and get Angelo out of the apartment, that would be no problem, but long-term he was a sitting-duck at present. He would have got in a whole heap of trouble back in London with the boy down at the docks had it not been for Father. No, what he needed was a wife, the boys were a lot of fun and he had certain needs, but a man in his position needed a family. Maybe he could look into tying the knot with what's her name...that Marjorie Penham-Smythe, the one who was always looking at him all doe-eyed at the Yacht Club. A good sort, good family who'd been here forever apparently, yes, she'd do, he'd better get to work on that one once this all died down. In the meantime, he had a lot of tidying up to do in the next twenty-four hours.

One week later, raids were made on numerous senior members of the Royal Hong Kong Police Force. Many officers and their families and associates were found to have hoarded millions of Hong Kong dollars in cash, property and luxury goods. Most notable amongst them was Chief

Inspector Peter MacFarland, who had amassed a fortune of 4.3 million Hong Kong dollars.

The most notable exception to the rule however was Deputy Inspector Mark Hayton, who on inspection appeared to live an almost frugal existence when compared to his colleagues. It looked like Mark Hayton was to be fast-tracked to the top, but he had a few scores to settle on the way, and Jock Torrence was at the top of that list.

CHAPTER SEVENTEEN

Pik Uk Prison, Clear Water Bay, 1997

Kwan Yo Hang rolled over on his bunk once more and began subconsciously rubbing his arm. This had been his second night in this cell and he seriously needed a hit of heroin or red chicken, as it was known to him. The doctors had prescribed him methadone when he had his entrance medical two days earlier but he barely felt the effect, and knew he was in for a long day if he didn't get a hit soon.

A couple of his Sun Yee On brothers had patted him on his back in the canteen before visiting hours yesterday, this had made him feel good for the first time in a few days. They told him that they would get him some red chicken as soon as the wardens let him out for exercise, but he was still being monitored for the next few days so he'd have to stay strong. The brothers had also told him not to speak to anybody about anything that had happened, especially his cell-mate who was at that moment snoring away peacefully in the bunk below him.

The visit from his mother had gone horribly from start to finish. She could barely look at him in the face for the whole thirty minutes and was constantly crying throughout. When he closed his eyes, he could still see his mother looking at him through the glass partition.

"Little one, tell me you didn't do this!" again and again she'd repeated the question.

He had just wanted to sweep his fragile little mother up and tell her everything would be alright. It was all a mistake and they could go home. Instead he tried to look strong for her.

"It will be OK, Mother. The brothers will take care of it," he said as he placed a hand on the glass, his voice breaking.

"Your brother is at school today. Those men are not your brothers."

Kwan had swallowed hard and could not look into his mother's eyes.

Outside his cell window meanwhile, he could see that dawn was breaking. He knew he had to go back for another interview with the turtles later today. He'd ask the lawyer man if the masters could send some money to his mother, yes that would be a good idea.

The lawyer man had also visited him yesterday after his mother, but Kwan had been so upset and unfocussed that the words had barely registered. He'd said that there had been new developments but all Kwan needed to do was keep quiet and he would do all the talking to the police. Kwan didn't care about the lawyer man, he just wanted all this to go away.

In the cold light of morning Kwan Yo Hang was hit by another wave of nausea and stomach cramps. The man on the bottom bunk told him to shut the fuck up.

*

Royal Hong Kong Police Headquarters Hong Kong Island, January 1997
Jackie Shuen had his back to Alex and Heidi Lim and the phone wedged on his shoulder. He then swiftly put the phone back on the cradle and picked up his jacket from the back of the chair.

"Rufus Chan wants to see us in the lab right now," he said with a sense of urgency.

Within five minutes the three colleagues were once again standing with their green scrubs on looking at the now familiar body of Darren Meakin, who was lying face down with his upper torso stripped to the waist.

"I think we have our weapon, officers," said Dr Chan holding a square metal object.

"What is it, exactly?" Shuen asked.

"I believe it's called a diving weight. Apparently, the divers use them in some sort of harness to weigh themselves down in the water. This is a 3kg lead weight, similar to the one that I believe killed the deceased."

Alex thought that the Director of Pathology seemed to be enjoying holding court, as he continued.

"Please take a look once more at the indentation on the back of the victim's head. Remember I said that I thought the weapon was rounded, well look at this."

He then placed the lead weight carefully into the broken part of the skull.

"A perfect match, I'm sure you'll agree."

"Did you get that weight from the airport, Dr Chan?" Alex asked.

"Yes, after looking at the suicide note, we were able to take one from the works container where there were dozens of them. Of course, we checked for fluids and prints on all of them, but came up with zero."

Alex added, "Presumably, if Goff did kill Darren Meakin, he would have thrown the weight and knife away somewhere."

Dr Chan looked over the rim of his glasses before replying. "Well, deduction is obviously your line of work, Detectives, but one would say that it is fair to assume that the weapons used are no longer at the crime scene."

"And any update on Goff?" Shuen asked.

"Well he's still dead if that's what you mean," replied Chan rather curtly.

"What I meant was…" Shuen paused. "…the angle and trajectory of the bullet wound you were talking about yesterday?"

The pathologist took a step to his right and placed a hand on the handle of one of the large morgue drawers. Alex hoped that he wasn't going to come face to face with a dead Andy Goff once more, but Chan paused as in contemplation.

"I've taken the measurements more precisely since returning to the morgue, and I believe the weapon would have been fired approximately twelve inches away from his face entering directly between the eyes causing instant death. Like I said yesterday it's a little strange, but I've seen stranger. Is that all?"

On the way back to the office, the three officers bumped into Karl Roberts in the corridor.

"Shuen, Wu Torrence, the chief wants to see you straight away," he said, completely ignoring Heidi Lim once more.

Alex then followed Shuen, as he had never been in Chief Inspector Mark Hayton's office, down the corridor to the lift, before pressing the top floor button. The two men remained silent as the doors closed. Alex subconsciously straightened his tie using the reflection in the lift door and Shuen broke the tension by mock-saluting Alex.

"It's like going to the headmaster, isn't it?" Alex half joked as the lift reached the top floor and the doors opened. The receptionist told them the Chief Inspector would see them immediately.

As they entered, Mark Hayton had his back to the two officers and was looking out at the bustling street in the Central District below. The office had a strong maritime feel to it with an assortment of yachting memorabilia adorning the walls and a golden anchor on the Chief Inspector's large oak desk. Alex also noted a masonic seal on a paperweight.

"I'm going to miss this, you know," he said without turning.

"Sir?" Alex replied.

The senior officer turned. "You'll be hearing soon enough, I suppose. I'll be leaving my post at 12pm midnight on the day of the Handover."

Alex knew that many of the senior people in Hong Kong Government and the civil service in general would be stepping down after the Handover, but this was the first he had heard about the Chief Inspector leaving. Hayton continued, "There will be a press release this week I'm told." He seemed to click back into the present. "But up until the 30th of June I intend to run a tight ship."

Instinctively Alex turned to his right and saw a large blown-up photo of Hayton, proudly steering a racing yacht with a crew balancing on the side. The yacht's name was THE CHIEF 3. Alex assumed quite rightly that Mark Hayton had upgraded from THE CHIEF and THE CHIEF 2 over the years.

"Do you know who will be replacing you, Sir?" Shuen asked.

"Well, Senior Inspector Karl Roberts would be the logical solution, in my humble opinion. He has been shadowing my duties and has been with me constantly for the last few weeks. But who knows? They may decide a Chinese face might be more politically correct?"

Alex was once more drawn to the photo of the yacht. One of the crew, all in matching uniforms, was Karl Roberts.

"Previously, the Governor and the outgoing Chief Inspector would decide, but this will be a decision for the incoming Hong Kong Chief Executive and presumably Beijing," he continued.

The Hong Kong Chief Executive was going to be the new head of Hong Kong replacing The Governor, after the Handover, and was seen by many as being in the pocket of Beijing.

Alex had no idea if the Chief Inspector had resigned, retired or jumped before he could be pushed. Hayton seemed to click back into life and clapped his hands.

"Right gentlemen, please give me the latest news on the Meakin stroke Goff incidents."

Shuen took the lead. "Well Sir, as you know Andy Goff appears to have taken his own life after admitting to killing Darren Meakin in his suicide note. The forensics corroborate this and that the murder weapon was a lead diving-weight. We also have the original suspect, Kwan Yo Hang, coming in for questioning later today."

"So, what's the story there with the triad boy?"

Shuen continued. "We're not a hundred percent sure, Sir. He was probably on-site that night, but we don't think he was involved in the murder. He was very vague about details at the first interview, there were no marks on him, and I felt the lawyer was instructing him."

"The boy is a Sun Yee On triad, correct?"

"Yes, Sir, correct."

"And do we have any indication why he took the rap in the first place?" Hayton asked.

"Well he's obviously been instructed to do so from higher up the Sun Yee On chain. They are at around half of the construction site, with the 14k triad on the rest, taking dry salaries – gambling, illegal money-lending – that kind of thing. But we're not sure exactly why they would make the boy take the blame for something as serious as this."

Hayton scratched his chin. "Maybe we never will. At least the family of Darren Meakin can get some closure. – They're Roman Catholics I believe. – You'll be returning the body tomorrow, I gather, Detective Inspector Wu Torrence."

This was the first Alex had heard of his impending departure, but masked this with a simple nod before Hayton continued.

"By the way, I bumped in to a sailing chum, Raymond Barnett, at the Yacht Club last night, Wu Torrence. He told me he'd made your acquaintance at the new airport."

Alex tried not to react and there was a brief pause before Hayton broke the silence once more.

"Do you sail, Wu Torrence?"

"Sir?"

"I noticed you looking at the photo earlier."

"It looks very intense, Sir."

"Yes, it is. That was the 1994 Royal Hong Kong Yacht Club. – Hong Kong to the Philippines challenge race."

Alex nodded.

"That particular manoeuvre is called upwind hiking. It's crucial that all team members move in the same direction, don't you agree?"

CHAPTER EIGHTEEN

December 1973, Sai Kung Police Station

It was a crisp, sunny Monday morning as Jock Torrence and Taff Williams pulled up outside the station in Taff's old red Datsun 100A. Taff already had the keys in his hand as the motor kept on running before juddering to an eventual stop.

Taff laughed. "It gets me from A to B!"

Jock agreed and patted the dashboard. "Aye, as long as it does the job, that's all you need."

Jock still tended to favour Fords, and his present model, Cortina, was currently being driven down to Temple Street by Lily for some last-minute Christmas shopping. Some ex-POWs made a big show of not buying anything Japanese, but Jock personally viewed them as nothing more than objects and had no problem with his kids watching the family Hitachi TV, for example.

As Taff laboured out of the small Japanese car, Jock noticed that his friend had put on a few pounds since his wedding the previous year. It also still looked a bit strange with Detective Williams being out of uniform, as was the case nowadays. Jock was pleased that his friend was now a detective and as much as he would hate to admit it, this did make social engagements and their out-of-work friendship a lot easier.

Taff spotted Black Tooth before his boss and nodded in the direction of the lychee tree that the triad had come out from behind.

"I wonder what that bugger wants," he said.

"I'm not sure, but just wait here for a minute will ye', Taff," replied Jock before walking over.

Black Tooth greeted Jock with a nod of the head which was returned.

"I need to speak to you, officer Torrence," the man said in English.

"Do you now?" replied Jock, intrigued.

"Yes, it is a bit delicate, but somebody high up in my organisation wants to speak to you personally in Tsim Sha Tsui."

"And why would that be?" Jock asked.

The man seemed to be quite uncomfortable with the encounter and answered earnestly, "I honestly don't know, but I am instructed to stay here until you return safely."

Jock knew this was a common tactic used by the older Chinese generation when trading and a big show of face for both parties. Merchants would put a son or a brother on the other trader's boat or property, until the deal was concluded, ensuring that nothing underhand would take place. Jock was also intrigued. Because of the structure of the 14k and its nature he was certainly interested in knowing who wanted to talk to him…and why?

Black Tooth continued. "One of our drivers can take you now."

Jock nodded and briefly explained the situation to Taff.

"Are you sure, Boss? It's all a bit sudden. Do you want me to come with you?"

"I think it will be OK, Detective. Mr Wan here has given me his word. Could you look after him, please?"

Slightly uneasily, Taff escorted Black Tooth into the station as Jock got into the back of a nearby silver Mercedes.

Black Tooth looked around the reception area. "Do you need me to go in a cell?"

"No, there won't be any need for that, Wan. Just sit there. But listen and listen well. If anything happens to my boss, you'll wish you had never been born. Understood?"

"Understood," he nodded.

*

Around forty minutes later, the Mercedes pulled up outside the Peninsula Hotel on the Tsim Sha Tsui waterfront. A bell-boy opened the door and Jock slipped him a few coins.

The driver looked over his shoulder. "Mr Chan will be in room eighty-eight. I will be waiting here."

The Peninsula looked magnificent in the morning sunlight. The fountains and lion statues at the entrance gave the place an almost regal look. The number eighty-eight also registered with Jock. The number eight is often seen as lucky by the Chinese, and this was certainly a sign of opulence on the part of whoever was waiting on the eighth floor.

Jock walked into the reception area and the woman behind the counter said immediately, "Good morning, Detective Inspector Torrence. Mr Chan will see you right away. The boy will show you the way."

Jock momentarily wondered if it would be prudent to call Taff and let him know his wherabouts, but the bell-boy had already pressed the lift button.

On the eighth floor, the bell-boy knocked on the door marked 88. Jock felt momentarily awkward as he realised he had no more coins in his pocket, but the boy's face registered no emotion as he turned away.

The door was answered by a tall, smartly dressed Chinese man with his hair slicked back as was the fashion nowadays. "Please enter, Inspector." He motioned courteously into the suite, as he let himself out.

Behind the desk sat a heavy-set Chinese man. He was also immaculately dressed in a tailor-made suit that would probably cost a month of Jock's wages. He was also wearing an assortment of heavy – mostly jade – jewellery and a fedora hat whilst smoking a large Cuban cigar.

If indeed this was the 14k Mountain Master sitting in front of him, that would be quite a coup for somebody like Jock Torrence. Intelligence shared at his ICAC meetings had said that the leader was unknown, but he could be one of three men, none of them named Chan.

"Detective Inspector, thank you for coming at such short notice," the man raised his large figure out of the leather chair and shook Jock's hand.

He continued, "Please be seated. May I offer you a drink, or a cigar perhaps?"

"No, thank you. May I ask whom I am addressing?"

The fat man laughed. "My name is not important, Inspector, but I insist you must try a wee twenty-year-old malt, from your homeland I believe."

The thoughts were racing through Jock's mind as the man turned to a globe-shaped drinks cabinet. He needed to register the man's physical details and mannerisms, which would be of help to his colleagues down the road. He had the room number and car registration all memorised, but doubted if they could be linked to the man opposite.

A large crystal glass was placed in front of Jock. "I am told they say in Scotland that the only thing that should be put in whiskey is more whiskey. Therefore, I have omitted ice, Inspector."

Jock took a sip and raised the glass. The whiskey even at this early hour was wonderful, and he savoured the mouthful. The man opposite seemed to be studying Jock's face and was smiling intently. Jock's uniform, whilst smart, did feel a tad out of place in the grandeur of the room and the Scotsman subconsciously felt the worn cuff of his shirt, and felt slightly uneasy.

"Inspector, we are not as different as you might believe."

Jock raised an eyebrow. "Is that right? In what way?"

"I know we are at opposite ends of the spectrum. I understand that parts of my business could be unpalatable to a man such as yourself." He paused and took a sip of whiskey. "But I think we both believe in order and structure. Discipline, should I say."

Part of Jock wanted to add that opium, prostitution, human suffering and extortion were not something he believed in, but felt there was more to be earned by remaining silent.

The large man chuckled. "You have a son, I believe, Inspector?"

Jock felt his hand tighten on the glass as he tried to maintain his composure. "My home life is nae' business of yours."

The man laughed again. "Inspector, inspector, please, you are here as my guest. I simply wanted to make a comparison. I too have a son."

Jock nodded, only slightly appeased.

"And any son is going to make mistakes," the fat man added.

"And?" asked Jock.

"Well, this is the purpose of our meeting, Inspector. My son has made a mistake and I need your help."

Jock raised his hand. "Look, I'm going to stop you there, Mr Chan, or whatever your name is. I'm a principled man, I've never taken a bribe in my..."

"Inspector," the man interrupted, "I would never dream of insulting a man such as yourself with something as ugly as a bribe, but please hear me out. My son, who normally is not a bad boy, has done something rather stupid, and he has done it in your district. I believe there was some sort of altercation at the weekend and he is currently at your police station. I need you to let him go."

Jock started to stand. "Look, if he's in my cells, he's there for a reason. I teld' you I am a principled man. The law is the law!"

The man laughed out loud and slapped the desk. "You've been sitting here for twenty minutes and you don't remember who I am..."

"I think I need to leave...."

"Do you, Tommy Soldier?!"

Jock collapsed into the chair as the man opposite rolled back his shirt sleeve to show a faded tattoo of a ship's anchor.

Tears immediately sprang to Jock's eyes. "Popeye, is that you?!"

The Chinese man was also crying as the pair embraced.

"I never got to say thank you!" said Jock.

"Now you can, Tommy Soldier. Now you can!"

*

Even by the time the Mercedes pulled back into Sai Kung police station Jock was still in shock. He glided through the front doors, passed Black Tooth who was reading the *Sing Pao Daily News*, and headed straight for Taff Williams' desk.

"Can I have a quick word, Taff?"

"Jesus, Jock...er boss....you look white as a sheet. Are you OK?" he replied.

"Aye, I'm fine. Are there three boys in the cells for an assault?"

"Yeah, nasty attack that one. I was the arresting officer but I haven't charged them yet as the other man is still in hospital."

"Listen Taff, I need the youngest to be released. I need you to make this one go away and I can't tell you why."

Unusually for Jock, he made physical contact and put his hand on Taff's arm. Taff looked at his friend. In nearly fifteen years of working together, Jock Torrence had never asked for anything remotely close to what he was asking for now. Taff knew instinctively that it must be important.

"Consider it done," he said. "If you are telling me that you are OK, then this never happened."

"Aye, I promise you, I'm fine." He paused. "Thanks Taff."

"For what?" replied the Welshman, as he headed towards the cells.

CHAPTER NINETEEN

January 1997, Hong Kong Island Police Station
Alex grimaced as he sipped the tepid, awful coffee in a Styrofoam cup while Jackie Shuen motioned Heidi Lim over to his desk, where the two men were seated.

"What time is the Kwan interview, Heidi?"

"He'll be here in fifteen minutes or so," she replied.

"And is everything in order as planned?"

"Yes, Sir," she smiled.

Jackie turned to Alex. "We have a little ace up our sleeve!"

Just then Alex's mobile began to ring. He could see from the caller ID that it was Chief Inspector McGregor back in Manchester. As Heidi Lim hurried off, Alex motioned to Shuen that he had to take the call as he moved in her direction towards the exit.

"Wu Torrence?" McGregor barked.

Alex couldn't help noticing Heidi's contour and tight skirt as she paced down the hallway.

"Er...yes, what's up, Boss?" Alex answered as he scratched the back of his neck.

"I hear you've been ruffling a few feathers this trip, eh?"

Alex paused, momentarily contemplating which way to answer. "How's that, Sir?"

"Listen, I've had a call from my opposite number, what's his name again?"

"Chief Inspector Mark Hayton, Boss."

"Yeah, that's the fella. He rang me earlier. He's not a happy camper. He said you've been asking questions at the new airport or something?"

"Well, I might have…"

"He kindly reminded me that my officer was there in an observation capacity and not as an investigator."

"Yeah, he wasn't happy that I spoke to one of his Yacht Club member friends from the construction site," he replied.

"Listen, I don't give a fuck what you do as long as you're out of my hair, Wu Torrence, but use your fuckin' noddle and try not to piss anybody off in the process!"

Alex raised his eyebrows, "Yes Sir, understood."

His boss's voice lowered a notch. "I hear you're back on tomorrow night's flight with the stiff, aren't you?"

"Yes"

"Listen Alex, take it from me. You're playing the away game here. I know dealing with these public-schoolboy types can be a bind, but let them do their job. We've got more than enough crime here in Manchester for you to get your teeth into when you get back, OK?"

Alex nodded. "OK, Boss, I guess I can't do too much damage in twenty-four hours anyway."

"You'd better not!" McGregor snorted, before adding. "Listen Alex, you're a good copper, just learn to choose your battles more wisely."

Clunk.

Alex looked at his phone's screen, unsure if he'd been scolded or complimented.

A short while later, Shuen and Alex were making their way to the interrogation room when the double-doors at the far end of the corridor opened and the now familiar figure of Kwan Yo Hang appeared, handcuffed and flanked by two uniformed officers. The swagger of three days earlier had disappeared, and the shaven head and prison uniform made the boy appear even more vulnerable.

"Watch this," whispered Shuen.

At the other end of the corridor, the opposite doors opened as Heidi Lim led a small, middle-aged Chinese woman by the arm.

"Mum!" Kwan shouted.

The small woman jumped with surprise. "Son!" she turned to Heidi Lim. "What are they doing with my boy?!"

The officers held Kwan tightly as he tried to get to his mother, whose legs appeared to have buckled.

"Mum!" he sobbed. "She shouldn't be here, she shouldn't be here."

Heidi Lim gently led the woman into a side room, as Kwan continued his protests and was forced into the interrogation room at the opposite end of the hallway.

Alex had seen this manoeuvre a few times in many different stations and situations. Two criminals meeting in a corridor can often produce insecurities, emotions and hopefully results, but Alex couldn't help but feel that this was quite harsh on the boy's mother, who was an innocent party in all of this.

"That was a bit naughty, Jackie," he whispered.

Shuen shrugged. "Sometimes you have to break a few eggs to make an omelette, as they say."

Karl Roberts was once more already seated behind the glass partition as Alex entered the darkish room.

"What was that friggin' circus going on out there?" he whispered.

"I'm not sure," answered Alex, choosing instead to concentrate on the other side of the one-way mirror.

The clearly agitated prisoner was refusing to sit down and had already kicked the plastic chair next to his lawyer; the same brief from three days earlier.

"Why was she here, she's done nothing wrong!" he cried.

Jackie Shuen sat down, crossed his arms, and said calmly. "Sit down, Kwan, and I'll tell you."

Shuen was taking charge and psychologically putting Kwan in his debt. Alex knew this, but doubted if Kwan had the mental capacity for very much even in a regular state, never mind the agitated manner he was now in. Kwan sat down like an adolescent who'd been sent to his bedroom. Shuen then pressed the recorder and recited the normal formalities in the direction of the tape.

He continued, "Kwan, your mother is very concerned about all of this, and you not cooperating and lying is causing her distress."

Before the boy could respond, the lawyer said, "For the record, I believe the detective deliberately engineered this meeting between my client and his mother outside the interview room, and in doing so has caused my client undue stress."

Kwan looked at his shoes. "Just leave her out of it, OK."

Alex noticed through the glass that the boy was rubbing his forearm. Alex had seen dozens of young triads craving a hit of heroin, and Kwan looked identical to them at that precise moment.

"For the purposes of the recording Senior Constable Heidi Lim is entering the room at approximately 14.47," Shuen said.

Heidi Lim sat down and shook her head whilst looking at the defendant.

"Your mum is really upset, Kwan…"

The lawyer interrupted. "Listen, we are not playing this game!"

Lim ignored the man and continued. "Kwan, we can make all this go away. We know full well that you didn't do what you confessed to."

Kwan glanced instinctively at his lawyer, who was staring icily at Jackie Shuen.

She continued calmly. "Just tell us in your own words what happened on the night of the incident, Kwan. We know you're not a murderer."

"I don't talk to turtles," Kwan said, but with a lot less conviction than three days previously.

Jackie Shuen blew smoke in the air and pushed the packet of cigarettes and a lighter across the table to Kwan. An offer he accepted greedily.

"Do you know *how* we know you didn't do it?" he asked.

The question was directed as much at the lawyer as it was at Kwan.

He continued, "The reason we know you didn't do it Kwan, is because we have a confession from the real murderer."

The lawyer was trying to hold his gaze, and his cool, but a slight tapping on the table gave away his annoyance.

"We just need you to tell us what you actually saw, and we can help you," said Shuen.

"Think about your mum, Kwan," added Heidi Lim.

The lawyer regained his composure. "And are you going to share this information with us, Detective?"

Shuen laughed. "What's the matter? Have your triad brothers not told you everything?"

"I object to this insinuation! I am a respected member of the legal profession, and I will not have aspersions cast on my character!"

Lim continued. "Kwan, think about it. Would your real friends let you go to jail for murder? If you tell us the truth, we can protect you."

Kwan again looked around nervously at the lawyer who was now red in the face and glaring at DI Jackie Shuen, who nonchalantly stubbed his cigarette out in the ashtray next to the tape recorder.

"Kwan, we can put you in protection, even get you a new lawyer," said Shuen.

"How dare you! I've never been so insulted!" the lawyer shouted as he stood up. "I suggest we take a recess and you learn some manners, Detective!"

Shuen spoke to the tape recorder and said nonchalantly, "DI Shuen, interview paused 14.53."

He then pressed the stop button before looking the lawyer straight in the face. "There is a boy's life at stake here, and you are more concerned about your reputation and fee, no doubt. When you call Sun Yee On in a minute, give them my regards won't you?"

The lawyer lunged at DI Shuen only to be restrained by the uniformed officer guarding the door. The man straightened his tie and spat. "I'll be back in five minutes!" he said as he straightened his suit and left the room.

Kwan looked up and said quietly. "I think I'm going to vomit."

*

Alex closed the toilet-seat lid and sat down as quietly as he could. He could hear Kwan dry-retching in the stall next to him.

"Have they given you any methadone yet?" he whispered.

The boy paused. "Yeah, but I need a hit soon."

"Listen, why don't you cooperate? You can get out of here and go home to your mum."

"Who are you?"

"You don't need to know that. But that lawyer isn't helping you, trust me."

The boy retched again. Alex passed a stick of gum under the stall.

Alex continued. "Do you want me to pass anything on to your mum, Kwan?"

"Just tell her I'm sorry..." he retched again. "Tell her I didn't do it!"

"Everybody knows you didn't do it, they just need your help. The gweilo who was killed had a wife and a little baby, Kwan. When you go back into the room, tell them the truth. You can plead innocent and go back to your mum, start again, and get away from the Sun Yee On."

"I'm not a grass, I don't snitch."

"I know Kwan, nobody is saying you are. But what is more important – going home to your mum, or saving face?"

"They said if I took the blame I would get paid and be promoted."

There was a knock on the door. "Are you finished, Kwan?" said an officer.

Alex cursed under his breath and left the toilet stall quickly and without making eye-contact with the uniformed officer, who was waiting for Kwan to appear. Upon leaving the bathroom he headed directly to Jackie Shuen's desk.

"Listen Jackie, I've just spoken to Kwan in the bathroom. You're right, the boy is in the pocket of the lawyer, but I don't think he's going to give you anything much today, he's scared stiff."

Shuen nodded. "What did he say?"

"Basically, what we know already, in that he's being told to keep quiet and follow orders."

"Did he give any details about the night at the airport?"

"No, nothing, the uniformed officer was outside so I only got a few seconds talking to him."

"I suspect that they'll be retracting the confession at some point. I just wish I could charge that slippery bastard lawyer as well."

A uniformed WPC put her head around the door. "Senior Inspector Roberts is asking when the interview will resume, Sir?"

*

The lawyer was whispering in the ear of his ashen-faced suspect as the detectives settled down on both sides of the mirror. The charged atmosphere of twenty minutes ago had reduced significantly.

The lawyer cleared his throat. "In light of the latest information, my client will be retracting his confession in writing as soon as possible."

"Does that mean I can go home?" asked a confused-looking Kwan.

The lawyer put a hand on the boy's shoulder, who was once again rubbing his arm.

Shuen spoke calmly. "Kwan, whether you stay or go depends on what you tell us. Three days ago, you sat in that very chair and said you killed Darren Meakin with a chopper because he was stealing copper-wire. Are you now saying that is not the case?"

The lawyer spoke first whilst still holding the boy's shoulder. "You have the right to remain silent."

"Come on Kwan, just tell us if you saw anything!" Shuen said.

The boy was in the crossfire and looked confused. "Can I go then?"

The lawyer spoke again. "It is my belief that the confession was beaten or coerced out of my client…"

"A confession that you typed up!" countered Shuen.

"Acting on behalf of my client I merely put the confession in written format without realising the fear that my client…"

"The only fear he has is from your paymasters!" Shuen leant forward. "Is that the best you can come up with?"

The lawyer sat back in his chair and crossed his arms, straining not to take the bait as before.

Kwan spoke rapidly. "The big gweilo hit that fat gweilo on the back of the head after he got out of the water but I didn't know he'd killed him. It was dark and I couldn't see very…"

The lawyer again put his hand on Kwan's shoulder but the distressed boy didn't seem to notice. "…much. He hit him on the back of the head."

"But why did he kill him?" asked Shuen.

"I don't know. Crazy gweilos, always drinking! The fat man was looking at a big box; then the big gweilo hit him from behind, that's all I know!"

"And why was he in the water?"

"I don't know! Every weekend the big gweilo was in the water when the other gweilos weren't there."

"And what was in the box?"

"I don't know. He brought it out of the water."

"My client is obviously in a distressed state and I'm not sure that this is admissible due to his…"

Shuen ignored him "So why did you confess, Kwan?"

Kwan looked sideways at his lawyer. "Like he said, the turtles beat it out of me."

"Really? You didn't have a scratch on you and you didn't say a word to anybody? Were you that scared, Kwan?"

"I'm not scared of anybody!"

"I think you're scared of whoever is paying your expensive lawyer."

The lawyer stood up. "That's enough. My client is being harassed and I am being continually insulted. My client will not be saying another word until I have drafted the retraction. Do not be surprised if you are reported, Detective."

"And don't be surprised if the ICAC pay you a visit anytime soon!" retorted Shuen.

Ouch, thought Alex from behind the screen.

*

Alex stood alone on the top deck of the Star Ferry, looking across Victoria Harbour towards Tsim Sha Tsui. It had been another frustrating day on the Meakin/Goff Case (*Number 2047, completed*) as it was now known and filed away under. Alex knew that, even with the crowds, he could get twenty minutes to himself on board one of Hong Kong's most famous and cheapest tourist attractions.

Alex remembered as a child, how he and his father had been travelling on the Star Ferry one day when a commuter had loudly spat on the deck. Jock had instinctively grabbed the man by his shirt collar and frog-marched him over to one of the crew. Alex chuckled at the memory.

"Is something funny, Detective?" a female voice asked from behind.

"Heidi! No not really, I was just thinking how nice it is to travel first-class." He laughed once more.

Heidi Lim leaned on the rail next to him. "It's been a strange week, hasn't it?"

"Yes, it certainly has. You don't come across many kids admitting to a murder they haven't done back home in Manchester."

She leant in closer to him. "I don't think you do anywhere, to be honest. I think sometimes you see these young men covered in scars and tattoos. They try to appear so tough but really, underneath, they're just scared little boys."

"Yes, I guess so. What do you think will happen to him, Heidi?"

"I can't believe they'll just let him walk away. I imagine he'll get charged with Accessory After the Fact for not reporting the murder and do six months or so. He's just a puppet really, long term he'll just be another wasted triad life."

Alex nodded and couldn't help thinking about his cousin Curly. When they had been nineteen or so and Alex would be on his yearly trip to Hong Kong, Curly would always have endless stories of girls, fights and fast cars. Approaching their forties, these stories seemed kind of pathetic nowadays.

The ferry let off a loud claxon as a sailing boat approached too closely below.

"Have you get time for a drink, Heidi?"

She hesitated. "Yes, but on two conditions…I'm paying…."

"And?"

She tossed her fringe like a certain young triad, "And no turtle talk!"

The Handover Murders   173

CHAPTER TWENTY

July 1974, Hong Kong

Jock handed the taxi-driver two notes and waited while the change was handed back (slowly and with bad grace) from the expectant driver. He had pulled up near the Standard Chartered Bank tower and he would walk the short distance to headquarters. He'd been called in two days earlier for a routine review which happened once or twice a year, as per police guidelines. The July heat was intense and shocking after the air-conditioning of the taxi, but Jock was dressed in his *civvies* and was in good spirits, both kids had come home with good report-cards the previous week from King George V Secondary school and had been promised a junk trip out to Tai Long Wan beach the following weekend as a reward.

His review last year had been conducted by old Porterhouse, and had been nothing more than a formality ending with a nice brandy and a chat about the following weekend's racing. Jock had a few incident reports tucked away in his briefcase. The recent ICAC work was highly confidential and not up for discussion. There had been a few land rights issues between different clans as per normal in the New Territories and a rise in burglaries (probably by illegal immigrants) but other than that, there was not much to report.

After a leisurely five-minute stroll, Jock was in the entrance of the Royal Hong Kong Police headquarters waiting to be told which office he needed to go to. Jock liked to visit the old place with its hustle and bustle, but he had to say that he much preferred the tranquillity of Sai Kung. Jock spotted a US sailor in full whites handcuffed to a radiator opposite him looking decidedly the worse for wear, like he'd been overdoing his R&R, whilst over from Vietnam on leave. Jock supposed that the US military police would be picking the young man up shortly. The sailor made eye-contact with Jock also.

"Hey Joe, you got a smoke?" he asked.

Jock laughed good-naturedly and lit a Lucky Strike which he then placed in the handcuffed sailor's mouth. He also put four extra *'smokes'* in the sailor's top pocket.

A receptionist leant over the counter. "Superintendent Torrence, Commissioner of Police Hayton will see you now."

This brought the American to life. "Hey Joe! You a cop? Can you help a guy out?"

Jock patted the man on the shoulder. "I think you've made yer' bed sailor, now you've got te' lie in it."

"Thanks for nothing, Pal!" said the sailor as he slouched down on the bench, the cigarette drooping out of his mouth.

Jock was still laughing as the lift doors closed and he made his way to the office of the new Commissioner of Police. Jock had looked at the ICAC raids the previous year pragmatically. Of course, the sweep had uncovered a few bad eggs and knocked a few noses out of joint, but on the whole, it had to be considered a success. The then Deputy-Chief Mark Hayton had proved to be whiter than white and had been quickly promoted, once his superior, Peter MacFarland, had been arrested in disgrace. Jock had to admit that even though he personally didn't like the man, things in Hong Kong were running reasonably well under the new boss.

The doors pinged open and yet another smiling receptionist told Jock in a sing-song voice to please wait. Eventually Jock was called through, Hayton was standing looking out of the window with a Napoleonic-style pose, before turning and addressing Jock.

"Torrence, Torrence, good to see you, old boy. "Thank you for coming." He then spoke to the receptionist. "Daisy, be a dear and bring us tea."

Hayton beckoned for Jock to be seated at one side of the large desk. Jock broke the ice. "Congratulations on the promotion, Sir."

"Why, thank you, Torrence, I've also got the old ball and chain since we last met, what?" he said, raising his ring finger.

"Well congratulations on that also, Sir," Jock said, already knowing full well, as the whole wedding had been splashed over the society pages a couple of months previously. Jock had always suspected that Hayton was a *nancy boy* but again, he was rather uninterested in the whole society scene, and wished him well.

The two men discussed the goings-on in the Sai Kung District with Hayton appearing to be paying half a mind to the conversation and only briefly thumbing through the papers Jock had placed on the desk between them. Eventually Hayton stood once more. "Now Torrence, as well as your annual report there is something rather delicate I need to run past you if I may…"

Jock raised an eyebrow. "Go ahead, Sir."

"Do you know a man called Wu Jianbin, Torrence?"

"No, Sir," said Jock shaking his head honestly.

Hayton looked Jock in the eye as the atmosphere changed. "Now, Torrence, think carefully, do you know or have you ever met a man called Wu Jianbin?"

Jock tried to rack his brain and hesitantly replied. "No…er, it, it honestly does'ne ring a bell, Sir."

Hayton sat down for effect and pulled a manila folder out of the top drawer of his desk. "We have been monitoring Wu Jianbin, who we believe to be one of the mountain masters of the 14k triad, for around a year now. So, imagine my surprise when CID tell me that one of our Regional Superintendents has visited him at The Peninsula Hotel on… er…" He opened the file. "…on December, the sixteenth of last year. – And you say you've never met the man?"

Jock's entire world was about to come crashing in at that very moment. It could only be the meeting with Popeye; he had no idea of Popeye's real name. He had somehow been seen with one of Hong Kong's leading triad bosses, and had nothing to say in his defence. Were there photos? Was the room bugged? A million questions rolled around in Jock's head but he opted to stay quiet for the moment as Hayton continued. "It seems that the officer in question was in a room with the suspect for a full thirty minutes before shaking hands with the man in the hotel lobby. Do you have anything to say, Torrence?"

Do you have anything to say? Do you have anything to say? Those were the exact words that Keije used to repeat over and over again when he was beating him. The worst time had been when Jock had been suspected of stealing rice. Jock had been kneeling for hours on a concrete floor with a bamboo pole behind his knees. Each time that Jock had refused to speak Keije had stood on the pole crushing his knees into the floor.

"I said. Do you have anything to say, Torrence?"

Jock crashed into the present. "I...er...."

Jock couldn't think. His instinct was to stay quiet. He didn't know how to lie and there were other people involved in this also. Not only had he been talking to a gang boss, he had also given instructions that a criminal be released. Taff Williams could be implicated in this through no fault of his own.

"Torrence, I know full well you were involved."

Hayton's voice had somehow merged into that of Keije's. Jock couldn't breathe. Think man, think! He finally collected himself and grabbed the side of the chair. "I'm sorry, Sir. That was me at The Peninsula but a cannae' tell you why I was there."

"Well, I see." Hayton paused for effect. "That leaves us in somewhat of a tricky situation, does it not?"

Jock could barely hear the words as the pain in his knees seared to the surface. He wanted to tell Hayton that he'd visited the bravest man he'd ever met, the man who saved his life. He wanted to tell Hayton to go to hell, but he couldn't. For the first time in his life he was morally wrong, caught red-handed. He'd done it; he'd done a deal with a criminal, let a violent man go and implicated his best friend Taff in the process. The room was spinning as the pain in his knees got worse and worse.

"May I remind you, Torrence, that I am Commissioner of the Royal Hong Kong Police Force. If you do not tell me exactly what happened there will be profound consequences. Do you understand?" said Hayton savouring the moment.

"Aye, I understand. But you can go to hell," said Jock at last raising his head.

Hayton tapped his fingers together. "Very well, you leave me no choice. I expect your resignation on my desk by o-nine hundred tomorrow morning. In view of your previous good record you will be allowed to leave honourably on the understanding you leave the colony immediately. If you were to stay or ever return I would not be so lenient, however. Dismissed."

Jock left the room with his feet not touching the floor. Being dragged out of a Japanese interrogation room by the hair had been less painful than what he had just experienced. Jock found the nearest toilet and threw up violently.

Meanwhile, back in his office, Commissioner of Police Mark Hayton was once more looking out of his window with a contented smile on his face. Subconsciously he rubbed a knot on a piece of rope on one of his displays, he could feel an erection rising under his uniform trousers and thought to himself that he must pay the boys a visit on *The Chief III* on his way home to celebrate.

CHAPTER TWENTY-ONE

January 1997, Sai Kung
Alex was still wearing yesterday's shirt as he woke up alone in his mother's spare room with one leg hanging off the side of the single bed. The Sunday morning dawn chorus of insects and birds seemed a lot louder than usual, and his pounding head and dry mouth made him momentarily regret the last couple of drinks on his previous night's impromptu date with Senior Constable Heidi Lim.

As his eyes grew accustomed to the light coming through the thin floral curtains, he could hear his mother deliberately banging the vacuum-cleaner around in the next room.

"Mr Important Detective man coming home drunk...singing like a Hakka...smelling like brewery...."

Instinctively he felt for his left breast-pocket and smiled as he felt the crumpled napkin with Heidi Lim's personal phone number, and something undecipherable written in Chinese. Like a lot of expatriate Chinese or Eurasian people, Alex could only manage rudimentary written Chinese, which had provided much amusement to Senior Constable Lim at the previous night's karaoke session and later when she slipped the napkin into his pocket and kissed him goodnight on the cheek at the MTR station.

"Does Frank Sinatra want bacon sandwich?!" Lily shouted above the vacuuming.

"You're a life-saver, Mum, thanks!"

Alex momentarily thought about asking Lily to translate the note, before realising what a terrible idea that could be.

Thirty minutes later, fed, showered and with two paracetamols working their way around his system, Alex decided to walk down to Sai Kung centre and pick up a

Sunday Morning Post. The day was sunny and clear; the case was just about filed away and he'd had a night out with a beautiful girl, but in all honesty, he now wanted to see the back of Hong Kong and get back to dreary Manchester.

The case, whilst filed away and supposedly finished, had left a bit of a bad taste. Whilst everything seemed tucked away and ordered, Alex couldn't help but feel that they hadn't really got to the bottom of things. Why was Andy Goff in the water on the night of the murder anyway, and why did he feel the need to kill Darren Meakin? Did he mean just to knock him out or to actually kill him? Who was Number Six? And did Goff really blow his own brains out? Alex shrugged absent-mindedly with the realisation that many of these answers went up in smoke with Andy Goff's death.

"Oy, ugly! You look like shit!" shouted Curly, who was leaning against a wire fence.

"I feel like shit, cuz!" he replied.

"You need something to give you a lift Mr Policeman?!" he patted his pocket jokingly.

Behind Curly was a group of five teenagers standing on plinths doing balancing exercises, they all had brightly-coloured trousers on with plain white vests.

Curly thumbed behind him. "Do you remember practicing for the Lion dance?!"

"God, yeah, I only did it once on the last Chinese New Year before we left for England. I think it was the year Uncle George dotted the eyes."

It was customary for a local dignitary to paint the eyes of the dancing dragon on the first day of Chinese New Year and Curly's dad had been given the honour that year, because of his social standing and for all the work he did for community.

"Yeah, that was special. He only saw one Chinese New Year after that, I think," he replied without emotion.

Chinese New Year lion dances, a bit like sport, were somewhat of a grey area in community/triad relations. Two or three triad groups usually entered competitions and kids with martial arts abilities were valued because of their balance and movements. The boys behind Curly may or may not have been fledging triads, but they could certainly move. Traditionally, after the contest, the lions would dance from business to business with a band behind them making as much noise as possible to ward off spirits and to take *lai see* (or lucky money) in red packets from the shop-keepers and restaurateurs, but this was done in full view and taken as a good-luck donation rather than protection money.

Alex saw someone else behind his cousin. "Christ! Is that Black Tooth? He looks about ninety!"

Curly laughed and before Alex could stop him shouted, "Hey boss! This one here wants to be the lion's arse!"

The old man stood up gingerly and walked to the fence. "Alex lah! I hear you are still English turtle! You can be arse for sure!"

Alex nodded and used formal Cantonese. "It's nice to see you, Uncle Wan. You look well."

"Ay yah....I look like shit, Alex lah! Too much good living. Black Tooth, black lungs, black cock, black everything!" he replied.

"You wish you had a black cock!" said Curly.

"Ha...you see this one still cheeky, Alex lah!" he laughed. "It's good to see you Alex lah, even if you still turtle!"

With that the old man turned and shouted something incomprehensible to the boys. Alex couldn't help but notice that in the broad daylight both Black Tooth and his cousin looked decidedly rough with their yellow teeth, cracked skin and cigarette stained fingers. Alex hoped that there was more for his cousin in life than this, but realistically he knew there wasn't.

"You got time for a coffee before I go, Curly?"

"Nah, I got more important things to do than be with you! When do you leave? I'm sick of looking at your face."

"Likewise. I'm off in a few hours."

"No worries." He came close to the fence. "Only joking brother, it's been good to see you. When are you back?"

Alex felt the note in his pocket. "Soon I hope. I'd like to come for the Handover. Hey listen, can you do me a favour, and translate this?"

He passed the napkin through the fence.

"Ha ha. It says you are naughty, drunk detective and need to go home!"

Alex laughed as the note was returned. "Hey, listen cuz. If you ever need a break, you are always welcome at my place in England."

Curly laughed. "What and leave all this?!"

"I'm serious. Look, I can pay for a flight for you...think about it."

Curly's bravado veneer dropped for a second. "Thanks, man. I appreciate it, but I've got Chinese New Year coming up, then the Handover but...you know...thanks."

With nothing left to say he turned and headed for the newspaper shop. Curly was a grown man and would make his own decisions, but Alex was reminded of a lecture that had been given during training when the speaker had likened gangs and triads in particular to a type of pyramid scheme. He had said that young men were lured in by the romance of money, girls, drugs and alcohol which were romanticised in the movies and exhibited by elder peers who had cash to spare, jewellery and flashy cars. But the reality of being in any gang was that only the top few percent benefited, and the remaining majority worked long hours for little or no pay, and were open to physical, verbal and drug abuse. The lecturer had concluded that, financially, and in the long term, most gang members would actually be better off working at McDonald's. Looking back over his shoulder, he knew that realistically, if Curly didn't make some drastic changes in his life, the best he could hope for would be, eventually to take over from Black Tooth, and the worst would be a wooden box.

*

Alex was having his third cup of tea on his mother's veranda and taking in the South China sun before heading back to dreary Manchester accompanied by a dead welder in the cargo section. The news that day was mostly about negotiations between the British and the People's Republic of China over the terms of the Handover, some celebrity gossip, and English football. The Darren Meakin case was merely a paragraph on page four.

On the night of Saturday 18th January, construction worker Darren Meakin (28), of Manchester, England, was murdered *at Chek Lap Kok, the site of the new airport construction site. Initially, eighteen-year-old, Kwan Yo Hang was charged with his murder but it now appears that the Englishman was killed by a compatriot colleague who later took his own life. Meakin's body is being repatriated to the UK, where he is survived by his wife and one year old son.*

One paragraph, yesterday's news, thought Alex, as he put the newspaper down and stretched. He decided to dress as smartly as his limited wardrobe would let him before his flight. Occasionally he would get an upgrade to business class on these flights due to the nature of the trip, but more than likely he would be looking at twelve hours in economy, courtesy of the Greater Manchester Police Force.

Alex had three texts on his mobile when he returned from changing; one from Heidi Lim wishing him a good flight, one from Jacky Shuen advising him that he would give him a lift to the airport shortly, and one all in upper case from Uncle Taff.

ALEX COME TO CLUB ASAP. HAVE SOMTHING TO SHOW YOU.

Alex couldn't help but feel slightly frustrated with the old man, as he tried to call Taff back as his mobile went to voicemail. He was just about to call the USRC when Jackie Shuen appeared on his mother's patio.

"Good morning, Mrs Wu Torrence; is he ready?" he said from outside.

"Good morning, Jackie. Are you hungry? Can I get you anything?"

Shuen patted his stomach. "No thank you, I need to be careful nowadays, unfortunately."

Alex placed his small suitcase in the doorway. "Good morning, Shuen. You really didn't have to drive me, especially on your day off."

"We just wanted to make sure you actually left," he replied jokingly, as he put the bag in the boot of the Honda.

Alex said his goodbyes to his mother and Aunty Ah Lam and was grateful for the blast of cool air-conditioning as he closed the car door and waved once more at the two little old ladies.

Shuen buckled his seatbelt. "You must miss them, Alex. Have you ever thought of moving out here permanently?"

Alex was still waving. "Maybe, who knows? I see them quite a lot, but you never know." He turned. "Is there any chance we could do a quick detour to the USRC in Kowloon, please, Jackie?"

"Sure, no problem. We have plenty of time to spare."

"Do you remember my dad's old colleague, Taff Williams? I told you he'd spoken to Goff in the Watering Hole, remember? He wants to see me urgently."

"Yes, I remember him from when I was a new recruit. People were a bit intimidated by him back then."

"I know, it's strange to see him old and frail nowadays. I remember thinking that he and my dad were giants when I was growing up."

The USRC had a slightly different feel to it as the two detectives exited the Honda Civic. While it was still a little too cold for the pool, a BBQ seemed to be in full swing, with many more families and children around than earlier in the week. A group of footballers were removing their dusty boots at the club's entrance whilst complaining about the referee.

Alex had hoped that it was just a quick visit and that Uncle Taff hadn't had too many early glasses of gin and tonic.

At reception Alex asked, "Is Inspector Williams around, please?"

"I believe he is in The Gunners Bar, Sir. One moment. Would you kindly turn off your phones and pagers?"

Two minutes later Taff was beckoning the two officers through to the bar.

"Alex, DI Shuen, thanks for coming over. You've got time for a drink, haven't you?"

Both detectives declined a drink and Alex felt slightly embarrassed as he could smell the alcohol on "Uncle" Taff.

"I'm in a bit of a hurry actually, Unc...er...Taff," said Alex.

"This won't take a minute, Boyos," he replied jovially. "Now DI Shuen, has young Alex here filled you in on my evening with the lovely Mr Goff?"

"Yes he did, Inspector Williams. He told me that Goff was extremely agitated on the evening before he attacked one of our uniformed officers and you spoke to him in the Watering Hole bar in Tsim Sha Tsui…"

"That is correct," he interrupted and raised his index finger.

Alex couldn't help but think that nowadays Taff would make a terrible witness in any court. The booze, old age, and possibly early dementia seemed to make Taff Williams a shadow of the man Alex used to know when he was growing up.

"Now if you two young men would follow me, I have something to show you near the trophy displays."

The old man gingerly lifted himself off the bar-stool and beckoned them with his walking stick to the exit of the small bar. Alex raised his eyebrows in an apologetic manner towards Shuen, but he didn't seem to notice as he followed Taff into the hallway.

"Now, did Alex also tell you that the big thug was muttering on about 'Number Six'?"

"Yes, he did, but we are not sure what exactly…"

Taff turned right towards the changing rooms and stopped. He tapped a framed photo in-between two trophy cabinets. Jackie Shuen stopped mid- sentence.

The photo was of a rugby match and the small plaque read: USRC vs Combined Veterans, Charity Match, 1993. In the photo, play seemed to have broken down from a scrum, and muddied, mostly expatriate men were huddling over the ball. In the centre of the scrum stood a younger, bloodied version of Andy Goff, and on the floor next to him, his team-mate was shielding the rugby ball. He was considerably slimmer and with slightly more hair, but there could be no mistaking the familiar figure of Senior Inspector Karl Roberts.

He was wearing shirt Number Six.

*

One hour later, Detective Inspectors Shuen and Wu Torrence were huddled over a two-seater table in an overpriced coffee shop at the no longer fit-for-purpose Kai Tak airport. The airport was totally packed with returning holiday makers and

Filipino domestic helpers, who all seemed to have as much luggage with them as humanly possible.

Alex leaned forward and then slightly back as Shuen's cigarette smoke stung his eyes. "What do you think it means, Jackie?"

Shuen inhaled. "Who knows for sure? It means that a murderer almost certainly knew one of my commanding officers. I mean it's highly unlikely that they would play on the same team and not know each other, but we don't know how significant their relationship or the number six is."

"Can you ask Roberts?"

"Hardly, he's looking towards promotion, possibly even the top job. He's not going to admit to anything other than playing rugby with him, is he?"

"True. Maybe Goff just drunkenly thought his team-mate could get him bail or help him out or something?"

Shuen shrugged. "His mobile was checked and there were no numbers that couldn't be accounted for. His wife and boss mostly. I checked personally at Tsuen Wan police station and the station chief was adamant that it was his decision to bail Goff."

"Taff was saying that when he spoke to Andy Goff, Goff insisted he needed to sort something out before Number Six found out. And remember, this was shortly before Goff tried to get back into the dive container, and when he attacked the Constable," said Alex.

Shuen rubbed his chin. "Look Alex…Taff Williams…"

"I know he's not the most reliable witness and he's a friend of the bottle, but he might be on to something. Who knows?"

"Maybe, like you say, who knows?"

Just then there was a tannoy announcement. "Would all remaining passengers for Cathay Pacific flight CX 253 to Manchester please make their way to gate eight…"

Shuen continued. "I guess all I can do at this end is…what's that expression in English…oh yeah…keep an ear to the ground."

The men shook hands warmly and Alex said, "Take care, Jackie. We also have an expression in English…watch your back."

PART TWO

CHAPTER TWENTY-TWO

April 1997, Manchester, England

Detective Inspector Alex Wu Torrence leant back in his chair and put his hands behind his head while stifling a yawn. Even though it was only five thirty in the afternoon it had been dark outside for over an hour, and the raindrops on the window-pane, highlighted by the streetlight outside, only added to the gloom of another Friday afternoon in Manchester.

Across the room, Alex's colleague, Trev Burnham, was preparing for the outside weather by putting his trench-coat on, "Quick pint, Alex?"

"No thanks, mate, I've got a bit of paperwork to finish."

Trev Burnham was only in his early forties but looked a good ten years older, and Alex knew full well that there was no such thing as a *quick pint* in Trev's world.

The Mancunian was wrapping a scarf under his double chin. "Well, if you change your mind, we'll be in The Swan."

"Have a good weekend, Trev," he replied.

Subconsciously Alex touched his own waistline and told himself once again that he ought to renew at the local gym. Since his last trip to Hong Kong back in January, he hadn't been even once, and his late-night diet of takeaways and cans of Carlsberg was beginning to show. Trev Burnham was probably only about ten years older than him and Alex hoped sincerely that he didn't turn out like his colleague, who had now been wearing the same egg-stained shirt for the last three days.

Burnham had recently separated from his wife of twelve years, Debbie, and even by Trev Burnham's low hygiene standards he'd let himself go somewhat in recent months.

Alex wasn't even sure where his colleague was living at present. Not being particularly close anyway and working on separate teams had meant that Alex's only window into Trev Burnham's private life was his increasingly bedraggled look, and the occasional downwind smell of stale body odour.

Alex's own love life hadn't been much better. Since his break up with Kate the previous November, Alex's only *romance* of any sort had been his impromptu date and a peck on the cheek from Senior Constable Heidi Lim over in Hong Kong.

His ex, Kate, was absolutely stunning, the sort of woman who turned heads when she entered a room. She was a legal secretary whom Alex's sister May had set him up with three years previously. His big sister had remarked at the time that her friend was "far too good for him so he had better not fuck it up," which of course was exactly what he had done.

One of the problems with any Detective's line of work is that you have to build a defence mechanism, a wall, as Kate used to call it. And even after two years of dating, Alex couldn't quite let her in; trivial things for other people, *normal people*, had proved major obstacles for Alex Wu Torrence. It had been over a year before he had given her a key to his apartment, and work talk was superficial and on the surface... "Good day, dear?" "Yes, we found a corpse that had been impaled on a steel bar and he'd had his tongue cut out, you could still see the agony in his eyes...You?"... Hardly. Work was for work and home was for home, but Alex had driven an insurmountable wedge between them that eventually came to a head with of all things, a kitten.

Kate and he had been walking past some industrial rubbish bins at the back of a nice Italian restaurant in Bucklow on a warm September evening the previous year, when they had heard meowing from under the bin. Kate had teased the little cat out with a bit of meatball from their doggie bag and immediately fallen in love with the little grey ball of fur. Pets weren't allowed at her shared house, so Alex slightly drunkenly agreed to look after it until a more suitable home could be found. They had named her *Lap Sap,* the Cantonese word for rubbish, and as weeks grew into a month and then two months, Kate had shown no signs of giving away Alex's new lodger. Things came to a head when Alex had done a double shift at work and the cat had taken a crap on his bed. He stupidly said that the cat would have to go, and Kate in reply had asked him how he could possibly commit to her if he couldn't commit to a cat. He didn't respond, up went the wall, and away went Kate and Lap Sap to a new life and a new apartment that did accept pets.

Alex sighed as he thumbed through a couple of manila folders consisting of his two most recent cases; the first one being a suspected triad assault at Cardiff University. Alex had driven down to the Welsh capital two days previously after two Hong Kong Chinese youths had attacked a mainland Chinese student, leaving him in intensive care. Cardiff CID suspected triad links and called in Alex, who immediately on arrival at the station in Wales knew that the two defendants had been watching a few too many Shaw Brothers movies rather than having any probable triad links. However, this hadn't provided much comfort for the injured boy's parents, who were waiting for him to regain consciousness and find out if he had any lasting brain injuries.

Alex was able to ascertain that the two young *Hong Kongers* had been extorting money from the other student, who was from Shanghai and apparently more studious, far less street-wise, and basically scared to death of them. When the money had run out, the two youths from Hong Kong had taken turns using the unfortunate student as a punch-bag in the University dorm-rooms and when they'd grown bored of that, they started with a variety of implements such as a lamp, baseball bat and an ashtray, plus for good measure they had stubbed out cigarettes on the poor boy's back and arms. Depending on the extent of the damage sustained, Alex suspected that the pair would be looking at between two and eight years in a British prison when they should have been studying mechanical engineering with their parents' hard-earned money. Personally, Alex hoped the little bastards got the longest sentence possible.

The second case was a bit closer to home; Blackpool, Lancashire to be exact, and Alex had seen this remit dozens of times before – two men have a disagreement which gets out of hand, one man reaches for a chopper etc. etc.

In this instance, a fifty-four-year-old chef had attacked his boss's son with a chopper in a fit of rage. Normally with random, unprovoked assaults by British people the first thing Alex would generally think of would be alcohol or substance abuse; with Chinese people his first instinct would be gambling, and in this instance, he was correct. The chef and the other man had been playing mah-jong for money on the previous Saturday night after a long shift at the family's Chinese restaurant when, according to witnesses, the chef flipped the board over, pulled out a chopper and proceeded to chop the other man twelve times before calmly sitting down and lighting up a cigarette. A doctor later told Alex that if one wound to the neck had been two or three millimetres deeper they would have been dealing with a murder rather than assault.

Upon questioning in the interview room, the chef had simply said to Alex that his boss's son had been *planting rice* (a type of cheating at mah-jong) and deserved exactly what he had got.

When Alex had first started at the Triad Liaison branch he had approached each case with vigour and a sense of achievement, especially when his manila envelopes had resulted in a conviction, closure, a full stop, or whatever you wanted to call it, but with weeks like the one he had just had and the open-ended way in which his last visit to Hong Kong had finished, Alex Wu Torrence was beginning to feel increasingly irritable, frustrated and ready for change.

Alex put both files in his bottom tray, rubbed his eyes, and internalised another *normal* week – two victims in intensive care, two families wondering if and how their sons were going to pull through, and three defendants in custody without a shred of remorse between them.

Just then the office door opened once more and Trev Burnham re-entered the room.

"I forgot my bloody wallet!" he said as he opened his desk drawer.

Alex stood up. "Hold on Trev! I think I'll join you after all."

*

Two pints at The Swan had been followed by two more and a whisky chaser in the snug at The Feathers, and the crowd of colleagues had thinned out until eventually it was just the two detectives facing each other over a beer-stained table. Trev placed four pints in front of Alex and bumped into a woman with her back to him.

"Sorry, love!" he said through a cloud of smoke. "Here you go, Alex, two each, let's get these down us before closing."

Alex blew out his cheeks. "I'll try Trev, but I'm struggling a bit, to tell the truth."

"Bollocks, lets sink these and hit a club!"

Alex looked at his colleague who, like him, was still in his work clothes with the ever-present egg stain on his shirt, and wondered if any man could look more like an off-duty policeman than Trev Burnham at that very moment.

"Takeaway and bed for me I think, Trev," he said.

"Suit yourself, some lucky lady could be getting even luckier tonight, methinks. Although, I could go for a burger!" Burnham laughed whilst rubbing his hands and dropping ash onto the froth of his pint.

Trev Burnham and his team had been working on a case known in the tabloids as *Manchester's Burger Wars*. Portable hamburger stalls had been a regular feature outside pubs and clubs in Manchester for years, but things had taken a more sinister turn since the explosion of Manchester's rave scene and in turn, the drug of choice, ecstasy. Burger vans had always been fairly profitable for stall-holders catering for late-night clubbers with the munchies, but it was now well known that ecstasy tablets could be bought at many vans for anywhere between ten and twenty pounds per pill. Profits were huge, which in turn had led to turf wars, gang violence and intimidation, and at least two deaths in the last twelve months.

"I think I'd give the burger vans a wide birth if I were you Trev," said Alex.

"Aye, maybe you're right, we could always grab a chinky..." He stopped. "Oh, shit...look, I'm really sorry, Alex, it's what we always called Chinese takeaways when we were kids... I shouldn't use that word...."

Alex raised his palm "Don't worry, Trev, it was a slip of the tongue. I've heard worse."

"Oh, shit mate, I feel terrible, I'd never call anybody a chink...oh shit I said it again...fuck..."

"Look Trev, if it makes you feel any better you can buy me a mixed fu yung from the Golden Dragon later, OK, pal?"

Thirty minutes and two pints (or in Alex's case, one and a third) later, the two dishevelled detectives were sitting by the large window of the Golden Dragon Takeaway and Restaurant waiting for their takeaway orders. A blue-flashing police light was reflected in the open glass door and they could still just about hear an ongoing argument that they had passed in the street five minutes earlier. Both Alex and Trev had served their time in uniform and Trev was telling him for the third time that night that the police were nothing more than human dustbin men.

"Dregs, human waste that's all they are. Smashing some other blokes face in 'cos he bumped into you or spilt your pint...."

A middle-aged man moved slightly away from them and Alex trained his ear to some of the Cantonese being barked from the kitchen...*too slow...order 43...more vegetables....*

Alex had deliberately asked for the takeaways in two bags as he felt the need to rid himself from Burnham, get home, eat some crap Chinese food and above all, sleep.

"...and what do we have to do? Clean it up, Alex, clean it up...."

Alex and his sister, May, had spent a good portion of their adolescence working weekends in a Chinese Restaurant owned by one of Uncle George's cousins back in Morecombe. Alex had been a dishwasher, vegetable chopper and eventually a waiter, whilst May had been either a waitress or front of house. All of this ended abruptly for May when she came home crying from one shift, after a drunk had asked her if her fanny went sideways like her slitty eyes. This was too much for their dad Jock, and May ended up working on the tills at Woolworths every Saturday shortly after that.

"...They won't even have a clue tomorrow what they've done, and the girls are just as bad, if not even worse."

As a waiter, Alex had found the early evening crowds pleasant enough, families or couples out on a date. Set menus with a side order of chips – and maybe even a bottle of Lambrusco for the truly adventurous – were the order of the day. One or two Chinese families used to visit also, never venturing near the battered sweet and sour pork balls, chow meins or egg foo yungs, trusting instead that the waiters would bring them some authentic Szechuan dishes that didn't appear on the normal menu.

"...see, take them slappers out there....If they hadn't been egging their blokes on...."

The problems had generally come after 11pm, kicking-out time, last orders, the bell. Drunks, all sorts of drunks – happy, morose, tearful, angry at life – hanging over the counter, asking for extra spice in their beef curry and chips, or if there was cat in the black bean chicken. Alex had heard and seen it all before he even chose to be a police officer. Maybe it was the frustration of being a helpless fifteen-year-old boy that pushed him in that direction, maybe it was his father, or a combination of the two? Who cares?...Food and bed was all Alex wanted.

A Chinese teenager in kitchen whites and hat came through the alcove behind the counter, holding four tinfoil boxes. In Cantonese, he said to the woman who was serving customers. *Two chicken, one duck, one beef...."*

Alex knew the routine so well, the meats and veggies had been wok fried in the kitchen and the sauces – black bean, curry, sweet and sour – were then added, accompanied by egg fried rice, chips, prawn-crackers, placed in a white plastic bag and then, "Goodnight, enjoy your meal, next...."

Just then a large, fat man at the counter looked up from the sports section of *The Sun* and pointed at the boy. "Speak fuckin' English! It's not fuckin' Japan. This is Engerland."

The boy stopped in his tracks and looked momentarily stunned as the woman quickly filled the white bags whilst looking down. The man looked too old to be wearing the standard sports gear of a drinker-come-football-hooligan, and his belly was hanging out from under his Umbro t-shirt. His mates looked younger and embarrassed.

One said, "Come on, Dave, leave the lad alone."

"No, it needs to be said. This is my country and everybody must speak English." He poked his pudgy chest for emphasis.

The detectives stood up in unison and Alex beckoned the young chef to go back in the kitchen and in Cantonese said, "*Momentai* (OK), no problem, we will sort this. Spit in his food later, *panyau* (friend)."

The thug moved his drunken gaze towards Alex and once again pointed. "And you can fuckin' speak English anarll', my country, my rules...."

Trev Burnham sidled up to the yob and whispered, "Why don't you shut the fuck up before we send you out to those coppers outside, knob-head?"

The man stood up as upright as he could with arms outstretched. "Do you want some, do you?"

Quick as a flash Alex had the man's arm up behind his back and his head pinned on the stainless counter. Burnham produced his warrant card as the man's *friends* either sat down or looked at the wall.

Burnham read him his rights, "You have the right to remain silent, but anything…"

"Gentlemen," the woman behind the counter said, "Your food, enjoy your meal…next order please."

Burnham picked up both bags as Alex pushed the man outside, making sure he caught the man's forehead on the door frame as they exited with a satisfying crunch.

Trev whistled to one of the uniformed. "Hey Barry, cuff this one will you. Drunk and disorderly and resisting arrest."

"I didn't resist anything, this Chinky bastard," the man shouted as Alex twisted his arm harder. "Aaaargh…you're gonna break me' arm. Police brutality!"

Trev Burnham had half a prawn cracker in his mouth and the other half down his front as the uniformed officer took over and handcuffed the man.

"Like I was saying, Alex, we're nature's bin-men and that there is nature's rubbish. Shall we see if we can get a night-cap somewhere?"

Alex felt his head spin as the chilly air hit his lungs and he noticed a spray of blood on his work shirt, presumably from the yob they had just arrested. "No thanks, Trev. I'm going to get home."

"Fair enough, see you Monday." Burnham started to whistle and headed down the street tucking into his remaining prawn crackers.

Alex deliberately headed in the opposite direction. A shitty end to a shitty week, he thought, as the rain started to drizzle more and as one block of streets turned into two, then five then ten. His drunken logic was telling him to get away from the city centre, it was also taking him towards Kate's new flat.

When he eventually arrived at the apartments, he momentarily paused and remembered that he wasn't a hundred percent sure which apartment she was actually in. He'd helped her move in before his Hong Kong trip and things were done in a civil manner, with a few tears shed by Kate, and Alex himself had felt a little lump in his throat as little Lap Sap had explored his new surroundings. Was it 3A or 3B? He looked at the intercom button and sure enough Kate had put a neat, typed sticker on her button – *K. JENNINGS 3A.*

He pressed the button and waited for a good minute. Eventually a female voice sleepily answered. "Who is that?"

"Kate, it's me, I've got takeaway."

"Alex? Are you mad, it's nearly one in the morning."

"Kate, it's raining, can I come up? How's the cat by the way?" He could hear the slurring of his words.

"Alex, this is really not a good time. Are you drunk?"

Alex momentarily thought he could hear another voice, or was it just his mind playing tricks on him? He then caught sight of himself in the dull reflection of the lobby doors; his hair was stuck to his head, he had blood on his shirt and tired looking bags under his eyes...what was he thinking?!

"Look Kate, I'm really sorry, it was stupid of me to ask. I'm truly sorry."

"Alex," she paused. "Look just get home safe, and maybe call me later in the week, OK?"

"OK." He let go of the button and rested his forehead on the cold, glass, lobby door.

"Nature's bin-men," he said to himself, before heading off once more into the cold Manchester night.

The Handover Murders   197

CHAPTER TWENTY-THREE

The following day, Alex had felt suitably guilty about the previous night's drinking session, so that he had dragged himself from his sofa and daytime TV and was now watching the full-time score come in on Saturday Grandstand as he was cycling on the machine at the gym (whilst sweating stale garlic and beer). Both United and City were playing away that Saturday, so at least the charge room at the station would be a little more quiet than normal, thought Alex, as he wiped his brow.

On the soundless TV, Des Lynam was stroking his moustache and laughing as the tele-printer below brought in the scores....

DERBY COUNTY 2 ASTON VILLA 1.....SOUTHEND UNITED 1 BRADFORD CITY 1....

Only two or three years earlier Alex would have been playing himself, but had finally given up when he felt he had lost his edge. Football was all about winning for Alex, and when he started to lose more than win he had decided to call it a day.

...BARNSLEY 4 CHARLTON NIL...HEARTS NIL ABERDEEN NIL...

Also, two or three years ago, he would probably have been having a quick drink after the game and arranging to meet Kate for a nice dinner or the cinema. After last night, he really wouldn't blame her if she never spoke to him again, to be honest. Did he even want her back? He'd had his chance, and did he even truly love her? Was he capable of loving anybody for that matter?

When they had broken up his big sister May had flipped, and given him both barrels as they had sat drinking coffee in Starbucks. "You total fucking dick, Alex," she had said. "You've just thrown away the best thing that could possibly happen to you, and over what? A cat for fuck's sake, a cat! I should be buying a wedding hat for the summer, and you can't even commit to looking after a fucking cat. Poor Kate, that's all I can say!"

But she could say more...lots more in fact. May, it seemed, had inherited their mother's uncanny ability for telling the absolute truth without the slightest hint of tact. He'd promised his big sister that he would go back on bended knees to Kate and beg for forgiveness, but he'd never quite got around to it, until the previous night that is.

Alex took another swallow of water and on the screen, reporter Stuart Hall, clad in his sheepskin coat, was talking into the microphone as the score from Ewood Park came in; Blackburn losing 2-3 to Man Utd, with United looking like strong contenders for the title this year. Strangely, Alex had a thought that Darren Meakin would be happy with that result, before shaking his head and turning the cycling machine up a notch.

The gym was playing some terrible eighties music compilation crap and the rhythmic boom of Bros was keeping tempo with Alex's thumping head. He made a note to bring the Stone Roses or The Smiths on his Walkman for the next time he visited, when out of the corner of his eye he saw, rather than heard, his mobile ring.

"Hello, Alex Wu Torrence..." he cupped his other ear.

"Er, hello, is that the policeman?"

"Yeah, yeah... sorry, one sec, it's a bit loud where I am," he said whilst heading through the double doors with a towel over his shoulder.

"Hello, can you hear me? It's a bad line," said the voice.

Alex mopped his brow and inhaled. "Wu Torrence."

"Yeah, mate, look I'm not sure if you remember me? It's Wayne Harris, the diver from Hong Kong."

Even with the bad line Alex instantly recognised the voice of the big Australian. "Yes, yes of course I do, Wayne. What can I do for you?"

There was a pause at the other end of the line as Alex tried to find a quieter corner near the gym reception.

Harris continued. "Listen mate, I'm in a bit of a mess over here and I don't know where to turn.... It's just that you gave me your card, remember?"

Alex could sense the distress in the man's voice. "Wayne, I can help you, are you OK?"

"Listen mate, it's late here and I don't want to sound like a wuss but I'm worried. It's all a mess!"

"Just calm down, Wayne, and give me some details. You can tell me in confidence, I give you my word."

"That's the thing, right? You're a Pommie copper, right? You're independent of the Hong Kong police, right?"

"That's right," he replied.

"I need help..."

"Alex, call me Alex."

"Listen, it's like this. I don't give a shit about myself, I can take care of myself, but I've got a girlfriend and a little baby now. He knows where they live..."

"Who knows, Wayne?" he asked, as two women in lycra walked passed him.

"Number Six!"

The name took him off guard. Alex stopped in his tracks and put one hand on a gym notice board. "Who's Number Six, Wayne?"

"Look, it's a long story, started by me doing something fuckin' stupid, alright."

"I'm in no rush, Wayne, start from the beginning."

"Well, look, it's like this, you know, after you left, things started to settle down and they let us start diving again in the tunnels at the airport. Anyway, one day I was doing some repair work and found a box underwater. Well you know we find all sorts of shit underwater; porn, electronics, hash, you name it...."

Alex said, "Go ahead Wayne, this is between me and you only, I give you my word."

"Well, we find stuff but it's kinda like finder's keepers. So, what I did was, I didn't say anything to the blokes topside on the comms, I just tied it to a ladder on one of the inlets with a rope and went and got it later."

"And what was in it?"

"Well that's the thing, I was hoping for some DVDs, cameras, that kind of thing, but when I opened it, it was like winning the fuckin' lottery, mate. There were four luxury watches, kosher not copies, and some jewellery. Plus, stacks of cash, US dollars in bundles, and some pills, I don't know what they were, I threw them away."

"And the other things?" asked Alex.

"Well this is where I got stupid. My Filipino girlfriend was eight months pregnant at the time and I took it as a gift from heaven, if you know what I mean."

Alex coughed whilst collecting his thoughts and listening intently.

"I shoulda' just buried the shit out of sight and took it when I left Hong Kong, but you see – the cash! It meant I could get a little rental place for me, the missus, and the little baby, you know, off-site. I'd been sleeping in a fuckin' hut for nearly a year at this point, by the way. I was stupid: I got a nice car, and wore one of the watches on weekends, a Rolex Speed master. I must have lost my mind!"

Alex sensed there was more to come. "So, what happened, Wayne?"

"You see, well, one of my mates from the hut, Dave. Well, he slept over at the new flat one weekend after a session. I just told my workmates I'd been saving for the baby and the watch was a fake, that kind of thing. Well you see normally I'd catch the bus in, the car is a red BMW 3 series, I didn't want to drive it onto site and draw attention to myself. But anyway, that Monday morning we'd been up late the night before and me and Dave, we're still half pissed and running late. Look, and if I'm being honest, I was showing off a bit to Dave, but the other fuckin' stupid thing is, that I've still got the fuckin' Rolex on from the night before."

Alex could almost hear the relief in the man's voice at being able to get all of this off his chest.

Harris continued. "Well, rather than park near the dive site, I thought I'd be fuckin' smart and park near the offices, you know, blend in with the bosses' cars. Jesus, I'm such a dick! Anyway, I'm just locking the BMW when I literally run into a copper, face to face. The big gweilo copper who was on-site after big Darren got murdered."

Karl Roberts, thought Alex. Senior Inspector Karl Roberts, aka Number Six.

Wayne continued. "Well, he clocked me straight away. A fuckin' scruffy diver with a bloody sports car and two months' worth of wages on my wrist. So, he says to me all calm and the like, that he thinks we need to have a little chat."

"And what did he say?"

"Well, my mate Dave's done a runner at this point, and this copper gets in the passenger side of the car, and we go to a quiet part of the site and he's all calm whilst I'm shitting a brick. So, he asked me where I got the watch and the car, so I says some bollocks about saving money and the watch being a copy watch from Tsim Sha Tsui kinda' thing. I can't remember what I says exactly, but he stops me dead in my tracks and says he knows exactly what I've done. And bear in mind I'm shitting myself at this point, there's watches, cash and jewellery all sitting in my flat."

So, what happened then?" asked Alex.

"Well, it's like this, he says I've been a naughty boy and he knows all about the box, but we can do a deal."

"What kind of deal?"

"Well, this is the thing. I might be a bit rough around the edges Alex, but I'm no criminal. He says that I have two choices: I can go to jail, or I can give him back whatever I've got left and make three or four deliveries for him, and this will all go away."

Alex scratched his head. "Did you say deliveries, Wayne?"

"Yeah, this is the thing. Andy Goff was doing the deliveries before he died, and I must have stumbled on one of the boxes underwater. You see the tunnels should be mostly dry by now, but they're all leaky as fuck. There's all sorts of stuff coming in and out, right under the noses of everybody, and this cunt Number Six is in on it."

"Do you know his real name, Wayne?" asked Alex.

"Mate, I honestly don't, I've only met the fella two or three times. The first one, like I was telling you about, the second one, to give me a mobile phone for instructions, and the last one was today. I need help Alex, I don't know where to turn. The baby is here now, my missus has overstayed her visa, it's all a mess!"

"Look, just explain the deliveries and we can work from there. What are you delivering exactly?"

"I don't know. I really don't, it could be anything, they're in sealed waterproof boxes. I just get two numbers, one with the inlet where I collect the stuff, and the second is where I have to leave them. Plus, there is always one box like the one I found which I guess is his kick back."

"And what do you do with that?" asked Alex.

"That one goes off shore, there are some inlets a few hundred meters away from the runway, and they must pick them up in a boat or something. You see, once everything's dry, any muppet could do this, but with the exception of that one inlet, all the others should be dry. Stuff could come in and out by plane or boat and never see the light of day."

"And how many deliveries have you done underwater now, Wayne?"

"Well, that's the thing. He said if I did three or four he'd write off my debt, maybe even pay me a bit. But I've done over six now, all at night, and I was getting twitchy, so I texted and said I'd had enough…." Harris paused.

"And what did he reply?" prodded Alex.

"Fuck, mate, it was horrible. We arranged to meet up near Castle Peak, a quiet road and all. That was stupid, I should have insisted on an MTR station or somewhere busy. Anyway, when I get there he beckons me into his car and there is this other gweilo cunt in the back, sunglasses and cap on, not saying a dickie bird. So, I says I was really sorry about the first box and all, but I've done all they asked and that I've got a baby now and responsibilities, and I wanna' stop. And this is the horrible part, this Number Six cunt, he says he knows I've got a baby, and he hands me a polaroid of my missus and the little fella. What kind of sick cunt would do that? And then he goes off saying he's trying to be all reasonable and all, whilst this cunt is sitting in the back saying fuck all," Wayne exhaled and took a nervous breath.

"So, what else did he say?"

"It gets worse, mate. Before the baby came, I was thinking I could just go to the Aussie consulate or ship out on a junk or something, but there's my baby to think about now, they know where they are! My missus has no papers, the baby isn't registered yet. They're sitting ducks," he cried.

"Try and stay calm, Wayne. You said it got worse?"

"Well, my mind is all over the place at this point. I don't know who's involved or who I can trust. So anyways, he tells me to shut up, but I try begging with him to be reasonable. So finally, this bastard in the back chirps up, pommie as well, I reckon. He says that I *will* do the deliveries, up until Handover day…. And then I realise the cunt's got a fuckin' gun on his lap! And he says, if I don't do as instructed, I'll end up in the same way as Andy Goff!"

Alex rubbed his temple. "Did they tell you that he shot Goff?"

"I don't know if they did or not, I honestly don't know, but that's what they're threatening me and my family with! I need help, Alex!"

Back in Manchester, Alex's head was spinning." Listen Wayne, I can help you but you're going to have to trust me. I'm going to get one of my Hong Kong colleagues to call…"

"Oh fuck, I can't trust…"

Alex interrupted. "No listen, I give you my word, I trust this man. His name is Jackie Shuen, he was with me at the airport. Talk to him and nobody else, understand? He will call you tomorrow, and we will work something out."

In the background, Alex could hear a small baby crying, and he could sense the tension on the phone line.

"Jackie Shuen, you say? Look I'm going to have to go…I shouldn't have rung."

"Listen Wayne, you did exactly the right thing, we can help you, trust me."

"I hope so, I really do."

After he ended the call, he quickly dialled DI Jackie Shuen's mobile number in Hong Kong.

"Hello, Alex, long time, no see."

"Hi, Jackie, are you sitting down?"

CHAPTER TWENTY-FOUR

May 1997, Police Headquarters, Central, Hong Kong

Senior Inspector Karl Roberts settled onto the black sofa in the now familiar office of Police Commissioner Mark Hayton, as his boss was involved in some nondescript conversation on the telephone. He had mixed feelings about Hayton. Even after all these years of working together he still didn't know exactly how he felt about his boss, more so now with the Handover on the horizon. On the one hand, he had certainly helped him career-wise, especially in the last few years; with an introduction here and there, either at work or the Masons or the Yacht Club, and he was definitely pushing him for promotion once he retired after the Handover. But like a lot of people, he couldn't help feeling that Mark Hayton only cared about Mark Hayton and would trample over anything or anybody to get what he wanted.

The money from their *little deals* (as Hayton liked to call them) had also helped him out substantially, and with his little beach-house in The Philippines, his salary and his pension due in a few years, Karl Roberts had been looking forward to a nice future before all this broke out with Goff and the bloody airport; but in the end, everything had seemed to work out. He'd got the Australian on board for the last few *little deals* and everything looked to be back on track.

Roberts couldn't remember exactly when the *little deals* had started, but with hindsight, Hayton had been testing him prior to any *little deals* being made. The odd bit of confidential information; a snippet had been told to him in secret, and at the time he had felt privileged to be trusted by his boss; the introduction at the Lodge and the vows of secrecy also gave him a feeling of importance and one up over his colleagues. Karl Roberts was a man who could be trusted, a "good egg," as his boss would put it. That was ten years ago, and then later, the secrets had turned into tasks, maybe an odd errand here and there, perhaps a warning to somebody to back off discreetly or to lose a case file: nothing too much, just a bit of greasing of the wheels. And in return the promotions came, plus the odd envelope with a bit of tea-money inside. Hayton knew that Roberts wasn't flash or stupid and he wouldn't get too greedy or slip up. He also knew that Roberts wouldn't ask too many questions about his private life as long as the envelopes kept on arriving. In truth, the thought of what Police Commissioner Mark Hayton did on his yacht or over in The Philippines truly disgusted Roberts, and over the years there had been a succession of "boat-boys" on *The Chief*, small, effeminate, and seemingly younger and younger. When they had sailed down to Puerto Galera on numerous trips over the years, Roberts had deliberately turned a blind eye to the goings-on of his boss, it was never spoken of openly, and when they did arrive in the Philippines the two men normally went their separate ways to their own villas. In public, Mark Hayton was a pillar of the Puerto Galera expat community, with donations to the local school and orphanage, but the rumours in the bars about the creepy Hong Kong policeman with the yacht had made Roberts's skin crawl. There was talk of a syndicate of old greasy expatriates doing all sorts of unspeakable things to kids as young as six or seven years old.

As a copper, both in the UK and in Hong Kong, nothing turned your stomach more than sex offences involving kids, but in the Philippines, Roberts, to his own disgust, simply chose not to notice. He blanked the rumours completely, took his tea money from the little deals, and buried his head in the sand.

*

Hayton was just listening to the last few words of the conversation on the phone whilst watching Senior Inspector Karl Roberts out of the corner of his eye. The caller on the other end of the line was talking about policing arrangements and extra officers for Handover night, blah blah blah… After Handover night, it wouldn't be his problem anymore and he honestly couldn't be bothered with organising anything within the last twenty-four hours of his watch before he would be leaving this God-forsaken place.

"Yes, yes that sounds fine, Cheung," he said. "Go ahead with whatever needs to be done."

In truth, the only thing that the soon to be former Police Commissioner Mark Hayton was bothered about on Handover day would be going to receive his OBE at Government House from Prince Charles. The letter from Buckingham Palace had arrived the previous week and his wife Marjorie had nearly laid an egg when it had arrived. Poor old, saggy, dependable Marjorie had put the letter next to a glass of champagne for when he arrived home from work. In truth, they had both thought a knighthood was in the offing, but one couldn't be too down in the mouth about an Order of the British Empire after all. Obviously, Marjorie would have been overjoyed at being called Lady Hayton at one of her coffee mornings, bridge games or whatever ghastly boring things she got up to now the children had fled the nest, so to speak. Tristram at Harrow, and Victoria, studying law at Trinity College, Cambridge, both doing the family proud; dull as dishwater the pair of them, but doing well, all the same. But either way, the OBE would certainly lift Marjorie's dull and dreary existence, for a short while at least. They hadn't shared a bed for over ten years now, thank God, and after the Handover and all the pomp and glory, Marjorie would be heading to the family home in Buckinghamshire to be closer to the children, whilst he would be getting his independence in The Philippines at last. Of course, divorce would be totally out of the question at their time of life and social standing, but with retirement and mainly separate lives on the horizon, Hayton finally felt a sense of freedom beckoning.

Cheung was trying to elaborate more on the line, but Hayton brought the call to an abrupt end. "Yes, yes Cheung, whatever, just do whatever you think with whatever resources it takes, goodbye."

He then spoke in the direction of the sofa. "Christ knows what they will do without us British, eh Roberts?!"

"Indeed, Sir. But remember some of us will still have to put up with them after your ship has sailed, so to speak," said Roberts, pleased to have thrown in a sailing reference also.

Hayton put the phone down and headed over to the drinks cabinet, and raised an empty glass towards Karl Roberts. "I believe the sun is over the yard-arm, Senior Inspector, is it not?"

Roberts nodded in the affirmative as his boss placed two large malt whiskies in front of him and joined him on the sofa.

"Well, only two months to go now, Roberts. Of course, you are still OK for the final voyage on the 1st of July aboard the good ship *The Chief III*, I presume?"

"Absolutely, Sir. You seem in rather a good mood, if you don't mind me saying," added Roberts.

"I've had a little something in the post from Buckingham Palace, but mum's the word, eh," Hayton tapped his nose and savoured the malt. "Between you and me, one will be paying a visit to Government House on Handover day."

"Congratulations, Sir."

"Thank you, Roberts."

With that the Police Commissioner sat back on the sofa and savoured the aroma of the fifteen-year-old malt they were now sharing. Hayton thought to himself that Roberts had done a decent job for him, all things said and done over the last ten years or so, but he couldn't help feeling that, like the local Chinese, Karl Roberts would struggle without direction and leadership. Every ship needed a captain, so to speak, and Roberts was more of a first mate type of chap.

"How's the whisky? It's nice Scottish malt from a friend of mine at the lodge," he said.

"Excellent Sir, thank you. I'd better stop at one though, as I have rugby training tonight."

Hayton could see Roberts in the scrum now, all pushing and shoving, but no direction. It would be up to the scrum-half or centre behind him to dictate the play and make decisions. He'd enjoyed rugger himself when he'd been at Harrow like his son Tristram today. He'd been a speedy little winger who had enjoyed the camaraderie, not to mention the communal showers. Hayton dug down in his memory and tried to remember where exactly Roberts had been at public school – Loughborough or somewhere terribly provincial and dull, he couldn't remember where exactly. In the beginning, he'd made a few calls and asked the right people before they started on a few *little deals,* years earlier, and Roberts had been rewarded suitably, a shoe-in at the lodge and the Yacht Club for starters, a thing that would normally have been above his social standing, if truth be told. And then there was the money, but money, of course, was no substitute for class, it had to be said.

"Just another little one more for the road, Senior Inspector, don't you think?"

"Just a small one, Sir. You've twisted my arm."

You see the thing about good leadership was about letting people go about their jobs and only getting involved when it was absolutely necessary. Margaret Thatcher was a case in point, the greatest leader since Churchill, it had to be said. It was all for the greater good. Chaps like himself did their jobs, were rewarded, and then gave instructions to oiks like Roberts who in turn were rewarded also, and in the end, everybody prospered. And look what we have now with that pleb Blair almost certainly in Downing Street, and the communists about to take over the crown colony. He shuddered.

The whisky was warming him nicely as he once again looked over at Karl Roberts. He'd looked at Roberts as some sort of tool or another cog in the machinery previously, but now he was going to become more of an insurance policy. Since he had been informed by Government House that he would be stepping down as Chief of Police, he had been educating Roberts with a view to him taking over; whether that would come to pass was out of Hayton's hands after the 30th of June, but it would be wise to have a friend as high up in the police as possible. At present of course, Hayton was well-respected and protected within the judiciary, civil service, the press, you name it, and he knew that nobody could touch him. But he certainly wouldn't want any of his little deals or his private life ever to come out, either now, or in the future, as this would be a terrible embarrassment to him, and more so for Marjorie. And Senior Inspector Karl Roberts was his little insurance policy, somebody to keep things ticking over whilst he would be enjoying the sun, his retirement, and his little brown boys in The Philippines.

Just then there was a knock at the door as DI Jackie Shuen entered the room.

He said, "The files you asked for, Sir."

"Thank you, Shuen. Is everything done and dusted?"

"Yes, Sir, quite straightforward. You can read my report," he replied.

The case had been quite a tedious one, with an American housewife killing her bonds broker husband. It looked pretty straightforward, but the press and the American Consulate were sniffing around it, so Hayton thought he'd better take a look.

"Yes, it looks pretty cut and dry, but you know what these Americans are like, what! That will be all, Shuen." With that, Shuen was dismissed with a wave of the hand and the smell of whisky in the air.

The thing at the airport had been an annoyance earlier in the year, and in fairness, Shuen had only been doing his job, but when the English boy, Jock Torrence's son, had started sniffing around also, this had proved rather an annoyance at the time for Hayton. Roberts had initially vouched for that meathead Goff, but then because of one thing and then another it had all started getting rather choppy. Nonetheless with Hayton's good leadership and judgement, he had finally navigated them into calm waters, and at the end of the day, the only two men who knew exactly what had happened were now seated in this room.

*

Jackie Shuen thanked the Police Commissioner's secretary and adjusted his eyes to the stark tubed lighting of the corridor as he made his way back down the hallway. The phrases "cut and dried" and "done and dusted" came to mind. Why couldn't they just say "settled", or even "finished", for that matter? It was almost like they had a third language to keep the "riff raff" – as Police Commissioner Hayton would say – down. As a young detective, Shuen had written all these strange English phrases down in a note-pad and worked out their meanings either from a book or at language classes, which at the time had given him an edge professionally. Good English-language skills had helped him immensely, whilst many relatively good police officers with poor English had been held back. Shuen had tired of English classes nowadays, but noted how his younger Chinese colleagues were scrambling to learn Mandarin Chinese before the Handover.

Being close to forty himself, he and his wife had discussed maybe Australia or even New Zealand as an option as both were advertising for ethnic Chinese officers to cope with the increasing Chinese populations, but Hong Kong was home to them, their kids were settled in good schools and three of the four grandparents were still alive and well, so they "had put a pin in that idea" – again as Police Commissioner Hayton would say. Jackie Shuen was third generation Hong Kong Chinese, his grandfather had arrived in Hong Kong from Shanghai after the Second World War and Chinese civil war, but before Chairman Mao's Great Leap Forward had really taken hold on the mainland. His grandfather, a successful tailor, had hated the communists and moved his whole family and business to Hong Kong. The old man used to joke that the British thought they made Hong Kong but it was the Shanghainese who did the work for them. Both Jackie and his father before him considered themselves Hong Kongers not Shanghainese, and it was Jackie's father who had insisted that he stay in school rather than become a simple tailor in the family business.

It had been a few weeks since the call from Wu Torrence in England, when initially Jackie Shuen's head had been spinning by the sheer magnitude of what had been said over the phone. Two senior policemen not only implicated in corruption but in murder also. He had corroborated the story at a clandestine meeting with the scared Australian where he had given the man his personal mobile number and assurances that he would do all he could to help. The problem was, linking both police officers to the fraud with little to go on other than the Australian's word and a few text messages consisting mainly of numbers. The second problem was one of resources, for a full-scale surveillance of the airport and Wayne Harris's movements, he would need the approval of his bosses, who in this instance were implicated also. He briefly thought about going to the ICAC but Hayton especially was so well connected that this would be out of the question. As far as the Andy Goff murder went, Shuen had barely anything to go on; the Australian had said that he had been threatened with a gun but that was all, the man had very few details and he didn't even know Karl Roberts's real name. Shuen and Wu Torrence had nothing concrete and certainly nothing that would stand up in – or even get to – court. The Goff case had been signed off as suicide one month earlier and he, Goff, was listed as the probable murderer in the Meakin case, but Jackie knew that linking either Hayton or Roberts to the Goff or Meakin cases without further evidence would be impossible. Meakin and Goff were dead, the Australian was scared stiff. He himself had no manpower and his only ally other than Heidi Lim was in Manchester, England.

The Handover was only six weeks away and Police Commissioner Mark Hayton would be sailing out of Hong Kong on the 1st of July for good. Jackie Shuen and Alex Wu Torrence needed to think of something…and fast.

CHAPTER TWENTY-FIVE

May 1997, Manchester, England

Alex Wu Torrence turned the desk lamp on to give extra light on the papers on his desk, as the daylight faded once more in gloomy Manchester. Alex had felt better lately since cutting down on the booze and hitting the gym more regularly, but the Hong Kong case was still gnawing away at the back of his mind. He'd been in contact with Jackie Shuen a few times but it was fair to say they had reached a bit of an impasse.

He felt like they needed a break or a change of luck before anything could move on, and there seemed to be a sense of resignation about the whole case. Trying to look at the whole thing objectively, it was fair to say that they were in a bit of a Catch 22 situation. Two senior police officers in the Royal Hong Kong force were both implicated in corruption and possibly a murder; but without the say so of said officers, the resources needed to investigate couldn't be provided. Currently the Australian diver, Wayne Harris, was in touch with Jackie Shuen, and to his knowledge the only other officer who was in the loop was Heidi Lim.

At one point, Alex had thought of passing on Taff Williams's details to Jackie Shuen, but what use would an old man with a drink problem and a walking-stick be in this situation? In one moment of madness he'd even thought of approaching his boss McGregor, before quickly realising that he would tear him a new arse if he knew what he was up to.

Alex was looking out of the window absent-mindedly as Trev Burnham entered the office with his usual good grace. "It's fuckin' pissin' it down out there, Alex. What's the matter with you? You look like you've fell in a bucket of tits and come out sucking your thumb!"

Alex laughed. "It's just, you know, that case in Hong Kong, back in January?"

"The murder of that Manc' welder? I thought that was all signed off," said Trev, as he pulled a Mars bar out of his pocket.

One of the plus sides of working as a Triad Liaison Officer was that, other than an occasional meeting with McGregor, he was pretty much left to his own devices. The down side being exactly the same thing; he was mostly left to his own devices.

"It was, but…listen Trev, have you got half an hour? Could I run a few things by you, mate?" he asked.

"Sure, I was going home to a microwave meal and tossing one off to Carol Vorderman, but I guess that can wait! What can I do for you?"

Two hours later the two officers had a whiteboard full of names, arrows, and the occasional post-it note, all connected with the Meakin/Goff case. Because of his recent appearance and smell, Burnham had become a butt of office jokes, but here in an empty office and with a clear mind Alex could appreciate what a competent copper he actually was. Even with little or no knowledge of Hong Kong, he had grasped the complexity of the case and was throwing around ideas, questions and suggestions at a rapid rate, whilst pacing the room.

"So, what happened to the Chinese boy, in the end?" he said.

"He'll be out in few months. They charged him with wasting police time but he'll be back inside before long, that's for sure."

Burnham nodded. "And we've got these two public schoolboy plums sitting pretty whilst they're on the take and possibly involved in a murder."

"We don't know that for sure, but it's highly probable," Alex replied.

"But on the day Goff shot himself (or was shot) the Police Commissioner has said that Roberts was with him all day."

"He said something to the effect that Roberts hadn't left his side for weeks."

Burnham added, "It sounds like this Roberts is a right arse-kisser to me."

"I agree," smiled Alex.

"And this Aussie bloke, he's doing these runs for them now? Can't you put a wire on him?"

"We could, but he rarely if ever speaks directly to Roberts. He just picks up and drops off where he's told to via text message using a pay-as-you-go sim card. He's so scared I'm not even sure he's a credible witness."

"But couldn't you monitor the pick-ups of these boxes?"

"We could but the ones coming inland go to triad groups we believe, and we'd only nick lower ranking kids like Kwan Yo Hang anyway. And the boxes with the kickbacks go off-shore, so we'd need marine police surveillance or at very least a boat, which can't be authorised without Hayton's say so."

The two detectives carried on bouncing ideas off each other until Alex looked at his watch; 22.34, and rubbed his eyes.

"Hey Trev, I really appreciate you having a look at this, but you must be knackered and hungry now."

"No, it's all good mate," he stretched. "I'm happy to help. In my book, there is only one thing worse than a bent copper and that's a kiddie fiddler, and it looks like our friend Hayton could be both."

Alex stifled a yawn. "It's just good to have a different set of eyes running over this. Thanks."

"No problem. It seems to me that your biggest obstacle is, that whilst this posh boy Hayton is in charge, you're screwed. But I've thought of a couple of things…."

"What's that?"

"Well, when I was a bit green and new to all this, I had an old mentor in the force called Ted, a brilliant old fella, he never missed a trick, old school, you know. Anyway, this one time I was really focussed on this spousal abuse case and I was beginning to take it personal. This nasty bastard had broken into their old house and threatened her, but she was scared stiff and wouldn't testify and we couldn't really pin anything on this bloke who was knocking her about. Anyway Ted, my mentor, he tells me about his Al Capone theory...."

Alex interrupted. "Where they couldn't pin anything on the world's biggest mobster until they looked at his tax records!"

"Exactly, Al Capone didn't go to jail for murder, robbery or violence, he was sent down for tax evasion!"

"And what about your wife-beater?"

Burnham took a sip of tea. "I did him for stealing a five-quid lock. When he'd broken in he'd pocketed the backdoor lock, so we charged him with theft rather than assault. He was on probation for something else so we managed to send him down for two months, and during this time his ex-wife built her confidence up and agreed to testify about the violence. He ended up doing a few years bird as I remember."

Alex nodded as he knew exactly where Trev Burnham was coming from. His dad had also told him on more than one occasion that there were different ways to skin a cat.

"Trev, you mentioned a second thing?"

Burnham continued. "Well, this Hayton bloke. You said he's untouchable whilst he's in charge?"

Alex nodded.

Trev Burnham paused before adding, "Well, he's not in charge after June the 30th, is he?"

As the evening's work drew to a close Alex absent-mindedly tidied up the white board and his desk before declining a *swift pint* with Burnham. Once he was on his own, he looked around at the drab, grey office. Sometimes he wondered if he really belonged here, but then when he was in Hong Kong he felt exactly the same in reverse. He didn't quite fit in at either place, he guessed.

Before putting his coat on and turning out the light Alex wrote two post-it notes to himself which he stuck on his computer monitor:

RING JACKIE SHUEN ASAP and BOOK FLIGHTS TO HONG KONG.

CHAPTER TWENTY-SIX

30th June 1997 (Handover Day), Hong Kong
With only twenty minutes to go until midnight and the Handover beckoning, Lily looked over at her big handsome son standing tall in the middle of the crowd under the Tsim Sha Tsui ferry clock, with the new Convention Centre lit up for the occasion across Victoria Harbour on Hong Kong island. The Convention Centre was filled with all the big-wigs from Britain, China and Hong Kong, all smiles and pomp, whilst the general population were huddled outside in areas such as Tsim Sha Tsui, Central and Wanchai.

Ah-Lam and herself would have been more than happy to have watched it all on television, until Alex had surprised them with an unannounced visit, two days previously. He'd convinced them both that events like the Handover would happen only once in a lifetime and he would treat the girls to dinner and a taxi if they agreed to come. The same couldn't be said for Ah-Lam's son Ay-Yun (or Curly or whatever he was calling himself this week). He'd been invited but had said he had more important things to do. Extorting parking money off good people, no doubt. She could feel the reassuring arm of Ah-Lam next to her as the volume level in the crowd went up a notch or two as somebody shouted, "Ten minutes to go!"

Lily looked again at her son. Gazing intently out to sea, he was taller and darker than Jock but just occasionally he had exactly the same stare as his father, distant but intense, not unkind, but completely focussed on what was in his mind. He'd been out and about for the two previous days supposedly "seeing friends", but being a policeman's wife for over thirty years, she knew that something was afoot. In her younger days at functions or at the USRC with the other officers' wives, the women would be recalling some case or police gossip that had been in the news. People's lives ruined by murder, robbery or violence was just tittle-tattle for those women, simply to pass their boring days around the club pool or in the school yard. But not Lily, not Jock and Lily. Once her man was home for the day with his coat on the hook and his slippers on, he was her Jock not the Royal Hong Kong Police Force's Inspector Jack Torrence, and that's how they both had liked it. Jock would have been so proud of Alex as he was today. He wouldn't have been able to tell him of course, but *she* would have known; a look, a gesture or a moment would have told her everything she needed to know, he had been an extension of herself for all those years and now, sadly, he was gone.

Lily had mixed feelings about the Handover itself. Britain had leased the New Territories for ninety-nine years when Great Britain had been the biggest empire the world had ever known, probably thinking that Britain would go on to even greater things with China begging them to keep Hong Kong British in the future; who knows? In fact, nowadays, mainland China was growing at an incredible rate whilst Britain seemed, at least to Lily, just to be stagnating.

Back in the seventies, when Jock abruptly resigned, Lily had been alarmed by the harsh realities of the northwest of England. She hadn't been naive enough to expect something out of her beloved *Pride and Prejudice* and of course she had visited Britain on their honeymoon after all, but actually living there day in and day out with the weather, the heavy, greasy food and the early dark nights had all come as a shock to Lily. She could still remember vividly the day when Jock came home and said that he had resigned; he was white and looked like he'd seen a ghost. She knew her man, probably better than he knew himself in truth, and if he said they had to leave then they had to leave, no question. May, who was going through the terrible teens at the time, had barely spoken to either of them from the moment they told the kids until they started school in Morecombe. Little Alex had been a lot easier and had looked on the whole thing as a big adventure, especially as his dad had promised to take him to a football match when they were settled in England. In the end, they all "made a good fist of it" as Jock would say; May found the Bay City Rollers and some spotty boy called Daniel, Alex always had football, and Lily did her best to throw herself into housework and the English way of living.

But it was her husband Jock who had worried her the most. It used to break Lily's heart seeing Jock arrive home from his security job every day. For years previously he'd been held up as a pillar of society in Sai Kung; the boss, a man people recognised in the street and openly thanked. Now he was just another working man doing security, with only his torch and a box of sandwiches to keep him company. A chum from the USRC, back in Hong Kong, had set him up with the job and initially they had thought it would be in an advisory, management type capacity. But when the dust had settled and with the packing cases still un-packed in their rented semi-detached in Morecombe, it became quite apparent that Jock would have a more hands-on role with his new job. He spent countless hours walking around deserted factories and mills, a stark reminder of Britain's industrial past, looking out for petty theft and vandalism. Even today, back in her Hong Kong, the thought of it could bring a tear to her eye.

Lily briefly wondered what Jock would have made of Britain handing over the keys to communist China. The way Lily saw it, Hong Kong didn't belong to politicians from Britain or China, it belonged to people like her, people like her father before her, and also to people like Jock who had made huge personal sacrifices, so other people didn't have to, in the future. Lily looked again at her handsome son; she had no doubt that part of Hong Kong belonged to him too.

Nearby somebody in the crowd stirred, "Ten seconds to go."

People joined in. "Ten, nine, eight, seven…"

*

"…Six, five, four, three, two, one!"

Fireworks went off at the far side of the harbour as Alex gave his mum and auntie both a peck on the cheek.

He raised his voice and joked, "What now? Do we sing Auld Lang Syne or something?"

After all the build-up, the actual count-down seemed a bit of an anti-climax even with the fireworks and cheering. Close by a WPC was drawing attention to herself as she changed her metal cap badge from the Royal insignia to the new "Bauhinia Flower" design which the incoming government had chosen as Hong Kong's new emblem. A man next to her cheekily asked if he could have the old one, which she politely declined.

Heidi Lim had said to him previously that she found it quite ironic that the new government had chosen a sterile, endangered plant as its new emblem, before adding that at least it was better than the communist stars.

Alex spoke again and joked. "What shall we do now, Ladies? Do you fancy a night out, clubbing and dancing?!"

His mum laughed. "Not for me, Sweetheart. I think a taxi, a cup of tea, and bed for me."

Auntie Ah-Lam nodded in agreement as Alex helped the elderly ladies through the throng of party-goers towards the huge queue of people waiting at the taxi-rank near the Star Ferry entrance.

"Give me Sai Kung any day," Ah-Lam said as they stood in line. "All these people, ay yah!"

Alex could still see the fireworks from his vantage point where he was standing. He felt alert and focussed after the two previous days covert planning. Other than his mother, only three people – Jackie Shuen, Heidi Lim, and Uncle Taff – had known of his arrival, and he had deliberately kept as low a profile as possible.

Back in Manchester, his late night brainstorming session had reignited his resolve on the Meakin/Goff cases, and after a little bit of tweaking and a long-distance phone-call, Alex Wu Torrence and Jackie Shuen had formulated a plan of sorts.

He told his mother that he'd only been back for two days when in truth he'd been in Hong Kong for nearly a week, planning and running through the potential scenarios with both Jackie Shuen and Heidi Lim. He'd booked a few days holiday from the UK without telling anybody where he was going or what he was doing.

Eventually, Alex and the two old ladies found their way to the front of the taxi rank and Lily was immediately embroiled in a heated argument with the taxi-driver who was demanding double the metered fare because of the occasion. Alex was by now tired, a little jet-lagged, and more than a little nervous about what was going to happen the following day, and would have been more than happy to pay the extra money, but knew better than to interrupt his mother especially when the principle was at stake. People behind them in the queue were starting to become agitated, but Lily was standing firm.

She pointed at the scruffy man. "If you knew who my son was you wouldn't be trying to rob us!"

He replied, "No-one trying to rob you lady. Go in another taxi if you can get cheaper!"

Whilst Alex knew that Lily was more than capable of holding her own, he had an early start and a busy day tomorrow. Subtly and without fuss he opened his wallet and showed the taxi-driver his UK warrant card, which up until today had looked remarkably like a Hong Kong one also.

"Ah sorry, Sir," said the man as he opened the car door for Lily, "Just a little misunderstanding, *lah*."

Forty minutes later and with a comfortable bed beckoning, Alex slipped the driver a hefty tip as they exited the taxi and headed for his mother's Sai Kung apartment. The driver might have been rude earlier, but he was working on Hong Kong's most historic night, reasoned Alex.

As his mother searched her handbag for her door key after saying goodnight to Ah-Lam, Alex's phone vibrated in his pocket.

There was a simple one-line text from Jackie Shuen. "WAYNE HARRIS HAS DELIVERED THE FINAL BOX. SEE YOU TOMORROW."

Alex replied with a simple OK and spoke to his mother. "I'll be out and about before you get up tomorrow, Mum. I've got a few things to sort out."

Lily laughed and brushed his cheek. "We both know that's not likely, Son." And then added, "I don't know exactly you're up to, Alex, but please be careful."

Alex Wu Torrence simply nodded and headed for bed.

CHAPTER TWENTY-SEVEN

1st July 1997, Hong Kong

The crickets were starting their customary dawn chorus as the sun rose over the New Territories outside his mother's apartment. Alex liked this time of the day with very little traffic or people around. He collected his thoughts and waited for DI Jackie Shuen.

Exactly on time, Shuen's Honda Civic rattled up the small steep lane. Alex swiftly entered the passenger side. "Greetings comrade!"

Shuen looked slightly puzzled, not understanding the British humour. Alex momentarily thought about explaining the communist reference but instead handed Shuen a paper bag. "My mum sent supplies. A bacon sandwich, I've had mine already."

"Oh thanks, you eat some strange things for breakfast," laughed Shuen as he turned the car around and started on the sandwich whilst still driving. "I think everything is in place, Alex. There is potentially a lot that could go wrong today, but we've done our best."

"You texted about Wayne Harris last night?" said Alex, opening the window a crack to let in some fresh air to replace the stale cigarette smell.

"Actually, this is good!" Shuen commented on the sandwich before adding, "Yes, he did an underwater delivery last night. The box is in place with a tracking device in it, and we gave Harris a recording device also. We're going to see him first thing and then we'll go to the marine police where Heidi Lim is waiting. The racing yachts will be heading out to the Philippines about 10.00am, so we can't hang around."

Over the last few weeks Shuen and Lim had been working tirelessly, piecing together Alex's plan, even Uncle Taff Williams had been involved and in some instances, invaluable. Through his old boys' network it had been Taff who had confirmed details about Hayton and Roberts joining a post-Handover sail to the Philippines today. They just had to hope that they made their pick-up before heading to the start line which they believed was at the new airport bridge.

"Where are we meeting him exactly?" asked Alex.

"There is a lookout place near where he lives. He's in the lay-by near Tsuen Wan, already waiting. I think he just wants the whole thing to end as swiftly as possible and to get out of Hong Kong as quickly as he can," replied Shuen.

"And we have offered to give him immunity?"

"Yes, we've taped his statement and he's promised to give evidence against Roberts, but as you know we've got nothing concrete on Hayton at this point. The thing with Harris the diver is, that he was more concerned about his girlfriend and their baby, especially since the woman is here illegally, having overstayed her domestic helper visa. But I've given him assurances that they'll be safe until we can get all three of them out of Hong Kong, and they are currently in a hotel."

Alex had never met Wayne Harris's girlfriend but did know that, for a lot of Filipino, Thai or Indonesian domestic helpers or *amahs,* finding a Western husband was a ticket away from the drudgery and sometimes borderline slavery of domestic work in Hong Kong. Some women worked up to twenty hours a day for peanuts with just one day off a week if they were lucky. For the unlucky ones amongst them, cases of abuse, violence and even rape were fairly common within the domestic help occupation, which was sometimes compared to modern-day slavery. So, it was hardly a surprise that a lot of these young girls headed to the night clubs of Wanchai every Sunday to meet British, American, or in this instance an Australian man.

Shuen continued to talk as they joined the road to Tsuen Wan. "I spoke to a friend in immigration and he's issued a stay of execution on her visa as a favour to me. They're actually getting married tomorrow as soon as the registry office re-opens after the Handover public holiday, and then they'll be on a flight out of here on the same night."

"And who says romance is dead?!" joked Alex.

Shuen again didn't seem to spot the humour, as the new airport bridge came into view, with the unforgettable figure of Wayne Harris leaning against a red BMW in the foreground. Alex hadn't seen the man since back in January and was taken slightly off-guard as the big Australian gave him a bear-hug, lifting him off the ground.

The words seemed to spill out of him. "Hey thanks, Alex man! I was so sorry for ringing you in England but I'm glad I did in the end. This fella has been great and I'm outta' here tomorrow!"

"So, I hear. Congratulations on the wedding, by the way," he said, whilst nursing his arm.

"Yeah, she's a cracker! And the little man…here, take a look at them," he said as he opened his wallet.

The photo showed a healthy, chubby baby on the lap of a pretty young woman. Alex thought that Wayne Harris must weigh at least double the weight of his soon-to-be wife.

Wayne continued. "Yeah, a quick honeymoon in Bali and then a normal life back in Brisbane. Ninita, my missus, she'll love it, and my folks can't wait to see the little man."

"And what about the BMW?" asked Alex, whilst admiring the car.

"Oh, my mate Dave is gonna' see what he can get for it and wire me the money, he's my best man tomorrow. He doesn't know anything about what's been going on recently but he's a good cunt and if you can trust a man whilst you're underwater with him, you can trust him with a few dollars that's for sure."

Jackie Shuen interrupted the pair. "Sorry Wayne, we are in a bit of a hurry. You made the drop last night, yes?"

"Yeah, the site was empty 'cos of the Handover so I moved the last of the boxes. The one with the electronic thingy is in the normal place offshore attached to a small orange buoy, as usual."

"Good, good," said Shuen. "And what about the phone-call?"

"Yeah, he was pissed off when I rang, that's for sure. He said I was never to ring him again blah, blah, blah. I don't give a shit anymore 'cos I'll be out of this shithole tomorrow."

"Did you record it?" asked Alex.

"Yeah, it's here, listen. It's a bit distorted, I think he was at a Handover party or something. Could a' been drunk, I reckon. Here."

Wayne Harris passed the hand-held recorder to Alex who immediately pressed, "Play":

The Australian spoke first. "Hey it's me, Wayne. I did the drop."

"Listen you fucking idiot. I told you never to call me unless it was an emergency," answered the unmistakable voice of Roberts.

Alex immediately agreed with Wayne's assessment of Robert's sobriety. There was music in the background and Roberts's voice had an aggressive slightly-slurred edge to it.

Harris spoke again on the recording. "Yeah. Well that's the thing. It is an emergency. Kind of. I'm done man, I want to stop…"

"Listen you prick, you'll be done when I say you're done, do you understand?"

"Yeah, but I thought we agreed four or so deliveries. I've done loads more than that…"

"And you've been rewarded handsomely, not to mention me forgetting about the theft of the first box."

The Australian then paused. "But you said if I did as you said, which I've done…" another pause "…that we had a deal and I wouldn't end up like Andy Goff…"

"Listen and listen clearly!" Roberts replied. "I'm not talking over the phone, so don't call me again. I'll be in touch."

The sound of the voice-recorder then went quiet as the tape continued turning in Alex's hand.

He pressed "stop" with his thumb. "Thanks for trying Wayne, it doesn't give us much, but it all adds up."

"Yeah, I tried to get him to take the bait on Andy Goff but he wasn't biting," replied Harris, before adding, "Listen I didn't like the cunt, Goff I mean. Nobody did, but he didn't deserve what happened. Do you really think they topped him?"

Alex replied honestly. "We're not a hundred percent sure what happened at the yard, but hopefully by the end of today we might be."

*

Ten minutes later and with a wedding invite kindly refused, the two detectives were on their way to the Gold Coast marine police headquarters about twenty minutes north of their previous location. The Gold Coast was quite an ambitious title on the part of the developers, as the golden beaches of the Mediterranean or the Caribbean didn't exactly spring to mind as they approached the purpose-built high-rise blocks near their destination. Shuen was crunching through the gears on the small Honda and Alex hoped he would get them safely to the boat without crashing.

Alex broke the silence as Shuen lit yet another cigarette. "I'm going to give Taff Williams a quick call and see if anything's happened yet."

Shuen simply nodded and inhaled deeply.

"Uncle Taff, it's me, Alex. Anything yet?"

Taff was sitting on an unmarked junk with three plainclothes officers near the pick-up point close to the new airport, and had been there since before dawn. To anybody passing by boat or on land they looked like recreational fishermen.

"No, nothing, Boyo! The fish aren't biting, but then again I've got no bait on my rod!"

Alex opened the car-window a crack, trying to release the smoke. "Any yachts around yet?"

"Nothing so far, but the racing boats don't necessarily have to pass us as they can go straight through Victoria Harbour to the bridge. These plainclothes boys have said that *The Chief III* left the Yacht Club twenty or thirty minutes back with four men on board."

"That's not many people for a racing crew," interrupted Alex.

"It's no witnesses, either," replied Taff. "We think it's probably only Hayton, Roberts, and Hayton's two little bum boys."

"Right, thanks Uncle Taff, keep us posted and stay safe. We're just pulling in to the marine police port now. Remind the boys on the boat that it is zero radio contact from now on, and call us when you ID *The Chief*."

"Will do, Boyo! I haven't had this much fun in years, and don't worry about me, I've been doing this since before you were born!"

Back at the Gold Coast, Senior Constable Heidi Lim was beside the car door even before Jackie Shuen had turned off the engine. Alex noted that this was the first time he had seen her out of work clothes. The tight jeans, sports jacket and trainers look worked just as well as the skirt and blouse combination. Alex wound the window up and reminded himself to focus on the job at hand for the next few hours.

"The yachts have left the Royal Hong Kong Yacht Club with the majority heading directly for the bridge, but two boats including *The Chief III* have gone around the opposite side of Lantau Island." She paused and only then did she greet the pair. "Oh, and good morning."

Alex also noted the sexy way her hair was tied back as Shuen asked, "Is our boat on standby?"

"Yes, we have the marine police on board plus two divers in case they throw the box overboard."

"Good, good, and no radio contact just in case Hayton is listening in," said Shuen. "Now all we have to do is wait."

*

Taff Williams was in his element on the small junk, a traditional local style boat, and he was definitely enjoying his moment in the sun. As he looked out over the South China Sea, he remembered what an old retired colleague once told him years ago, when Taff was still a relatively young man. He had said that when you retired from the police it wasn't like leaving a normal job, and part of you always remained a copper. Taff had probably dismissed it at the time but now, well in to his seventies and with his best years behind him, he couldn't agree more. Being involved in this case and getting the blood pumping through his veins had brought Taff to life for the first time in months, possibly years.

Betty, God rest her soul, was long gone, and these days, his days tended to consist of the *South China Morning Post*, horse racing, lunch, and various bars and expatriate clubs. He guessed it could be worse; he could be back in Wales having his arse wiped in some sterile nursing home. He had to be grateful, he guessed, that his body wasn't too creaky for a man of his age. Incredibly, his liver still seemed to be holding out, and he got that nice young Thai lady in once or twice a month for a bit of company and "how's your father". In fact, the only slight worry for Taff was that he had noticed that his memory was starting to slip; he could remember conversations between himself and Jock Torrence back at Sai Kung headquarters from over thirty years ago, but some days he couldn't remember what he'd had for breakfast that morning.

One of the crew handed him a cup of tea which he gratefully accepted in perfect Cantonese whilst adding. "Not long now, men."

"No, Sir," replied the young officer.

Yes, it was nice of young Alex to involve him in all of this. He liked the boy, just like his dad character-wise; tenacious and not likely to back down. Interestingly, Alex had asked him back in January after the murder of the welder if he had known why his dad, Jock, had been forced to leave Hong Kong. At the time, Taff had replied to Alex honestly that he wasn't sure, but that night when he got home Taff tried to rack his brains as to why his closest friend really had left the place he loved so much. Of course, Taff had asked Jock at the time, when he had said he was leaving, but Jock Torrence could be a closed book at times. Taff guessed that, in part, it was because of what he had gone through with the Japs and partly because he was an old-school copper like himself. Men like Taff and Jock buried their emotions and secrets away in tight little boxes never to be opened, but Taff remembered distinctly at the time that he had tried to get Jock to open up to him, to see if he could maybe help his friend. There had been loose talk flying around at the time of course, that Jock Torrence must have been on the take or corrupt and that he jumped before he was pushed, but Taff knew that was a load of old tosh. Jock Torrence wouldn't have let his own grandmother out of a speeding ticket, never mind being corrupt, he was that kind of man. In fact, the only thing Jock had done in all the years that they had worked together that was in any way not totally kosher, was when Jock had asked him to hand over that young triad from the cells to Black Tooth, which had been a huge shock to Taff at the time. Of course, it went without saying that Taff had done as he was told without question and it was never mentioned again; he had trusted his boss and friend implicitly; if Jock Torrence said he needed to be released there must have been a bloody good reason for it. Unbeknown to anybody but himself, curiosity had got the better of him after he released the thug to Black Tooth, and he had positioned himself outside of the cell door and listened to the two remaining villains talking in the cells. They were complaining to each other that young Wu had only been let out because his father was a mountain master and it wasn't fair that they would have to take a hit for the crime, when it was young Wu who had attacked the other man. At the time, it had all seemed very strange, and the only thing that Taff could conclude was that Jock must have met with the boy's father before he was released. Taff knew that Jock wasn't intimidated by anything or anyone and even a mountain master wouldn't be crazy enough to threaten a senior gweilo police officer. He also knew that a man with no stains whatsoever to his character could not possibly be blackmailed. It was a strange one, it had to be said. Jock Torrence did one dodgy thing in his whole police career and it was he, Taff Williams, who had helped him.

In the next few months after the dust had settled and with Jock, Lily and the kids safely in the UK, the detective inside Taff Williams had got the better of him. He had flicked back through the station diary; one of the last engagements Jock Torrence had had before resigning or taking early retirement, whatever you wanted to call it, was his annual review at police headquarters. Taff had known that these were generally quite straight-forward things usually involving a nice brandy with old Porterhouse, but Taff made a couple of discreet enquiries here and there and one of the secretaries, a gorgeous little thing called Daisy, had told him over a couple of gin and tonics that it was in fact Police Commissioner Mark Hayton who had conducted his final review. Within forty-eight hours Superintendent Jock Torrence, one of the finest men Taff had ever met, had left the force, and that bastard Hayton was somehow behind it.

In the present, the young officer interrupted Taff's thoughts by handing him some binoculars. "Sir, twelve o'clock. Two racing yachts are coming around the headland."

"OK, let's just hope they make the pick-up," he replied.

Sure enough, the two boats came closer and closer into view and agonisingly closer to the inlet. Near to Taff on the deck, another officer was hiding under a blanket with a camera with a long-range surveillance lens at the ready. Taff held on tightly to his fake fishing rod and you could hear a pin drop on the junk as the two sailing yachts inched closer.

On the deck of *The Chief III* somebody motioned to the other boat to carry on before the two yachts changed course from each other. Then finally the moment came; *The Chief III* dropped anchor next to the nondescript inlet and a dark-skinned sailor leaned over the side, and hooked a small orange buoy from inside the concrete block before pulling up the rope and eventually, a metal box.

The camera clicked into life and Taff could hardly breathe on the junk as he gripped the rod and said under his breath to the young officer, "You better call Jackie Shuen. Tell him we've caught a big one."

Back in January when young Alex had asked Taff about his dad leaving Hong Kong, he had replied that he thought Jock might have been protecting someone. What Taff hadn't said was, that he had a horrible feeling that the person he had been protecting was his best friend, himself, Taff Williams.

*

A uniformed marine police officer was showing off the large grey and blue police boat to Jackie Shuen, Heidi Lim and Alex Wu Torrence from a pontoon, when Jackie's mobile phone rang, interrupting the young man.

The talk had been impressive with lots of marine terms that Alex didn't understand at all, but reassuringly the crew looked focussed, well trained and ready to go. Alex wasn't exactly sure how fast the 'forty-five knots' that the officer had mentioned was, but he hoped it would be sufficient for the job at hand.

Jackie Shuen gave everybody the thumbs-up sign and motioned to the footbridge for them to board the impressive-looking boat whilst continuing with the call.

Finally, he put the phone in his pocket and said, "Right, everybody! The box has been lifted, we have a go situation. Let's do this!"

As he was climbing aboard, Alex asked over his shoulder. "Did Roberts or Hayton physically lift the box, DI Shuen?"

"Unfortunately not. It looks like it was one of the boat-boys, but we have photos, and Roberts and Hayton are definitely on board," he replied.

Alex nodded and wondered how much sleep Jackie Shuen had actually had over the last few days. Alex knew that Shuen had an arrest warrant in his pocket for Karl Roberts from a magistrate in the New Territories whom he was friendly with and wouldn't ask too many questions. The warrant had been signed at 1.00am that morning, once Police Commissioner Mark Hayton had become the *Former* Police Commissioner Mark Hayton.

Alex knew that Jackie Shuen and Heidi Lim would never have dreamed of undertaking what they were all doing at that very minute even a week earlier. Everything had been done with extreme secrecy, and whenever possible, left until the last minute. The boats, crew, and divers, for example, had been commandeered by Shuen under the pretext of manoeuvres, and other than one or two close friends of Shuen no-one had been told until the last moment exactly what the plan was.

Mark Hayton, up until the day before, had had too much power and had been too well connected. With the slim evidence they had, Alex and Shuen had both come to the conclusion that they couldn't apply for a warrant for Shuen's former boss. As the large boat powered out of the marina they had to hope for a large slice of luck for today's plan to work.

CHAPTER TWENTY-EIGHT
Divide and Conquer

1st July 1997, Hong Kong

The police boat was under the shadow of the new airport bridge and within minutes Alex could see around six racing yachts to his left, which he assumed were part of Hayton's farewell entourage, before the edge of the new runway came into view.

The police crew on-board were intense and focussed as two things happened almost simultaneously.

The open radio station 14 crackled into life. "Mark, it's Russell aboard *Splash*. The marine police are passing our portside. Over."

"Shit!" said Alex under his breath.

Hayton's recognisable crisp voice replied almost immediately. "Thanks Russell, old bean. It's probably just a farewell party. Start without us, we'll catch up!"

Just then Shuen's phone rang and Alex could hear Taff's voice loud and clear. "The box has been thrown overboard!"

"Don't worry Taff," he replied. "Get a visual on it, we have the divers on board, we're about two minutes away. Stand by."

One of the police crew, a diver, nodded and headed to the stern of the boat as the captain increased speed. As they rounded the northern corner of the runway *The Chief III* finally came into view.

At last, the moment they had all been waiting for came, as the large police vessel arrived alongside the sleek racing yacht. From his vantage point, Alex could clearly see all four crew members in their matching red and white uniforms.

Former Police Commissioner Mark Hayton was gripping the boat's wheel and had a face like thunder.

The captain of the police vessel spoke into the handheld device and the megaphone blasted out above their heads. "*Chief III*, *Chief III*, this is the Hong Kong marine police. Cut your engines, I repeat, cut your engines."

On the deck below, one of the police crew was throwing a mooring line to one of the Filipino boat-boys aboard the *Chief III* to catch. The young man looked nervously over his shoulder at his boss Hayton, who nodded that it was OK to do so.

Jackie Shuen patted Alex on the shoulder as he passed him heading towards the lower deck. "Right, let's do this!"

Within seconds, Alex Wu Torrence, Jackie Shuen and Heidi Lim were standing shoulder to shoulder on the lower deck of the police boat which was a good metre higher than *The Chief III*. Mark Hayton purposefully walked onto the bow of his yacht. Alex thought that the man looked slightly ridiculous with his skinny legs showing beneath his white safari shorts. He was also wearing deck shoes and a garish red and white polo shirt with THE CHIEF III adorning the pocket, which added a slight comedic value to the proceedings. Alex thought that yachtsmen, like golfers, seemed to choose the most ridiculous clothes.

Hayton placed his hands on his hips and addressed Shuen directly. "You had better have a bloody good reason for this, DI Shuen."

Alex noticed the Chinese junk with Taff Williams approaching the scene also, as Jackie Shuen replied, "We are coming aboard *Mister* Hayton."

Hayton looked momentarily perplexed as his use of the word "Mister", rather than "Sir", hung in the air.

The two boats were now firmly secured next to each other as Jackie Shuen, followed by Alex, both climbed over the railings of the two vessels. Again, Hayton puffed out his chest and repeated, "You'd better have a bloody good reason...."

With a uniformed officer at his side, Shuen completely ignored his former boss and spoke directly to Senior Inspector Karl Roberts. "Karl Roberts, I am arresting you for the murder of Andrew Goff and for soliciting favour and corruption as a serving member of the Hong Kong Constabulary...."

Roberts immediately went completely red in the face. "You are fucking joking, Shuen, I swear I will ruin you unless you turn around this minute!"

"...You have the right to remain silent but anything you do say..."

"You little Chinese bastard!"

Roberts half lunged at DI Shuen as the uniformed officer deftly turned the big Englishman around and cuffed him with a minimal amount of fuss.

Alex spoke for the first time. "The box you just threw overboard has a tracking device in it, by the way, Karl. The divers will be picking it up shortly."

Karl Roberts looked at him with another deathly stare as Mark Hayton involved himself in the proceedings once more on the now cramped deck. "Myself and Senior Inspector Roberts have no knowledge of either of these charges, and as my colleague just said, we would strongly advise that you turn around and get off my property this minute."

DI Jackie Shuen stepped towards his former boss, looked him straight in the eye and said calmly, "It doesn't work that way anymore. You don't advise me to do anything."

Hayton replied. "I may not be Police Commissioner as of twelve hours ago, but I still hold a lot of power and can *and will* cause you a lot of problems, believe you me!"

Again, Shuen completely ignored the man, and as planned, instructed the crew. "Men, take Senior Inspector Roberts to the junk and Mister Hayton aboard the police boat. Thank you."

*

The plan had been worked out as meticulously as possible but the speed and intensity of the situation took Alex by surprise as he walked across the deck of the junk, with his heart pumping and the adrenalin flowing, towards the now seated Karl Roberts. As planned there were now only three men on deck; Alex, Jackie Shuen and the handcuffed Senior Detective.

The big man looked up at Alex. "I don't know what the fuck you are doing here, Wu Torrence, but believe me if these cuffs weren't on me you would be in big fucking trouble!"

Alex rubbed his chin and took a calming deep breath. "You see, the thing is, Karl, I've been in contact with a friend of yours for the last few months. A diver called Wayne Harris. Well, when I say friend, he thinks you're a complete prick and has told us everything that you have been up to."

"I've never heard of him," Roberts replied immediately.

"Is that right, because we've got dozens of texts to him from someone called 'Number Six'. What's your number at rugby, Karl?"

"I'll repeat. I told you I don't know him. You two might as well throw your careers away."

"Now let's move on to Andy Goff," Alex continued. "He liked his rugby too, didn't he? Now, you and him, you had a little deal worked out, didn't you? He was the man on-site at the new airport. He did the deals and moved the merchandise around whilst you and Hayton turned a blind eye and took your cut."

Roberts sat impassively as Alex paused for effect before continuing. "Now everything was going fine until Goff started getting greedy. He was skimming off the top and starting to open the boxes and help himself to a few bits and bobs. Currency, luxury watches, all types of stuff that should have been going to the Philippines aboard *The Chief III*. Am I right Karl?"

"You can address me as Senior Inspector Roberts. And no, you are fucking not right, you cocky little twat!"

Alex continued, pleased that he seemed to be getting to the man. "So, everything would have been OK, more or less, except that on the night of the 18th of January, poor old Darren Meakin came home from the pub early and stumbled across your old rugby pall Andy Goff, who was helping himself to some of the contents of your box. Goff then lost his temper and hit the man over the head with a diving weight."

"You know as well as I do that Goff killed the welder and then killed himself. End of story."

"Now that's where you and I disagree, Karl. Andy Goff was a loose cannon and he could have spilt the beans on everything that you and your boss Mark Hayton had been up to, especially after we had him in custody. So, you and your pal Hayton pulled a few strings and got him released on bail. Then you waited until he returned to the lock-up in Kam Tin and you shot him in the face in the dive chamber with no sound and no witnesses to disturb you. Unless Goff was a contortionist, somebody else shot him, and that somebody was you."

"I was with Police Commissioner Mark Hayton all day, all week in fact."

Jackie Shuen spoke for the first time. "*Former* Police Commissioner, Karl. Who has just had a box full of contraband pulled on to the deck of his boat while being filmed. Do you honestly believe that he won't let you take the fall for this, Karl? He has just retired, and is on his way to his villa in the Philippines with all the young boys he can lay his grubby hands on. He doesn't care about your welfare any more than the welfare of those two Filipino boat-boys. You're dispensable, Karl."

Karl Roberts sat motionless as he appeared to assess his options.

Alex added, "Now here's the icing on the cake, Karl. Our diving friend, Wayne Harris, he came across the box of goodies that had got Darren Meakin killed in the first place. Goff must have thrown it back down an inlet to collect later on. Handy thing, isn't it, water? Everything goes unnoticed down there doesn't it?" Alex motioned to the water's edge where the police divers were now in clear view. He continued. "Now, the box was like a lottery win for Wayne, except he's not the sharpest tack in the box. He started flashing it about, the BMW, the Rolex. So anyway, you were visiting the head of construction, Raymond Barnett, a fellow mason I believe. Maybe to ask him if any boxes had been found, who knows? And then you see our mutual friend Wayne Harris in his shiny new red car, and bingo! What a stroke of luck, your deal is back on again except with a new mug to do the deliveries!"

Roberts spoke angrily. "You're out of your mind, Wu Torrence! This isn't fucking Scooby Doo, you know. You and I both know that there is nothing on me and Hayton is untouchable."

Alex replied. "Well, here's the thing, Karl. We have Harris in a safe place and he has already testified that you threatened to kill him like you killed Goff, plus the texts, plus the film today. Plus, they'll be pulling up that box any minute now. You're screwed, Karl."

Roberts sat back on the bench. "Like I said, I was with Police Commissioner Hayton all day."

"Yes, we heard you the first time. And in about ten minutes your alibi will be sailing off into the sun. Do you really believe he would set foot back in Hong Kong after all this? To help you, Karl? Think, has the man ever helped anybody but himself? Tick, tock, Karl, ten minutes."

Jackie Shuen walked towards the man. "On the day of the murder in Kam Tin, the murder you committed, we know a few things now. Firstly, that the murderer was let in by Goff, the gate was ajar and there was no sign of a struggle. And secondly, the suicide note, who types a suicide note by the way? A confession-stroke-suicide note, convenient, isn't it? And whoever wrote it said, 'Tell Melanie and the kids I love them.' Melanie Speed told us two concrete things. Andy Goff hardly knew how to turn a computer on, and secondly, in over ten years together, he had never called her 'Melanie'. Only 'Mel'."

"You're clutching at straws there, DI Shuen, and you know it!" interrupted Roberts.

"Eight minutes, Karl," said Alex.

"So, we took another look at the suicide note. Now print-outs have a time and date on the top. The time of the print-out was 14:50."

"So?" said Roberts sullenly.

Alex sat down next to the man on the seat. "Six minutes Karl."

"So," said Shuen. "So, we know a hundred percent, that our officers were at the crime scene at 14:44 exactly. Andy

Goff was already dead when you were disturbed and writing the note, wasn't he Karl?"

"Four minutes. Tick tock."

Roberts was once more scarlet in the face. He turned to Alex next to him in a low voice. "The thing is though, we both know that whoever was there shouldn't have been there, don't we Alex? What would an unauthorised British detective be doing at a Hong Kong crime scene? A man could lose his job for something like that. Goff got what was coming to him and if you knew what was good for you, you would turn around and fuck off back to Manchester right now!"

The man's voice was so quiet that only two other sounds were audible; the light splashing of the sea, and the whirring of the tape recorder in DI Wu Torrence's top pocket. Roberts looked down aghast as he realised what had just happened, and clumsily head-butted Alex clean across the bridge of his nose. Both men hit the floor as the tape recorder flew across the deck towards the water. Even whilst hand-cuffed, Roberts was able to manoeuvre himself across the deck, knowing that if the recorder went in the water so did the last piece of evidence. Alex could only watch through the tears and blood as an old man in a khaki suit came around from the bridge and prevented the recorder from reaching the water with his foot.

"There's nothing worse than a bent copper," said Taff Williams, before hitting Karl Roberts clean over the head with his walking-stick.

*

As Karl Roberts was being ferried off on the junk to the runway, the men paused briefly before entering the bridge of the large police boat and part two of the plan.

"That's going to sting a bit tomorrow, boyo," said Taff, as he passed Alex another tissue.

"I've had worse," grimaced Alex.

"What happened?!" said Heidi Lim as she came out of the bridge to meet them. She touched Alex lightly on the arm.

"Roberts rugby-tackled me," laughed Alex.

She removed her hand self-consciously. "The Former Police Commissioner is on the bridge with the Captain. As planned, the Captain is playing for time and checking the yacht's documents. Hayton is very irate."

Alex's head was beginning to throb. "I don't give a shit if he is irate. He can throw himself off the bloody boat for all I care."

Jackie Shuen flicked his cigarette butt overboard before addressing the group. "OK, focus everybody!"

As they entered the yacht's bridge Hayton spoke immediately. "DI Shuen, I assume you are behind all of this. Even as your *former* boss, I would strongly advise that you stop this charade, give me back command of my vessel and we'll be underway."

Shuen didn't respond directly to Hayton but simply nodded to the boat captain, who in turn whispered something to his second in command. Hayton's two boat-boys watched on subserviently, seated behind their boss, who was sitting cross-legged facing away from the table whilst trying to master as much authority as possible.

Hayton seemed momentarily distracted as the noise of the propeller broke the silence, before continuing. "And you Wu Torrence, I have no idea on God's earth what you are doing here, but believe me I am still well connected in the UK. You're a damn pain in the arse, just like your father!"

Alex laughed and examined the blood on yet another tissue.

"Jock Torrence was worth ten of you, Hayton!" said Taff Williams, entering the proceedings.

Hayton laughed. "My God! Is that Sergeant Williams?! One assu͏̶ d you'd have drunk yourself to death by now, m͏̶

hang around to see you get what's coming to g nancy boy…"

hand on the old man's skinny shoulder, lacate him. Alex could feel the pent-up ff but knew they all had to keep cool ull this off.

ce more. "This is quite a merry band I Shuen. Of course, I will be making

239

a note of all the procedural errors for your superiors. Acting out of your jurisdiction with a British detective and a retired drunk Welshman. Unless of course you come to your senses and send me on my way immediately."

Alex spoke. "You don't appear to be too concerned regarding Senior Inspector Roberts's predicament, do you Mark?"

"You can address me as Sir or Mr Hayton."

"I'll address you how I please, Mark. You've just had a box full of contraband pulled aboard your yacht in plain view of undercover police and yet you are throwing insults at myself and my two friends. Tut tut, Mark."

"Don't you tut me young man! Crossing me is not a wise move, as your father would testify!"

Alex was secretly enjoying his discomfort, but tried to stay focussed. "Karl Roberts has just been charged with the murder of Andy Goff and numerous charges of corruption…"

"None of which has anything to do with me, or you either Wu Torrence, for that matter!"

Alex paused as the boat continued to motor. "Well that's the thing you see, *Mark*. My department in the UK, the Triad Liaison Office, is linked to the Organised Crime Bureau and I've been doing a little historical research with the help of some of my colleagues."

"Is that right? Congratulations," replied Hayton smugly.

"Yeah, I got to wondering why a young, shining light of Scotland Yard would take a backwater posting in Hong Kong when he could have been fast-tracked to the very top in London, what with all his family connections and old school tie and the like."

Hayton laughed and shook his head. "Wu Torrence, you are your father's son, that's for sure. Totally clueless and chasing shadows."

Taff Williams took a step forward but was restrained once more by Alex. "Now, there were a few nasty goings on around West London. Boys, young boys mostly, the rumours were that these orphans or children's home boys, sometimes with behavioural problems, were being passed around l'' rag-dolls to politicians, civil servants, and of course officers."

Alex paused for effect before continuing. "Now, these were powerful men, and to them, the boys were just worthless objects. Nobody would have believed them, of course. Old boys' club and all that. But there was one sick bastard who always took things too far, sticking objects inside children. And get this, he also had a thing for ropes. Rope-burns, pain, torture."

One of the young men behind Hayton moved in his seat uncomfortably.

"So, it transpires that events got a bit much even for some of his hardened paedophile chums, and a young Mark Hayton was given a get-out-of-jail-free card and sent to the Far East."

Hayton sat upright once more. "You are on very thin ice here Wu Torrence. I am an upstanding member of society, and a happily married man!"

"You're a bloody nonce, Hayton!" shouted Taff. "What are those two behind you?!"

Alex continued. "Now for years, Deputy Inspector and later Police Commissioner Mark Hayton outwardly appeared to be a pillar of the Hong Kong community and the Royal Hong Kong Police Force. But you still needed to get your kicks didn't you, Mark, and that's where the Philippines came in handy. Always one or two young boat-boys discreetly hidden away in the Hong Kong Marina on your own yacht, but your real pleasure came with the younger kids passed on to you down in Puerto Galera. Helpless little things with no protection. Now this is the interesting part...."

"Oh, do pray tell, dear boy," mocked Hayton.

"Well, the Filipino government is trying to clean up its act with sex tourism, scumbags, lowlifes, that kind of thing. And they seem ˌ think there is some sort of paedophile ring in and ˌ e Mindora region, mostly old German and They actually have two suspects in custody being very co-operative apparently. Plus, what? Nearly all the victims have given ˌ of an old skinny English man who gets All of them reporting exactly the same and ropes."

"You sick bastard, Hayton. Is that what he does to you, boys?" Taff nodded in the direction of the seated Filipinos. "Or are you too old now? What are you? Eighteen, nineteen?"

"Nineteen, Sir," said one, before being interrupted by Hayton.

"Keep quiet, Nanoy. You don't need to talk to that old fool."

Alex cleared his throat. "And you see it's not just the sordid stuff that makes one's skin crawl, it's also the money you have been funnelling out of Hong Kong all these years. Only a fool would leave a paper trail of cash whilst in the public eye, so you did it all in currency and goods, didn't you Mark?"

"Every penny of my salary and assets has been audited by the ICAC for the last twenty years, as well you know."

"In Hong Kong, yes, but in the Philippines, that's where it gets a bit murky. Even a senior policeman like yourself couldn't afford the lifestyle you lead. Two full-time rent-boys, the house on the Peak, the villa in Puerto Galera. So we did a little digging. You don't own the villa in Puerto Galera do you Mark? You rent it…strange that?"

Shuen carried on. "Now you rent it from a network of companies who actually own the house, none of whom you are linked to. Did you boys ever sign any legal papers?"

The taller boy spoke again. "We signed our contracts."

"Shut up!" shouted Hayton.

"Now, Nanoy, is it?" continued Shuen. "We believe the papers you signed were for properties in the Philippines. Foreigners are only allowed to own fifty percent of a business, so your boss here got you to sign partnership papers that you probably didn't understand, am I right?"

The two young men looked confused before Alex continued. "Don't worry boys, you are not the first. Mr Hayton here has been doing this for years. He gets two or more of his young friends to sign for maybe twenty-five percent of a property or business, independently of each other, and then when he gets bored with them, he dismisses them with a few dollars and they go away, not knowing they are actually quite wealthy. What do you think Nanoy?"

The Handover Murders

Hayton interrupted. "You are just like your father, Wu Torrence. All huff and puff but no evidence. You know back in January when I said your father was a good man? Well he wasn't. He was linked with senior triads and I had the enjoyable job of asking him to leave the Royal Hong Kong Police force back in the seventies."

Taff countered. "Utter rubbish, Alex. Your dad helped start the ICAC, and my hunch was that he was getting too close to this scumbag's goings on!"

"Is that right, Williams? Well, all of you, ask yourself this; why was whiter than white Jock Torrence in so much of a hurry to leave Hong Kong in the first place? We had compelling evidence that he was in contact with one of the heads of the 14k triad. However, I gave him the option to leave honourably and quickly, which is exactly what you should be doing to myself now, gentlemen." He paused before addressing the captain behind them. "Are those documents checked yet, captain? I would like to be on my way."

Alex had so many unanswered questions swimming around in his head but he needed to focus on the job at hand.

The boat captain didn't respond as Taff Williams spoke once more. "Like I said, Jock Torrence was worth ten of you, Hayton...."

"Yes, yes, yes, Sergeant Williams, we've all heard your drunken ramblings before. Does he really need to be here, Wu Torrence? I find him terribly tiresome."

Alex re-focussed. "Captain. How fast can this boat go again?"

"Forty-five knots at full speed, Sir."

Alex ...tled. "I haven't a clue about what that means but it ... ...loesn't it Mark?"

...'t know what your game is, Wu Torrence, but ... the wrong man. I won't stand for this; do

...e captain again. "And how long until we ...aters?"

..." he replied.

...once more and edged closer. "You ... You'll sit down and do exactly as I

244

say. You are a crook and a paedophile. Have you not figured out what's going on here yet?"

For the first time an element of confusion surfaced in Hayton's demeanour.

Alex continued. "Like you said, you are too well connected in Hong Kong – police, judges, politicians, you name it. We would have little or no chance of a conviction. Fortunately, the Filipino authorities have issued a warrant and a reward for their *'rope man'*. If you look on the horizon you can just about make out the outline of a boat. They'll be taking you to Manila."

"You're bluffing."

"Oh, I never bluff. I'm a Torrence. And, by the way, they'll be seizing your boat too."

Mark Hayton began to stand up before being handcuffed by a junior officer.

Jackie Shuen spoke. "The men on the boat are professional bounty-hunters, everything is perfectly legal." He then spoke to the boat-boys. "They'll be helping you find a lawyer also, so you can find out what you're entitled to."

Hayton was red in the face. "I will have your badges for this, I swear."

Alex walked slowly towards Hayton, and calmly whispered into his ear, "You messed with the wrong family."

CHAPTER TWENTY-NINE

2nd July 1997, Hong Kong

"Good morning sleepy-head."

Alex opened one eye and then two as he surfaced from a deep, deep sleep. Heidi Lim was silhouetted against the morning sun as she drew open the hotel curtains. As she turned to face the sleepy detective he could see her slim figure outlined, naked under his blue work-shirt.

"God, I haven't slept like that in months," he said as he rubbed his eyes.

"I'm not surprised with all the excitement of yesterday!" she teased. "How is your nose?"

Alex placed his index finger tentatively on the bridge of his swollen nose. "It's still there, I guess."

She placed a tray next to him and gently stroked the contour between his eyes. "I ordered us some breakfast and a cup of ice. I'll make you an ice pack in a minute."

"Thanks, Heidi. Coffee would be great," he said, noting how fantastic she looked even with no make-up on and just his scruffy old shirt covering her modesty.

As she poured him a coffee without breaking eye contact he remembered the simplicity and intensity of the previous night. After everything had died down and they had arrived back on dry land, he had suggested a drink or dinner, and without much forethought he suggested getting a hotel room over dessert and coffee, to which she agreed without any hesitancy.

The reception staff at the Hyatt Regency may or not have raised an eyebrow at his bruised and battered face, but he didn't mind as they swiped away half of his month's salary on his visa card before heading to the room.

"Milk, no sugar," she said.

"You remembered," he smiled.

She manoeuvred herself and sat opposite him on the end of the bed. "I was up early thinking about yesterday. What do you think will happen to Roberts and Hayton?"

Alex laughed. "I thought you would have been thinking how fantastic a lover I was?!"

She slapped his foot playfully. "That too! But seriously, what do you think will happen to them? Do you think we did enough?"

Alex raised himself up against the pillows. "I think we did the best we could in a unique situation, Heidi." He sipped his coffee. "I think Jackie will secure a conviction on Roberts. – We have plenty on him and his alibi – Hayton – is now far away in The Philippines. – Hayton himself is a different matter entirely. He's a slippery, well connected bastard – excuse my language."

She laughed. "It's OK, we've seen each other naked, you can use bad language."

"Well, I was hoping we might see each other naked again shortly…"

"Focus, Detective! We have all day. What about Hayton?"

"Well the thing is, with men like Hayton, they are only bothered about two things; power and money, which have turned out to be his weaknesses also. Jackie is right, there was no way in a million years that we would have got a conviction in Hong Kong. He's too well connected and it would have been an embarrassment to so many people, he would have walked free. Will the Filipino police get a conviction? Who knows? Here's hoping! But what I do know is, that at the very least, his power and money will be severely diminished whilst he's under arrest. The villa will be gone once all of the boat-boys, past and present are connected, and legal fees and possibly bribes will drain all his ill-gotten gains. With what he's accused of, he's unlikely to be treated with any sympathy by the local police. Plus, hopefully the wife won't be able to stand the shame, and perhaps will testify against him in an effort to distance herself. Like I said, I think we did the best we could, and I can't imagine he'll be welcomed back to Hong Kong or the UK."

"And at best?"

Alex made a move for her wrist which she playfully slapped away.

"Oh, very well. At best, he will be spending a lot of time in a Filipino jail. Now enough turtle talk, senior constable. I have some particulars I would like you to take down!"

They moved closer and he kissed her lightly. She kissed him back and they rolled over in the large bed with the Hong Kong island skyline looking down on them in the distance.

CHARACTERS

Angelo – one of Mark Hayton's first boat-boys
BARNETT: Raymond Barnett MBE – Head of construction at Chek Lap Kok airport
BURNHAM: Detective Inspector Trev Burnham – Manchester colleague of Alex Wu Torrence
CAMPBELL: Captain Campbell – camp leader of Jock Torrence, father of Alex Wu Torrence
CHAN: Elsie Chan – Lily Wu's father's secretary
CHAN: Mr. Chan – Lily Wu's family driver
CHAN: Dr. Rufus Chan – Director of Pathology, Hong Kong Government
Curly/Ah-Yun Wu – cousin of Alex Wu Torrence and triad member
EDWARDS – of the Immigration Department/ICAC. Rank and first name unknown
FRANCIS: Miss Francis – Lily's teacher.
GOFF: Andy Goff – commercial diver
HAMASAKI: Corporal Hamasaki – Japanese soldier
HARRIS: Wayne Harris – commercial diver
HAYTON: promoted to Commissioner of Police (CP) Mark Hayton (NB the CP at the time of the handover was a local man and Mark Hayton is a completely fictional British expat.)
JENNINGS: Kate Jennings – ex-girlfriend of Alex Wu Torrence
Keije – Japanese soldier (rank unknown)
KOIZUMI: Major Koizumi – Japanese camp commander
KWAN Yo Hang – Triad and suspected murderer
LAM: Ah-Lam/Helen – Aunty of Alex Wu Torrence
LEE: Mr Lee – office manager for Lily's father

LEUNG: George Leung – Uncle of Alex Wu Torrence

LIM: Senior Constable Heidi Lim – Colleague of Alex Wu Torrence

Lin Lin – Lily's amah

MACFARLAND: Chief Inspector Peter MacFarland

MCCRAY: Bill (William) McCray – Best friend in the army of Jock Torrence, father of Alex Wu Torrence

MCGREGOR: Chief Inspector McGregor – Boss in Manchester of Alex Wu Torrence

MEAKIN: Darren Meakin – First murder victim

Nanoy – Filipino boat-boy

Pancho – one of Mark Hayton's first boat-boys.

PENHAM-SMYTHE: Captain Penham-Smythe – Captain in the Hong Kong Volunteer Defence Corps

Popeye – A member of the East River Guerrillas and later 14k Triad boss

ROBERTS: Senior Inspector Karl Roberts

SAITO: First Lieutenant Saito – Japanese soldier

SHUEN: Detective Inspector Jackie Shuen – Lead detective in the Hong Kong murders.

SMITH: Reverend Smith, Vicar at the Torrence family church

SMITH: Officer at Sha Tin police-station/ICAC. Rank and first name unknown.

TAM: Big Brother Tam – Deceased head of 14k triad

TORRENCE: Jock Torrence – Corporal in the Royal Engineers and later a Superintendent in the Hong Kong police force. Alex's Father.

WILLIAMS: Uncle Taff Williams – Former sergeant in the Hong Kong police and family friend of the Torrence family.

WILSON: Philip Wilson. – Immigration/ICAC. Rank unknown.

WU TORRENCE: Detective Inspector Alex Wu Torrence

WU TORRENCE: Lily-Li Lai Wu Torrence – Mother of Alex Wu Torrence

YONG: Wan Li Yong/Black Tooth – Sai Kung triad boss

FICTION PUBLISHED BY PROVERSE

Those who enjoy **The Handover Murders** may also enjoy the following novels, novellas and short story collections (listed separately).

A Misted Mirror, by Gillian Jones. 2011.

A Painted Moment, by Jennifer Ching. 2010.

Adam's Franchise, by Lawrence Gray. 2016.

An Imitation of Life. 2nd ed, by Laura Solomon. 2013.

Article 109, by Peter Gregoire. 2012.

Bao Bao's odyssey: from Mao's Shanghai to capitalist Hong Kong, by Paul Ting. 2012.

Black Tortoise Winter, by Jan Pearson. 2016.

Bright Lights and White Nights, by Andrew Carter. 2015.

cemetery – miss you, by Jason S Polley. 2011.

Cop Show Heaven, by Lawrence Gray. 2015.

Cry of the Flying Rhino, by Ivy Ngeow, 2017.

Curveball, by Gustav Preller, 2016.

Death Has a Thousand Doors, by Patricia W. Grey. 2011.

Enoch's Muse, by Sergio Monteiro.
  Scheduled, November 2018.

Hilary and David, by Laura Solomon. 2011.

Hong Kong Hollow, by Dragoş Ilca. 2017.

Instant messages, by Laura Solomon. 2010.

Man's Last Song, by James Tam. 2013.

Mila the Magician, by Zhang Jian (Catherine Chin). 2014.
  (English/Chinese bilingual edition).

Mishpacha – family, by Rebecca Tomasis. 2010.

Paranoia (the walk and talk with Angela),
  by Caleb Kavon. 2012.

Red Bird Summer, by Jan Pearson. 2014.

Revenge From Beyond, by Dennis Wong. 2011.

The Day They Came, by Gérard Louis Breissan. 2012.

The Devil You Know, by Peter Gregoire. 2014.

**The Monkey in Me: Confusion, Love and Hope
  Under a Chinese Sky**, by Caleb Kavon. 2009.

The Perilous Passage of Princess Petunia Peasant,
  by Victor E. Apps. 2014. (Young adult fiction.)

The Reluctant Terrorist: in Search of the Jizo,
  by Caleb Kavon. 2011.

The Village in the Mountains, by David Diskin. 2012.

Three Wishes in Bardo by C. S. Feng.
  Scheduled, November 2018.

Tiger Autumn, by Jan Pearson. 2015.

Tightrope! A Bohemian tale, by Olga Walló.
Translated from Czech by Johanna Pokorny, Veronika Revická & others. Edited by Gillian Bickley & Olga Walló, with Verner Bickley. 2010.

University Days, by Laura Solomon. 2014.

Vera Magpie, by Laura Solomon. 2013.

SHORT STORY COLLECTIONS

Beyond Brightness, by Sanja Särman.
November 2016.

Odds and Sods, by Lawrence Gray. 2013.

The Shingle Bar Sea Monster and other stories,
by Laura Solomon. 2012.

The Snow Bridge and other Stories,
by Philip Chatting. 2015.

Under the Shade of the Feijoa Trees and other stories,
by Hayley Ann Solomon. Scheduled, April 2019.

FICTION – CHINESE LANGUAGE

The Monkey in Me, by Caleb Kavon.
Translated by Chapman Chen. 2010.

Tightrope! A Bohemian Tale, by Olga Walló.
Translated by Chapman Chen. 2011.
Chinese translation supported by the Ministry of Culture of the Czech Republic.

The Handover Murders